MacBRIDE

CW01511993

Veronica had gone to Dermid MacBride's sheep station on a business trip, to buy some antiques from his aunts—but it all turned out very differently when instead she found herself masquerading as his fiancée! And as time went by, it became more and more difficult to tell him the truth...

Books you will enjoy
by ESSIE SUMMERS

SEASON OF FORGETFULNESS

To get away from the humiliation of seeing her ex-fiancé married to another girl, Valancy had gone off to work as secretary to the author Godfrey Carmichael, who was also embittered by the break-up of *his* engagement to the gentle Kathleen. In due course he suggested that Valancy should marry him—but how could she? How could she coldbloodedly marry a man who was so obviously still hankering after someone else?

A MOUNTAIN FOR LUENDA

With two little sisters and a brother to take care of, Luenda was at her wits' end for money, when out of the blue came an offer to live for a year on a New Zealand hill station—*and* with half the income for herself! It seemed like the answer to a prayer. But the dour Gwillym Vaughan, who owned the other half of the property, didn't see it that way at all ...

A LAMP FOR JONATHAN

It wasn't because she had stopped loving Jonathan Lemaire that Camilla had broken off their engagement, but because she couldn't face the disillusionment of knowing he was dishonest. Now, five years later, he had come back into her life. And now, even if Camilla didn't want him, it was obvious that Dilys Cranbourne *did*!

MacBRIDE OF TORDARROCH

BY

ESSIE SUMMERS

MILLS & BOON LIMITED
15–16 BROOK'S MEWS
LONDON W1A 1DR

All the characters in this book have no existence outside the imagination of the Author, and have no relation whatsoever to anyone bearing the same name or names. They are not even distantly inspired by any individual known or unknown to the Author, and all the incidents are pure invention.

The text of this publication or any part thereof may not be reproduced or transmitted in any form or by any means, electronic or mechanical, including photocopying, recording, storage in an information retrieval system, or otherwise, without the written permission of the publisher.

This book is sold subject to the condition that it shall not, by way of trade or otherwise, be lent, resold, hired out or otherwise circulated without the prior consent of the publisher in any form of binding or cover other than that in which it is published and without a similar condition including this condition being imposed on the subsequent purchaser.

*First published in Great Britain 1984
by Mills & Boon Limited*

© Essie Summers 1984

*Australian copyright 1984
Philippine copyright 1985
This edition 1985*

ISBN 0 263 75211 9

*Set in Monophoto Times 9 on 10½ pt.
01–1185   67967*

*Made and printed in Great Britain by
Richard Clay (The Chaucer Press) Ltd,
Bungay, Suffolk*

Life holds many magic moments, and a great number of mine came from poems I read and kept, many of them first published in the *Australian Woman's Mirror*. As I was writing this novel, a letter came to me from a nursing Sister who told me of keeping a poem of mine from years ago and quoting it at meetings. Recently she had found the address of another poet whose verses she had kept, and rang her. I too had delighted in her poems years ago. She wrote under the name of Thelma Irene Elizabeth Smith. They now found they both read and collected my novels. So, to Thelma and to Marjorie Olive Burns of South Australia, I dedicate this book.

Wordsworth said what I would like to say to them:

'Dreams, books, are each a world, and books we know
Are a substantial world, both pure and good;
Round these with tendrils strong as flesh and blood
Our pastimes and our happiness will grow.'

The author would like to record her thanks to the *Australian Woman's Mirror* for permission to use the poem by Joan Pomfret. Also to Peter and Anne Presland of Minaret Station, Lake Wanaka, who so generously brought me up to date with my previous knowledge of an access-only-by-water sheep station on the far side of the lake. Anne, like my Fiona Campbell, possesses a helicopter pilot's licence.

CHAPTER ONE

VERONICA BLAKENEY took the curve below the crouching outline of Mount Iron on her right and saw, for the first time, Lake Wanaka. She had plenty of time to catch that launch up-lake, so she drew into the side of the road and revelled in the scene ahead ... the cornflower-blue waters, immense and calm, cradled in the arms of vast, tawny hills with, to the west, snow-shawled peaks.

She told herself she was lucky to be tied no longer to showrooms of antique furniture and rows of valuable but musty books. She was free now to roam the full extent of the South Island picking up pieces on commission. It had been well worth the rigorous saving of the last two years to give her enough security to venture out on this, and already it was paying off. She was keeping her firm well supplied and so far the commissions earned had modestly exceeded her former weekly wage. True, it had been rather more uneventful than she'd hoped for, but it was glorious really to be roaming the country viewing treasures in their own settings and often retrieving them from mouldering in old lofts and barns.

This was the farthest venture yet, going up to Distaff Bay to see the Misses Maude and Adelaide Shaw. Even the name was apt—sounded like a dower house for the spinsters of the family! They seemed pets, from their letters. What an ideal situation for a prospective buyer of antiques! Or almost ideal. Adelaide had added, 'We have just told our nephew, who lives in the big homestead over the hill, Tordarroch Station, that we are giving a young friend of some Christchurch friends of ours a holiday. No need to upset him beforehand. All the chattels are ours, left to us by our mother, to do with them as we wish, and seeing we'd like to travel before we shuffle off this mortal coil, this *is* what we wish. So we are keeping him in blissful ignorance till you have a look. It may be you won't

7

want any, in which case he won't be disturbed. But if you like them, it will make a dream come true for us. In any case I'm sure you'll enjoy a few days up the lake in idyllic solitude in spring. The daffodils and bluebells are out.'

It sounded like heaven ... a quiet little bay with only mountain ranges at the back of it and not even a road leading to it to bring anyone to disturb the peace. She wouldn't be greedy; she would assess, choose, advise. She'd love to buy enough to let the poor old dears do a spot of globe-trotting. They were probably right under this nephew's thumb. They sounded quite old, so he'd be some grizzled son of the soil, in his fifties, someone who'd never heard of equal rights and women living their own lives, doing what they wanted to do. They'd probably always been stuck up there in an isolation that would naturally tend to be a man-dominated kingdom all its own. Veronica had heard about some of these isolated communities tucked away at the far sides of the southern lakes, reached only by launch—in fact not even communities, but one-family estates. Adelaide and Maude had probably never even got away to school, would have had a governess, known very little freedom.

Now she must look for this garage where she was to leave her car for the week. She ran down past the low, wide hotel in a sweep of emerald lawns and gardens where the Queen Mother had stayed, and later Prince Charles, for the trout-fishing. There were already a lot of tourists wandering about; small craft were bobbing at anchor, and down at the small jetty a launch looked ready to take off. Well, it wouldn't be the one she was to take, because she had more than a couple of hours to fill in. She'd explore the lake foreshore on foot when she'd left the car.

Ah, here was the garage. She pulled up, got out, went across to a man who'd just filled up a petrol tank. 'I have to garage my car here for the next week or so, while I'm staying at Tordarroch Station. My name's Veronica——'

A broad grin split his face, 'It's Veronica, is it? They're all in such a tizzy up there they said Victoria. Well, it's not much different, and we're damned glad you made such good time.

I'll put the car away after and run you down to the jetty now and Gus will cast off. It means Theo won't have a chance of getting up there before you do. I'm all in favour of spiking his guns. He's a mean sort of bloke, with a dirty temper. And of course, as for Lucy, it's just the sort of pickle she *would* land Dermid in. Come on, we've got to hustle. Gus decided to take tourists too, but he's ready to cast off at first sight of you.'

Veronica felt a little dazed and not a little apprehensive. This nephew . . . was he Theo or Dermid? And such a tizzy? Had he, whichever one he was, found out the aunts were going to sell some antiques and turned nasty? A mean sort of bloke? She hoped she was not going to be too involved. Still, perhaps he just didn't want them cheated. She'd a good mind not to go, but those sisters had sounded sweet and somehow pathetic, and they longed to travel. But Lucy? Who was she? Another old-fashioned name. Perhaps there were three maiden aunts at Distaff Bay. Was Lucy the odd one out who didn't want to travel and was trying to spike her sisters' guns? She hadn't time to think much or ask questions, though. It was so short a distance that only the fact that she had a case had made him almost throw her into an ancient two-seater and roar down the garage approach and across the road down a track to the jetty.

He whisked her out, her case and holdall were handed out and down, so was she. There seemed to be two family parties aboard. They were getting off at Minaret Station, Gus the pilot said, and he closed one eye in a broad wink Veronica took to mean, don't give away the fact that there's a tizzy going on at *her* destination.

She hadn't been prepared for the journey to take so long or the lake to be so vast . . . there was so much of it out of sight, with numerous arms of the lake cutting back into the mountains. The ones for Minaret Station were from the North Island of New Zealand, so Gus, finding this was their first visit to Central Otago, kept up an excellent commentary as they cut through the blue waters. He had both contemporary and pioneer history at his fingertips. She noticed that quite frequently he cast a swift but searching glance behind him. Decidedly odd.

Presently, as the group fell to chattering, she came to stand beside the pilot. He cast her a quick look, then said in a very low voice, 'You're a good sport to take this on. We hoped you'd waste no time on the way up. You must have travelled some to get here so soon. We hoped you'd make it early.'

Veronica instinctively dropped her own voice. 'I didn't exceed the limit. After all, it's a tricky road when it's your first time—that gorge! But tell me, does it really have to be so hush-hush?'

'Sure does. It's a small world, the lake community. Everyone knows everyone else. One hint and the balloon would go up. Look out, the others are coming over. No more now.'

It wasn't till he landed them at Minaret Bay with the lovely formation of Minaret Peaks above it, soaring up into the sky, and had sailed out into the body of the lake again that she was able to say anything further. She said, 'I take it their nephew has got wind of what his aunts are up to. He must be a colossal spoilsport, to disapprove of them even getting their treasures valued! They told me they were their very own possessions. I'm not likely to take advantage of them; in fact, if they like, I can value them and they can get their nephew to look them over in the light of my estimates and even get another opinion if he likes, say someone up from Dunedin. The two old dears just long to travel, and I can't see the good of hanging on to stuff they're probably tired of, anyway, and denying themselves the chance of seeing London and Vienna, Saltzburg and Venice and Rome ... the way Miss Adelaide spoke of those places in her letter was really touching.'

Gus gazed blankly at her. 'I haven't the foggiest notion what you're taking about. It sounds to me as if Anne hasn't explained in detail at all. Beats me. Did she just shove you off in a great hurry, tell you that you had to pretend you were Dermid's fiancée, and not even brief you on your lines?'

Veronica's stare was even more blank. 'Anne? Who is Anne?'

Gus swung round from the wheel. '*Who is Anne?* Why

Dermid's sister, of course. But you know her. You act with her!'

Veronica gulped. 'I know nothing. I think you're all mad! Who is Dermid?'

Gus's mouth fell open. 'Dermid? But that's who it's all about!'

'All *what's* about? If you don't tell me from A to Z, I'll scream! All I'm sure of at the moment is that I'm an antique buyer who was engaged by Miss Adelaide Shaw, unknown to her nephew whose name was never mentioned, to value some antiques because they want to travel a bit before they peg out, to put it crudely. I'm Veronica Blakeney, of Early Colonial Antiques in Christchurch, working on commission for them. So what's cooking?'

Gus pushed his peaked cap back, scratched his grizzled poll, then said in a flabbergasted tone, 'They were right about the name after all. They *did* say Victoria! My God, what's Mac done?—the chap at the garage. Look ... Anne is in a small professional stage group in Dunedin. She said she'd get a member of it, who wasn't going to Australia with them, to pretend she was Dermid's fiancée to get him out of the hole. The hole Lucy got him into. She was to say she'd been at the motel that night too.'

Veronica was sure her eyes were going glassy. 'Lucy? Who *is* Lucy? And what did she do?'

Gus said rapidly, 'Lucy Baring. She married Theo Baring, rather a tough hombre. She's a gentle little thing, but always in a flap over something. She stayed up at Tordarroch a lot before she was married. Her parents were separated and she was a bit pathetic and Tordarroch became a second home to her. Theo had a homestead across Lake Hawea that's even more isolated than Dermid's because it's up a river at the far side. Lucy and Theo quarrelled, and Lucy rang Dermid, but his housekeeper told her he was in Dunedin at a motel, on business. Damned if she didn't turn up there after midnight— she'd had trouble with the hired car. Those sort of things happen to Lucy. It was a motel with one bedroom and a divan in the lounge. Dermid shoved her in the bedroom, while he slept on the divan. He sorted her out next day and sent her back. The silly wench let it out to hubby, who is the jealous type. Hot-headed too.

'So they had another flaming row. What does she do but flee up here? Dermid had this bright idea . . . why not get one of Anne's actress friends to come up and pretend she was engaged to him? Anne rang back to say she had the very one, a bobby-dazzler who'd put Lucy right in the shade. Theo would know Dermid wouldn't look Lucy's way if he was engaged to her. Only she was Victoria. And you're not her, worse luck! What in hell do I do?'

Veronica said faintly, 'You'll have to drop me at Distaff Bay and go back for her. Perhaps like Lucy she's had car trouble.'

'Too late. Theo found out Lucy was up here. She came up with me in a public launch, so someone must have mentioned it. He phoned the farm, the housekeeper let out she was there, Dermid took over the phone, and Theo wouldn't believe there was nothing in it and said he was coming to haul Lucy back by the ear! That's why we wanted Victoria. We put on an early launch. I've got to get back, sure, for other bookings, but Theo could be catching that one. He'd leave his own launch at Hawea and get someone to run him to Wanaka. Imagine having him and this Victoria on the same boat! It's the only one they can take, because the other launches are on all-day cruises. So it's the only way he can come, unless—but I hardly think he would.'

'Unless what?' asked Veronica fearfully.

'Unless he's so flaming mad he brings his own launch across from Lake Hawea. He might reason it'd be a lot more private than the public one. He's got a phone, so he could have arranged for someone at Hawea township to meet him this side of that lake, with a boat trailer to transport it across the Neck. He'd be so furious he'd brook no delay.'

'The Neck?' asked Veronica, stupefied. What a conversation!

'The narrow bit between Hawea and Wanaka. It's a shorter trip across then. Ah, here's where we turn in. Tordarroch Inlet coming up.' He looked over his shoulder and groaned. 'I'm almost sure that's him coming across now. Look, we can get there before him . . . just. For sure Dermid will be on their jetty. I implore you, if he is . . . make out *you're* Dermid's fiancée. It's going to be an ugly situation otherwise. He'll be at Dermid's throat before you can say a word, but if he sees you throwing yourself into Dermid's arms, it'll give him a setback. It won't be for long. I reckon Theo'll hardly give Lucy time to pack her bags before he drags her off.'

Veronica made one last bid to escape. 'What about my name?'

'Theo may not have heard it. We've got to risk something. We can say he was mistaken on the phone. But I've an idea Dermid may have just said " my fiancée". I hope so.'

Veronica said, 'Dermid's going to be set back—I'm no bobby-dazzler.'

Gus must have been fifty-five, but he looked at the tall brown-haired girl in front of him with real male appreciation. Her cheeks had a heightened colour, her brown eyes were wide and apprehensive, coral lips were parted as if to protest; her lime-green dress had blown back in the lake breeze and had outlined her figure. 'You'd do me for one,' he said, 'and you'll certainly do Dermid.'

He came expertly about, and drew alongside the jetty. The group of people who had been rushing down the steep path to the water arrived on the planking. Someone seized the rope Gus flung and secured it. Gus leapt to the side, Veronica's hand in his, and another hand, rough and calloused, took her other one, and the next moment she was on the jetty, but it seemed to her as if the launch still rose and fell beneath her.

Gus hissed at the owner of the calloused hand, 'Theo's just coming round the headland—he must have transported his boat across the Neck. We've no time for explanations, though. This is *Veronica*. Yes, I know you said Victoria, but her name's Veronica. Veronica, embrace him. Now, Dermid, kiss her as you've never kissed anyone before!'

She looked up, saw a coppery jaw, a gleam of strangely brilliant green eyes and a head of dark chestnut hair then she was caught up in an iron embrace and kissed so hard she could feel the bones of his face.

If he had released her fully, she would have fallen. He seemed to realise this and retained a hold on her arms above the elbows. He said quickly, 'I must know the basics about you. What's your last name?'

Heavens, it must have been arranged quickly! He didn't even know this Victoria's surname!

'It's Blakeney. You must be Dermid Shaw.'

'Good grief, no. Did you think I was a stepbrother of Anne's? I'm Dermid MacBride, of course. Well, it's been all very rushed. How much do you know about the situation? I know Anne was just leaving for Australia, but I didn't realise she had hardly time to fill you in.'

'Just that someone called Lucy ran away from her husband and spent the night in a Dunedin motel with you, and Theo ... er ... Baring is furious, so you asked Anne to provide a makebelieve fiancée for you, who's supposed to have spent the night at the motel too. How much will this Theo know about your fictional fiancée? Quick, it sounds as if that boat is getting horribly near!'

He swung her round a little, away from the water, apparently looking lovingly down on her. He hissed intensely, 'He knows mighty little. He rang here, demanding to know if Lucy was with me this time. Said someone had seen her on the launch. I said she sure is, mate, and for heaven's sake get her out of my hair, that my fiancée was coming up and she wouldn't swallow Lucy twice. It was too much; she was a sport last time, and that I'd strangle Lucy if because of her, my wife-to-be thrust the ring back at me. Oh, lord, Gus, the ring!'

Gus, standing close, scrabbled in his pocket and said, 'Here it is, get it on ... keep your back turned.'

He thrust it between them. Veronica brought her hand up, and Dermid MacBride said, 'Wrong hand ... left one, dope!'

Colour flamed into Veronica's cheeks. 'I'll smack your face for that first time we're alone! This is a madhouse ... and you call *me* dope!'

All of a sudden the funny side of it swept over her, dispelling the anger, and to everyone's amazement she laughed out loud. It floated to the ears of the man coming alongside the jetty. It seemed to all the group the most natural and welcome sound in their world.

Dermid whispered, 'There's my housekeeper, Mrs Stephenson, and that's Lucy.'

Veronica saw a pale lily of a girl with hands clasped tightly in front of her, shrinking back against the housekeeper. Swiftly Veronica went over to Lucy, kissed her and said clearly and loudly, 'Lucy darling! Gus told me everything on the way up. Don't worry, everything's okay now I'm here.' She added with a note of amusement, 'It's all out of character. I wanted a man who'd rescue me from all the dragons. I've got a romantic slant. I thought Dermid was going to be a twentieth-century St George, but instead I've got to be the one to rescue *him*! I shan't let him forget it for the rest of his life! Now, where's that great big bumbling husband of yours? I'll fix *him*!' And she wheeled round to face a giant of a man hastening along the jetty.

His face was a mixture of thundery fury and incredulity. He stopped three paces from them. 'What's going on?' he demanded.

Veronica put out a restraining hand as Dermid MacBride went to step forward. 'Please!' she commanded in a ringing voice that sounded convincing even to herself. 'Now listen, Dermid. You and Lucy have blundered enough. If you'd had the sense to hustle her off to some hotel miles from your motel, this would never have happened. Instead you woke everyone in my boarding-house by ringing me at that unearthly hour and demanding that I get along to you. My landlady's never been the same to me since! So I'm not going to let you meddle any more. Theo, Dermid was only scared *I'd* go up in smoke if I found a girl from up here had spent a night in his motel, so his one thought was to get me there. And let me tell you this . . . I don't suppose any of it would have happened if Lucy hadn't been terrified of you. What sort of a man are you, anyway, to get a girl into *this* state? You're supposed to be the one who promised to love and to cherish her. What sort of cherishing is this?'

She stopped, not because she was out of breath or imagination, but she was scared to death she might over reach herself and give the show away.

The effect on Theo was ludicrous. He'd come to browbeat and was being browbeaten himself by a slim slip of a girl he'd never met in his life before. It was just as if all the suspicion and anger had sloughed off him in one second and a sense of shame and abasement had taken its place. He was put on the defensive.

He said, 'But—but I *do* love her. I love her and I *want* to cherish her . . . I feel she ought to understand this . . . but I can't keep up the sweet talk all the time. I'm too busy and she gets so miserable—thinks I don't love her and imagines things. She's for ever comparing me with Dermid, and I was so sick of it. I don't know why she didn't marry him if she thought he was the better man . . . more moneyed too!'

Dermid laughed shortly. 'I can tell you why in one. Because I never asked her. Nor was I ever likely to. Hang it, man, she's like a little sister—she practically grew up here. So when she's in trouble, she comes home. Nevertheless, I had enough sense that I dare not keep her in that motel unless I had my fiancée with me. Not because I was afraid of you, Theo, but in case it upset my very new engagement. I couldn't believe my incredible luck when Veronica accepted me. I wasn't risking anything.'

Dermid swung round on Lucy. 'What the devil got into you to keep bringing me into any quarrel you and Theo had? Married people are bound to have some quarrels. All families have quarrels, but they don't have to last. But why on earth drag *me* in?'

Lucy looked down at her feet, the ashy-fair hair swinging forward to hide her face. Theo barked; 'Lucy, don't do it. You know it infuriates me. Look up, and for pity's sake give us an honest answer. If there was nothing in it why did you keep harping on about how differently Dermid would've treated you. There were times when I felt that if you mentioned him again I would choke you. Why did you?'

Slowly, the lily-pale girl lifted her head, looked him full in the face, and there could have been nobody else present but the two of them. 'I wanted to make you jealous,' she said. 'To stir you up, to make you go my way. To make you into the sort of husband I wanted—an articulate husband. And I've ruined it all!'

They weren't prepared for the light that sprang into the grey eyes of the big red-faced man. He took a step forward, then stopped, suddenly aware of the audience of four. Dermid said swiftly, 'This is our exit line, I think. Come on, Gus. Come on, Veronica, Mrs Stephenson, let them have it.' Then back over his shoulder, 'And when you've disentangled yourselves from what I hope is a massive reconciliation clinch, you'd better come up to the house and have lunch. I'm simply starving!'

Veronica clapped a restraining hand to her mouth. But it was no good, the laughter spilled out of her silently. Dermid MacBride took her arm roughly, hustled her on, muttering, 'Stop it this moment ... it's a big moment for those two ... and *not* funny!'

She whispered jerkily, between spasms, 'I know, I know, but really, it's your fault. To be hungry, after a confrontation like that, is too absurd. *I'm* gone at the knees!'

Mrs Stephenson said grimly, 'So am I. I've lived up here since I was married, and seen Dermid and his sister and brother in more pickles than I care to remember, but never one like this. Nor have I ever heard so many lies told. I can only hope you can remember all you've said.'

Gus said, 'Now, now, Stephie, it saved the day, and I'm damned if I know what else would have done just that.'

They rounded a huge cutting in the solid rock of the hillside and were out of sight of the pair still on the jetty. A few yards farther on was a low bank. Veronica freed herself, walked to it, and sat down. 'I just have to have time to get my breath back and some bone into my knees. You can't walk on jelly!'

They clustered round her, gave her a few minutes. She got up, pushed the hair back from her dewy forehead, then looked ahead to where, on a lake-terrace, like a plateau, stood a white stone house with a very bright red, very steep, iron roof. Later she was to learn that it was a good landmark for the helicopters and small planes of the area. As they climbed upwards she said, 'Do you think they'll come up for lunch, or will they be too embarrassed?'

Dermid said, 'Lucy has a case here, so they'll have to. Gus, we'll give you your meal right away, because you'll have to get back to pick up tourists, won't you?'

He nodded. 'I'll phone and say I could be a trifle late.'

Veronica looked down on the ring she wore, a modest square-cut diamond in the centre with three tiny ones shouldering each side. She said, 'Does this ring belong to your wife? When can I get it back to you? If you leave before Theo and Lucy do, I can't give it to you.'

Gus grinned. What a likeable fellow he was, and what a friend to this Dermid character. 'Mollie won't mind. She'd say it was all in a good cause. She'll keep mum about it. She's the proverbial oyster in things like this, bless her. Never do for you to be without it in the next little while.'

Veronica said, 'Tell me, is this reconcilation likely to last? The garage man said Theo was a mean sort of man, and I don't think he meant in money matters. I think he meant nasty. How mean? How long will it take him to be really sure of Lucy? Won't he be suspicious and give her hell if he thinks it's a put-up job? It could make him think it was more serious than it was if you've gone to such lengths to deceive him.'

It was Dermid who answered. He said roughly, 'Well, could you have thought of anything better? Something had to be done right away. He's a good enough chap at heart, and the ruthless streak in him seems to attract Lucy, but she hasn't got the gumption to handle it. He had a tough childhood and has a chip on his shoulder because of it, and he's unpredictable when his temper's up. If you thought it such a rotten plot why did you embark on it? Or did you do it to please Anne and now you're regretting it?'

Veronica opened her mouth to protest, to explain, but just as Dermid MacBride swung round to see if the reunited pair was coming, Gus gave her a rib-jolting nudge that stopped her before she got a word out. Gus mouthed at her, 'Don't say you're not Anne's friend!'

Dermid turned back, somewhat relieved. 'Oh, they aren't within earshot. I suddenly thought they might be. Go on . . . are you regretting it? Because if you are, at least keep it up till they're back on that launch!'

This so incensed Veronica she said with spirit, 'I was starting to say I wasn't regretting it. Look, nothing much has been explained to me at all—I had to leap into this situation too quickly. I feel pressganged into something I don't care for, but for the sake of a marriage that looks like going on the rocks otherwise I'll go along with it. I don't suppose any misgivings I might have can count against *that*.'

For some reason the man looking down on her positively boggled. 'Well, that's the last statement I'd have expected *you* to make!'

Veronica put a hand to her head gave it a little shake, then said dazedly, 'It's not the sort of remark I *expected* to make when I set out this morning. I feel as if I'm taking part in a very bad play, and I've forgotten my lines and am improvising.'

He gave a bark of laughter more derisive than mirthful. 'Yes, I can well imagine you've never thought along such lines before.'

Veronica gave it up. She looked back. 'They're catching up on us and they're hand-in-hand. Let's hope it lasts and we don't have to keep up this farce too long.'

Dermid said, 'Well, to start with it'll be only till they eat, pack Lucy's things and take off for the far shore, but you'll have to play it along a bit. Never do to take off too soon. Wanaka and Hawea are small places, and a new fiancée leaving as soon as she arrived would be suspicious in anybody's book. And with being on the phone, Theo could ring here, even ask to speak to you, and would think it strange if we couldn't put you on the line. I never thought I'd ever think it inconvenient to be connected!'

In answer to her mystified look he said, 'Not much over a decade ago, our only contact was by radio-telephone.'

It made Veronica shiver. 'That could be frightening at times.'

'Indeed it was. Especially in illness. And worse still before there was even that radio-telephone link.'

She thought, 'That would be what makes it so much a kingdom on its own. A man-dominated one,' a thought she mustn't utter.

He added, 'Besides, you'll have to stay for a while. Anne said you needed to be out of Dunedin for some time. Pity you couldn't have gone with the company to Australia. I mean, as far as *you're* concerned; as far as *I* am, you're a godsend.'

Veronica decided she'd better remain a godsend and sort it out later. It seemed a chancy situation and she'd do irreparable harm perhaps if she threw them into confusion by starting now to say she wasn't Anne's actress friend. She must be natural for the sake of this pair. She put a restraining hand on Dermid's arm and said clearly, 'Darling, look . . . we've got company. *Happy* company. Lucy, I guess you feel like a million dollars right now. Theo, next time you and Lucy have a tiff, don't let her get away.' She had an inspiration. 'My mother disapproves of Dermid quite enough without you complicating things. The idea of her darling city-bred daughter marrying someone on a vast sheep station that doesn't even have a road coming to its door has given her the vapours as it is, but if she thought he'd been harbouring another woman, a married woman at that, in his Dunedin motel, she'd be forbidding the banns! I've got a lot of talking to do between now and the happy day, believe me, to get her even faintly reconciled to the idea! My mother can never realise that though we love each other dearly, she and I are as different as can be. She lives a life that's a positive round of golf matches, bridge parties, and social engagements.

'She thinks country life dead boring, and to imagine I can make a success of marriage up here, with not even a road to bring the world to my door, is the height of folly. So please, no more complications. She made me promise to sample life in the way-backs before committing myself to the irrevocable step.'

She paused, having run out of breath and invention. She had to hand it to Dermid MacBride, he wasn't a bad actor himself. He said, reaching out for her hand, 'Aren't I the lucky one? A girl as beautiful as this, brave enough to take on a high-country man, say goodbye to the city lights, and defy her fond mama into the bargain? And just when I can't believe my incredible luck, Lucy here has to throw a colossal spanner into the works!'

Theo put a protective arm round his wife's shoulders. 'But it seems she had the best of all possible reasons ... if she wanted to make me jealous she certainly succeeded, and I'm tickled pink to think she cared that much. I'm not an articulate man, I know. She'll have to put up with that and believe I love her.'

Veronica began to enjoy herself, despite feeling she'd strayed into a stage scene without a single rehearsal. She said, with a touch of asperity, 'Theo! Wrong technique. Never tell a woman she'll have to put up with anything. If speech makes your Lucy happy, then you'll jolly well have to be articulate! Every woman deserves her man telling her from time to time not only that he loves her but *how* he loves her. It's the only way Dermid will keep me happy up here.'

The look she gave him would have done credit to a first-rate actress. Gus turned away quickly and coughed. Dermid chuckled, 'You're pretty articulate yourself, my love. Look, all this high drama is making me ravenous! Stephie, I hope you've got something really good for us.'

'I have, and if only we could leave all this lovey-dovey talk behind us, I'd have it on the table in a jiffy. I made a special dish for Veronica, but it'll have to be slapped out in a hurry if Gus is going to get back to Wanaka in time. Come on.'

Veronica had only a vague impression of a house with big hospitable rooms and windows that seemed to embrace blue view after blue view of the vastness of the lake. Gus went straight to the telephone, to be frustrated when it was as dead as mutton.

Dermid MacBride took it calmly. 'Oh, well, I've lived up here more years without a phone than with one, but when you get back, Gus, get someone on the jetty to let the Post Office know in case it's near their end. We can do an inspection of the lines round here if it lasts. We did have a terrible nor'wester lately.'

The big table was already set. Mrs Stephenson quickly set out an extra place for Theo Baring next to Lucy's and brought out an enormous ashet piled high with succulent venison cubes, sprinkled with chopped glacé cherries, ground almonds and parsley, and circled with snowy rice decorated with red and green peppers and pineapple rings. She put a tureen of mushrooms on one side and one of jacket potatoes on the other. 'Dermid never thinks rice is any substitute for potatoes, but I like the look of the rice and the varied ways you can serve it, so I tell him he's got to allow me some creative arts. I spent so many years being frustrated by cooking plain stuff for the shearing gangs, I refused to be dominated all my days with male prejudices in my department here!'

It turned out a surprisingly merry meal. They all did justice to Mrs Stephenson's apricot tart and finally her coffee. Gus rose. 'I must go for my life. Veronica, I've got a message for you from Mollie. It's a private one, so excuse us.'

'Can I come?' asked Dermid.

'You cannot. And don't get jealous like old Theo here. It really is from my wife.'

Something about the ring, she supposed. He whisked her into a side-room, shut the door. He shook his head. 'No. I know you'll take good care of it. It's——'

She broke in. 'Thank goodness you did this! Why did you stop me telling Dermid I wasn't Anne's friend? And what will you do if she turns up at Wanaka? She must have been delayed. It will never do to have her here now.'

'It's okay. Mac would bring her to my boat, none of the others, when he'd sorted out what had happened. I'll fix it. Mollie could put her up for the night, or two or three if she doesn't want to return right away. But my guess is that something's happened. Perhaps she got offered a good part somewhere and just gave up this idea. But I stopped you telling Dermid because it was too awkward a moment with Lucy and Theo almost on our heels. It would have thrown Dermid. He'd never have sounded convincing if he'd thought you were a perfect stranger and not an actress. As it is you've been splendid. He'd have had no confidence in your being able to carry it through. If I were you I'd not tell him till it's all sorted out. He'll be more natural that way.'

'But his aunts? They're expecting me. It sounds as if they haven't mentioned that a young friend of their friends is coming. I don't think you knew either. The name on the passenger list for the later boat wouldn't have meant a thing to you. But how do I let the aunts know?'

He thought rapidly. 'Mollie's coming down to see me at the launch before my next trip. I'll get her to ring the aunts. Their phone may not be out. On second thoughts, I'll call in at Distaff Bay on the second trip and let them know. I can't this trip because Theo might ask why. He'll be gone before the next one, of course.

There was no doubt Gus fancied himself as a conspirator. He said to Theo, 'Mollie can talk of nothing else but Dermid and Veronica's approaching marriage. You know what women are. And of course she saw a lot of Veronica when they were courting. There's always a lot of secrecy about styles of wedding-dresses, isn't there? Beats me. However, I'm a peace-loving sort of chap, and I've been married long enough to go along with what seems so important to the womenfolk, bless 'em.'

Veronica thought Dermid looked relieved. No doubt he was walking a tightrope and wanted no tumbles.

She felt more apprehensive when Gus had gone. He was the only one who knew she wasn't a friend of Anne's. Well, with a bit of luck, Theo and Lucy would be heading out across the lake and she wouldn't fear being tripped up by some wrongful allusion to or question about that night spent at the motel. She didn't even know which motel. What a situation!

She could have screamed when Lucy dilly-dallied over her packing. Possibly she was nervous about being with Theo again on her own. But he looked a different man now. He and

Dermid were chatting quite freely. High-country talk—
Altitude, Aspect, Access . . . they called them the three A's in
these across-lake sheep stations.

This was a different world from the farm holidays Veronica
had known as a child. They all had roads leading to them,
towns within reasonable distance, neighbours. Here they
reckoned in terms of square miles, not acres, and ranges of
hills and mountains and rivers were their natural boundaries.
A vast, lonely area that reached back into a never-never-land.

She dared not venture an opinion about anything, only
nodded agreement with Dermid from time to time. He
reached out once or twice to squeeze her hand fondly and say,
'That's so, isn't it, darling?' or 'that's what we intend to do,
don't we, Veronica?'

Mrs Stephenson took pity on her and said, 'While Lucy's
finishing packing, you can help me with the dishes, Veronica.'
She twinkled, 'It's not often that two women get on so well in
the one kitchen as we do. Just as well, as otherwise, in an
isolated area like this, we might fall to fighting. Though I
reckon I'll leave them on their own for a bit when they're first
wed. Nothing like young folk being on their own. I might go
to my daughter's for a month or two.'

What actors they all were! To her annoyance Veronica felt
warmth in her cheeks and noticed Dermid looking amused.
What was more, the thawed-out Theo noticed it too. 'I like a
girl who can blush,' he said unexpectedly.

Mrs Stephenson laughed indulgently. 'So do I. There's
nothing of the tough female about our Veronica, thank
goodness!'

Veronica realised that all of them, from the launch pilot to
the owner of this station, were starting to enjoy this
masquerade. It had become a prank to them. They heard
Lucy coming downstairs.

With great inner relief Veronica too rose to her feet. Theo
took his wife's case from her and slipped an arm round her
shoulders. 'Right, let's get going. Sooner we're home the
sooner I can beat the living daylights out of you and relieve
my feelings. What an idea . . . thinking I didn't truly love you

. . . trying to make me jealous! It'll serve you right if you get sick and tired of me trying to prove it to you every day that you're the one and only. Now as starters, and in front of an audience, how does that sound?'

The pale lily was now a rose, positively glowing, and sparkly-eyed. 'It'll do me,' she said, and very naturally raised herself on tiptoe and kissed him.

'For once,' announced Mrs Stephenson, 'I've got enough romance to satisfy me, and not out of a book either, and with Dermid going in off the deep end like this about Veronica, I've achieved what I've been trying to do for years, saved him from being a confirmed bachelor.'

Suddenly Veronica felt as if her head was swimming. It all sounded so ridiculously natural, she was almost believing in it. Well, it looked as if she might have earned herself a couple of weeks or so of a very pleasant holiday, seeing she had to stay on a certain time to give credence to this bogus engagement, and she might do some very profitable business on the side. Perhaps Dermid would be so grateful to her for saving the situation at a moment's notice he wouldn't cut up rough if his dear old aunts did want to sell off a few things he'd rather they should retain.

They all trooped down to the jetty to see Theo and Lucy off. Theo's launch was a beauty, trim in its white paint with a décor of the same cornflower blue as the lake. Lucy, eager to get away now, sprang on board, Theo turned to say once more how sorry he'd been to have arrived in such a flaming temper, and caught his toe on a coil of rope. He teetered dangerously over the edge for a few seconds in which they thought he was going to pitch into the lake, made a right-about turn and leap with a tremendous effort, and crashed down on the steps instead.

Dermid, Veronica and Mrs Stephenson expected a bellowing laugh from him, but Lucy, wildly alarmed, leapt back on the jetty, and to their combined horror, Theo's first movement to gather himself together resulted in a cry of absolute agony.

Lucy was kneeling beside him in a jiffy. 'Theo . . .?' she

asked, 'Theo, you haven't? Not again? You have?' She looked up at the ring of concerned faces. 'He's slipped a disc again!'

Consternation sat upon them all. Dermid recovered first, and dropped down beside him. 'Look, it may not be. It could be a twist, having wrenched the muscles badly. Lie still for a moment, then we'll try to get you to your feet.'

It was soon evident it *was* serious. Theo tried to be stoical, but great grunts of pain burst from him as they got him up on to the top of the jetty. He turned and looked at his launch, said, with a real bitterness of tone, 'And all I wanted was to get home!'

They were silent with dismay for him.

He said, 'But I couldn't now. Not to make it across the lake, to say nothing of waiting for transport across the Neck. It's beyond me. Oh, damn!'

Dermid said, 'Well, nothing for it but to stay here. We'll get the doctor up from Wanaka. It's easier here than at your place, that's one thing. Theo, can you make it to this seat? . . . though you'll have to lie, not sit. I'll go and get the Land Rover.'

His progress was painful in the extreme. Sweat stood out in great drops on his forehead. The lily-white creature who was his wife suddenly became a strong, supportive woman who'd coped with her man in agony before. They propped him against the rail of the seat. Dermid said, holding out his hand to her, 'Come with me, Veronica, it's up in front of the house.'

She realised he hadn't dared leave her there in case she put her foot in it and gave herself away. They hurried up past the bank where Veronica had tried to still her shaking knees. They were no less shaky now. They suddenly stopped, looked at each other in panic and horror. 'You're stuck with this pretence, Veronica, it's like that old film, *The Man who Came to Dinner*. It was a repeat on TV last year. Let's hope the doctor is good at manipulation and he can be taken to Wanaka to recover. And let's say our prayers backwards that we don't trip ourselves up in the meantime. We'll need a memory like computer!' Veronica realised this was no time to tell him she was not a trained actress.

CHAPTER TWO

VERONICA found it had all the qualities of a nightmare, but one from which, unfortunately, she could not waken. She experienced a moment of sheer panic till on their return, her eyes fell on Theo, sheet-white and obviously trying to suppress groans as they lifted him into the Rover. They'd just have to keep up this dicey masquerade the whole time he was here. And she would do nothing to undermine Dermid's confidence in her ability to carry it through.

The Rover crawled away, Dermid at the wheel, Lucy trying to support Theo to shield him from any bumps on a track that left a lot to be desired.

Mrs Stephenson and Veronica walked soberly up the rough way again. They paused, and Veronica said, 'This is going to be tricky. It's one thing pretending to be Dermid's fiancée for a short time, and in a good cause, but another keeping it up. How long will it take for his back to heal? I mean, if the doctor can get here and manipulate it, will it be instant recovery? Or nearly?'

Stephie answered slowly, 'He'll have to be very careful for a few days. They won't risk him taking his own launch back, it's too steep the other side—there's no jetty. And even if we got him flown to his place, he can't stay there without his launch. I think myself the doctor may take him back to Wanaka. In fact if it's very bad, he may take him to the hospital at Cromwell. He hurt it last shearing, I believe. These big husky high-country men make shocking patients. I wouldn't like to be Lucy. Pity it's happened right now when they've just made it up.'

Veronica said curiously, 'How come they got into such a tangle? It was stupid of her to flee to Dermid. That would make any husband mad. It does even if a wife runs home to her mother.'

27

Mrs Stephenson sighed. 'That's Lucy, I'm afraid. She's one of the well-meaning sort, but woolly-minded. She belongs to another century—the clinging vine type, rather pathetic. Her parents were separated so she went from pillar to post, never sure of herself, then in her Varsity days fell in with Dermid, who's given to looking after lame dogs. He's such a strong chap himself he positively attracts them. Same when he finally got away to boarding-school—in his high-school days—he used to bring up all the lonely boys.'

Veronica's voice revealed surprise. 'Varsity? I somehow had the idea his whole life had been lived up here.'

'Oh, it was Lincoln College, the agricultural one. Lucy was at Canterbury University. She seemed to fancy Dermid for a time, but then she fell with a bang for Theo. I think his more abrasive character fascinated her. But she hadn't a clue how to handle him. However, it looks as if she's learning at last. Well, you'll have to carry on with this mock-up of an engagement for a while. Isn't it fun?'

'Fun?' said Veronica hollowly. 'I feel I'm on a tightrope! Watch me every moment, Mrs Stephenson. I'd like to see this through successfully and speedily. It's bristling with hazards!'

Mrs Stephenson's grey eyes gleamed with laughter. 'I think it's a gorgeous situation. I wish something like this had happened to me when I was young.'

'Gorgeous? It fills me with horror—why——'

'Oh, come on. I'm sure you'll find compensations. Pretending to be engaged to a personable man like Dermid . . . looked on as one of the best catches in the district . . . *and* free. Perhaps like all of us when we were young, you're looking back to—to other attachments. Don't. There's only regrets in that. Enjoy every moment of this.'

Veronica blinked. What could the woman mean? And *free*. She couldn't imagine. She gave it up and found herself giggling. 'You know, this is the most surprising set-up. Perhaps it's as well Dermid MacBride's parents aren't around—they might easily not approve of a lark like this. But you're a good sport.'

The housekeeper's tone was indulgent. 'His parents

wouldn't turn a hair. They're in Australia for six months with their elder son who's a vet in Queensland. They're starting to retire from running Tordarroch. In fact they've relinquished it already, so Dermid is MacBride of Tordarroch now. Only Rhoda and Gregor haven't quite decided what they're going to do. But they'd have entered into this affair without turning a hair. A bay like this looks as if it would be nothing but heavenly peace, but the MacBrides and the Shaws weren't born for a quiet existence. The two boys were fair devils and Anne no better. Born to trouble, all of them, and I should know. I've been here since they were toddlers.

'They were fair rips as kids, reckless as grown-ups . . . not physically only but in relationships. Dermid's mother was terrified Lucy would be hung round Dermid's neck like the Old Man of the Sea, out of sheer kindness of heart. Bit odd too, when he's so tough in other things. And she knew Lucy would never satisfy him—she's too insipid. He needs a lass of spirit. Look, girl, we're nearly up to the house, call me Stephie as if you've been here before, and I'll watch you don't get tripped up. Later, when Theo and Lucy are settled down, I'll show you round the house so you don't put your foot in it, asking where things are. Though we can say you've only paid one other visit if you slip up. We've got three men on the place, two young ones and Algie, their cook. He cooks for the shearers too, with a bit of help from us, when needed. He's a good sport, Algie, and we've already primed him up about you. But we must make sure he knows you're Veronica, not Victoria. Trust Dermid to get mixed up with the names! Though I admit he didn't know if he was on his head or his heels at the time, with Lucy turning up like that. The line was terrible when he rang Anne, so that'll account for the mix-up with the name. I'm not surprised the phone's off now. We had a terrible old man nor'wester a few days ago—gale force really, and the line's been dicey ever since. Hope it's not for long so we can get the doctor up. It might be that the aunts' phone is okay. I guess Dermid'll get someone to ride across. Their name is Shaw, and they're Rhoda's aunts. She was a Shaw.'

Veronica felt wary but, she had to ask. 'Oh, and after she

married Dermid's father did her aunts come up here to live? If they weren't used to such isolation, that must have taken courage.'

She must know how the land lay. If they'd brought up their own mother's possessions, they were quite entitled to sell them.

'Oh, no, they've been here for ever. It's Shaw land, not MacBride, really. At least it started that way. That's why it's called Tordarroch, after the old clan stamping-ground in Scotland. The first Shaw here, Findlay, married, in Scotland, a MacBride woman, Euphemia. Rhoda, unfortunately, was the last of the Shaws, but history repeated itself. She took a trip to Scotland and married a very distant cousin on the MacBride side. She produced, among her three, Dermid, as like Findlay Shaw as if he was a reincarnation.

'That'll do you to be going on with. We'll go through this side door. It leads into a porch off the kitchen—place where I do my sewing and ironing. It's great boon, you don't have to put it away each time. Rhoda always kept a day-bed in it in case any of the children was sick and could be near her.' She pushed open the door and said, 'Oh, it's in use again. Now isn't that sensible?'

Theo Baring was on the day-bed, his face drawn with pain, and Lucy was beside him, bending over him anxiously, pulling up a light covering. Dermid, standing in the archway that led to the kitchen said, 'I brought him in this way as there are not so many steps. He took one look at the day-bed and wouldn't go a step farther. He's right too. He won't be as lonely and shut-off as in a bedroom.'

Veronica's stomach churned. She thought: He'll be right in the listening-post here . . . able to hear everything the rest of them say. She and Dermid were likely to be tripped up any moment. Heaven send that phone was working, they could get the doctor and it could be Theo would be removed. It wasn't working. She could have struck Dermid for taking it so calmly.

He took her hand and said, 'I've put something in your room I went you to see, love. Come along.'

The stairs were wooden and under the carpet they felt grooved in the middle where generations of Shaw and MacBride feet had pounded up and down. All the doors in the long passage above were open, and Veronica's eyes caught fascinating glimpses of antique furniture. Very much a family house, cared for and loved, with really mixed tastes and fashions as befitting succeeding years of change and personalities.

Dermid showed her into a dormer room that she knew instantly dated back to very early days, by its furnishings, and took her momentarily by surprise when he said, 'Anne said you liked everything of the most modern, but that's something Tordarroch can't supply. This house evolved. It wasn't bought and furnished completely to one set of values or fashion whims. Can you stand it? I'll pay you well, of course, if that's any compensation.'

It was ridiculous to feel ruffled. Veronica subdued the feelings, and said, 'I also like new experiences, not just furniture; could be I'll come to like this, and what matter anyway? Theo's disc has complicated things, but it can't be long at the longest.'

'No, as soon as we get in touch by phone, the doctor may come up by launch and take him back to Wanaka. Possibly to Cromwell Hospital, there's no hospital in Wanaka. It could have been worse. I'd not realised what a very good actress Anne was sending up. Thought seeing you hadn't been picked for the Australian tour you mightn't have been much good. But I found myself believing in your mother . . . objecting to her daughter imagining she could settle on a sheep-station that didn't even have a road at its door. I could practically see her living that socialite existence. But perhaps it was true, that you weren't inventing?'

He saw a deep dimple carve itself in the cheek nearest to him, the light of mischief flash into her brown eyes, 'My poor mama! She's a nursing Sister full-time, at the Princess Margaret Hospital in Christchurch, is the most completely *un*sporting person you've ever met, wouldn't know one golf-club from another, and if it comes to that, the only card game she can play is Happy Families with my nieces and nephews. I was proud of myself. It sounded convincing.'

He laughed back, then said, 'I hope you have a darned good memory. They say you need one to be a good liar.' Was she mistaken, or was there a drily derisive note in his voice? Well, what a hypocrite . . . he was the one who began this and she was lying on his behalf!

She said with an inflection in her voice he couldn't miss, 'Let's hope you have a good memory too, fellow-liar. You hatched the plot. I'm playing a part.'

He reacted immediately, 'Sorry, I didn't mean to offend you.'

Her lip curled. 'Of course you wouldn't. If I get mad I could blow the gaff. Better keep in with me, and if you don't like the glib way I responded, don't show it.'

An anxious voice behind them, Lucy's, said, 'Oh, dear, please don't quarrel over it! It would ruin everything. Veronica, if Theo got the faintest idea we'd cooked this up, he'd go berserk. And he'd never trust me again.'

They all three stared at each other. It was true. This thing was bigger than any petty disagreements they might have. Theo would have just cause for anger, not to say suspicions, if he had any idea that Veronica wasn't engaged to Dermid, that he had no fiancée, that there hadn't been a third person in the motel when Lucy spent the night there.

Also, only Veronica knew it would be even worse for Lucy and Dermid if they knew she had had no acting experience at all. Better not make a bad situation even a fraction more fearful, my girl, she thought, by telling them. They were scared enough as it was. Veronica felt lower than low.

She summoned all her courage, sorry for the real fear that peeped out of Lucy's eyes, gave a grin, said, 'We won't let you down, Lucy. Dermid and I will play it up like nobody's business. You've got your part to do, getting Theo better. I won't fight with Dermid, I'll be so affectionate I'll be positively cloying. Come on, *sweetheart!*'

So they went downstairs in a wave of genuine laughter that reached the ears of the big man on the day-bed, and he thought, despite gripping pain, that it was nothing to the desolation that had filled his being when he thought his wife had fled to the man he imagined she'd loved first.

He said to Lucy now, 'If only we could get the doctor up here, or even know he was coming! Why did that blasted phone give up now? He's a wizard at manipulation. It's like a miracle. One moment you're on the rack, the next in heaven. Ouch!' He caught his lip between his teeth and turned his head away carefully, embarrassed.

Lucy looked hesitant, then resolute. 'Theo, do you recall what the doctor said last time? The next time you put your back out he wasn't going to manipulate. That it seemed to slip out again so soon; that it would get to the stage where it did more harm than good because there could be nodules, calcified ones, that could snap off and cause even more trouble. That it might be a case of complete rest. You'd better be prepared for that.'

Theo looked appalled. Dermid, Veronica and Mrs Stephenson did too, but hid it. Theo said, 'But lambing's less than a month away, and there's the pre-lamb shearing. I've just got to be right. What did you want to remind me of that for? He said *weeks*!'

Stephie said firmly, 'That's quite enough of that. Lucy's facing facts, not hiding her head in the sand. The worst thing you could do, if he did manipulate, is to tackle either shearing or lambing. I know you always take a stand with the shearing, and a darned good shearer you are too. But it would be lunacy. Nobody's indispensable. You remind me of Dermid's father. He got taken with appendicitis on the eve of the onset of lambing, but we coped. We had to, but what a performance that man put on when the doctor put him on the launch! I told him he wasn't God Almighty, the world would go on just the same. And it did. It was a very good year, hardly any losses. By the time they got him to hospital he was so nearly a goner, he was glad just to be alive. Anyway, when we get hold of the doctor he just may decide to manipulate. Don't meet trouble head-on. You've got a full lot of men just now and a

jolly good head shepherd—he's my own cousin, so he ought
to be!' She grinned. Theo subsided.

Dermid MacBride said, 'I'll get you some pain-killers, man.
Veronica, come with me. You might as well make yourself
conversant with our well-stocked medicine chest in the
storeroom. We aren't often out of touch by telephone, but
even when we can raise the doctor, very often he just advises
us how to treat ourselves. If he's called out to these way-back
places, he's out of touch with other patients. And we use
helicopters only in emergencies. They cost a hell of a lot.
We're not bad at things like this. Old Algie put his back out
once . . . boasting to one of the shearing gang he could still
show him a thing or two, and we kept the pain down with
tablets and used a heat-lamp on him and later massage. We'll
do the same for you when you can stand it.'

Veronica was impressed with the range of medical supplies,
not only pills and potions, but also instruments. They made
her realise how self-reliant these people had to be, how self-
supporting, even if they thought the isolation nowadays was
nothing like it used to be.

Dermid nodded. 'We get a fair bit of practice attending to
animals. That's where my brother in Australia, the vet, got his
first love of his job. It means you've a fair idea how to go
about things if there's any accident to family or staff. Not that
we welcome experiences like that, but do it when we have to.

'I remember Edward Campbell, up at Belleknowes, when
his wife, Fiona, first went up there. She was only the
governess then but Edward was head over heels in love with
her. Despite the fact that the silly chumps were at
loggerheads. He had to stitch her arm and the poor blighter,
tough and all as high-country men are, was sick the moment
he finished. Well, let's put poor old Theo out of his pain.
These are pretty potent.'

They were. He fell into an exhausted sleep, with his wife
beside his bed. It gave them a respite. Stephie called them
to the kitchen, made a pot of tea and produced cookies.
They unwound a little. Dermid closed a sliding door to
cover the archway into the porch. He looked across at

Veronica, taking stock of him and getting caught at it. 'What is it?' he asked.

She made no apologies. 'I'm taking an inventory of your features, trying to assess what sort of a man I've got myself engaged to ... by sheer accident.'

He sat up more. 'Accident? Not really. It was plotted.'

Heavens, she'd nearly given herself away! She said vaguely, 'Well, you know what I mean. I'm playing a part, an impostor.'

His eye was keen. 'You sound as if you're reluctant. Can't you look on it as just another part? By the way, I must take you across to the men's quarters. They know about it, but they're as safe as houses and tickled pink, but it'll look more authentic if you know them by name, if they come across to see Theo. Come on.'

She studied him again as they drove off in the Land Rover. A very angular coppery-skinned jaw, overhanging brows, dark bronze, chestnut hair and the brilliant green eyes. Even the hairs on his hands, as he gripped the wheel, were coppery. There was a suggestion of whipcord toughness, muscular, a queer magnetism that somehow stirred her. She was very much conscious of him as a man.

She took herself to task. This was absurd, sheer physical attraction with a certain piquancy added because she'd been so suddenly flung into a romantic attachment with a strange man. She felt better for analysing it so soon. The man could be a positive clodhopper with a mind that couldn't rise above the price of wool and beef and have no appreciation of good music or literature. On the heels of that thought she had a sense of shame. What would Mother have said to that bit of intellectual snobbery? Oh, stop it, Veronica, you're only here for as long as it takes Theo Baring's disc to slip back into place, and if you can help those two dear old ladies realise their dream, so much the better.

She hid a grin. Maybe this man beside her would be so grateful to her for stepping into the breach he'd raise no objections to her helping them to dispose of a few pieces provided there were no sentimental reasons for retaining them.

A voice beside her said drily, 'I was trying to put you in the picture, but it seems to me you haven't registered a word I said about the landmarks you might be expected to know something about.'

She said hastily, 'Oh, sorry—that was stupid. I'm apt to go off into daydreams at any time. It can be disconcerting to people.'

'And quite dangerous in your profession.'

For a moment she was caught off-beam. 'My profession?'

'Well, wouldn't it be disastrous if you were taking the part of, say, Juliet, and when she leans over the balcony yearning for Romeo, she suddenly goes into a trance and doesn't hear him speaking to her from below?'

She couldn't help giggling. Daydreaming on a stage was too absurd. A thought struck her. A clodhopper, not interested in literature, had been her disparaging possible appraisal, and here he was quoting a scene from Shakespeare! Served her right. Nevertheless she said, 'I can't imagine me playing Juliet. She was too young. Wasn't she supposed to be only fourteen? I'm twenty-four. That's not one of my favourite plays, anyway. I like more mature heroines.'

Dermid rounded the Land Rover by some pines whose roots sprawled out on to the track and said reflectively, 'Possibly girls matured earlier than. They certainly married young. Perhaps it isn't my favourite either, because of the circumstances and the feeling you're left with of wasted lives, but the world would have been poorer if it had never known many of those lines. For instance, if Romeo had never said: "Night's candles are burnt out, and jocund day stands tiptoe on the misty mountain-tops." I've seen that so often here, especially at lambing-time, when you can long for a night to end.'

For an instant Veronica could see it … the dark, penetratingly cold night, lit with stars that suddenly burnt out and light struck the misty mountains above the sleeping lake.

She said, 'I feel abashed. I must read *Romeo and Juliet* again.'

Dermid laughed, said, 'I wish our old governess could hear

you. She'd think I'd benefited more than she hoped. She instilled in us a love of Shakespeare. She sometimes got the children from Belleknowes, our nearest station, to come here for a week so we could have enough characters to act some out. But tell me, what sort of characters are you cast for? And what is your favourite?'

She had a lightning recall of her one and only venture on to the stage. 'Well ... I think I could truly say it was when I played Dick Whittington's cat in a pantomime.'

He looked startled. 'And what made you enjoy that so much?'

A mischievous glint lit the pansy-brown eyes he looked into briefly.

'Because it had a mechanical device hidden under my black velvet paw that enabled me to twitch my long black tail and every time I did it a fellow in the front stall guffawed so loudly the entire theatre laughed.'

MacBride of Tordarroch's angular face relaxed even more. 'Well, at least you've a sense of humour.'

Despite that relaxation, something in his tone made her say tartly, 'What do you mean? At *least*?'

He paused noticeably before answering. Then, 'Just I thought from what Anne said you could be rather intense, dramatic, inclined to take things too seriously.'

She dared not take him up on that. She'd no idea of the character or the personality of Anne's friend. She ventured, 'Perhaps you thought of me as only taking dramatic parts. Spoiled the image, didn't it, admitting to being Dick Whittington's cat?'

He said slowly, 'No, I wasn't thinking of dramatic roles. I meant personally—in your private life. In fact I was a little apprehensive, but I was the beggar who couldn't be a chooser. I needed someone very capable of acting a part very convincingly and at a moment's notice. But I dreaded bringing anyone up here who might be all airs and capers.'

She suddenly felt touchy on behalf of Anne's friend, who, poor girl, could be anywhere. 'You've a very narrow notion of stage people. You might be surprised to find they're just ordinary folk with a flair for getting inside the skins of the characters they portray.' (What was there about this man that made her want to take him up, challenge his statements, his outlook?)

It glanced off him. He said, amusement colouring his voice. 'Like inside the cat's skin, for instance?'

'Yes. That's it. But your "at least" sounded quite derogatory to the stage in general. Qualifications can. Like one of my grandmothers. When I was a child she was always saying: "Veronica's eyes are her redeeming features." It used to make me study myself in the mirror and feel my face must be the plainest of all faces to need redeeming.'

At that he took a swift look at her and said, 'Then you must have been the ugly duckling who turned into a very beautiful swan.'

'Oh dear, I asked for that! Don't be absurd. Look, what building is this we're coming to? I'm supposed to be on a familiarisation trip.'

'It's the cookhouse. Down-lake these days the shearing is often done by contract and the farm owners don't have to provide a cook any more and the men go home every night either in their own cars or the Boss's transport. I should say men or women, because women rouseabouts are very common now. But up here, of course, where they must come by water they have to stay. Years ago they used to bring their own cooks with them, but we're lucky to have Algie. He's an institution. Cooks can be the bane of high-country sheep stations. They're often bad-tempered, unreliable, addicted to the booze, surly . . . they can upset a whole gang. Those are the shearing quarters beyond there in the shade of the chestnuts and poplars. The kennels are beyond. They're tough dogs really, but nights up here can be bitterly cold.'

Surprised comment was jerked out of her. 'I don't believe it! I've never seen flowers round shearers' quarters before.'

'Oh, that's Algie's doing. His hobby is gardening. The rocks were there, from time immemorial I suppose, left imbedded when the glaciers retreated at the end of the Ice Age, so he planted the alpine plants round them, the only things at first that would survive in this open stretch in the depths of winter, but he kidded round Dad to get the men to erect that shelter fence and he gets colour now all year round. Spring is later here, of course, so our daffodils are just coming into bloom, and the narcissi and the matcheads.'

'Matcheads?'

'Grape hyacinths to you, probably, but matcheads in Otago. They're pretty hardy. I'll tell him you commented on his garden. That'll soften him up. He didn't approve of an actress coming up here—told me I was crackers, that I'd come a cropper over this and make things worse, which did a lot for my confidence! But I had to give it a go for Lucy's sake.'

For Lucy's sake? How much did that mean? He had said to Theo that he'd never asked her to marry him, but that wasn't to mean he wasn't attached to her. Perhaps Theo had swept Lucy off her feet before Dermid had realised how much she meant to him. She was just the type to appeal to a rugged type like Dermid. He was certainly prepared to go to some lengths to rescue her from her own folly.

His other two single men occupied the best of the shearers' quarters, set in a long line, facing the north sun, with a good verandah running the full length, and with hitching-rails for horses at one side.

'In the old days, the rails were in front, but when Algie wanted his garden we moved them,' Dermid told her. 'He only tolerates them at the side because it means he hasn't far to shovel the manure for his precious roses and dahlias.' There were showers, a wash-house, a big communal room equipped with television and a pool table. Best of all, to Veronica's eyes, one end carried a row of bookshelves with hardbacks, magazines, paperbacks.

Algie eyed her suspiciously, but the other two were very teasing in their comments and were obviously enjoying what they looked on as a real lark. Veronica said seriously, 'I know it seems fun, but it's deadly serious for Lucy and, I imagine, to Theo. It could break a marriage if he got any inkling, or else set up nagging doubts in his mind. So be sure not to make remarks with double meanings when you're near Theo, won't you? We aren't letting on I'm an actress. I don't think he'd ever dream I'm only a bogus fiancée, but if he got the faintest suspicion, an actress would be really suspect. Don't even tell your girl-friends about this. It could get back to him.'

Geoff Lang grinned. 'Too right we won't! Our girl-friends mightn't mind the chief's real fiancée coming up, but an alluring actress incognito ... oh, no, we've too much sense. They wouldn't like the competition.'

She joined in their laughter, spread her hands out in deprecation. 'Well, the adjective was yours. I'm simply doing a job for as long as it takes.'

Geoff looked sly. 'If the boss knows his onions, he'll carry out the whole thing. What better way of convincing Theo than to wed you, eh, Dermid?'

MacBride grinned a little but said quite seriously, 'Hardly ... I can't think of anything worse than a MacBride with a wife who'd always be yearning for the footlights. Like the lady said, it's a job like any other. I'll make the pay worthwhile and give her a good holiday out of it, that's all.'

Very final-sounding.

As they drove off Veronica said, 'About this pay—I don't want any, thanks. I'll look on this as a holiday. I've always loved farm life. Though my childhood holidays were in places less remote, mainly in the Auckland province where we lived when my father was alive. Then we moved to Christchurch and didn't know many people in the country. It will be lovely to stay here till Theo's disc decides to behave, but I refuse to take anything for it.'

There was a silence. Had she offended him? Then he said slowly, 'But when you get back into work you'll be on your own this time. Nobody to pay—at least nobody to share the rent. Wouldn't it help to be earning now?'

What had Anne told her brother about this out-of-work actress's circumstances? It was awful to be in the dark. She said lightly, 'I don't usually find it hard to find someone to live with. When I'm in work I usually put a bit aside for the lean times.' She thought that ought to fit in with the precarious life of an actress.

He said, frowning, 'But if you take no pay it puts me under an obligation.'

She reacted strongly to that. 'That's frightfully starchy. I've never thought obligations and favours can be measured out equally. Sometimes one is a taker, sometimes a giver. I had the chance of free board and in turn can help you out by acting a part. Let's leave it at that.'

Dermid agreed. 'And if it helps you to a new start and a better way of life, that'll even the score.'

What could he mean? Perhaps in the eyes of MacBride of Tordarroch, life in a city, especially on the stage, couldn't compare with life up here. There might have been great ructions when Anne settled for the theatre. They rounded the track corner by the old stone stables, and the hills opened out on to a huge expanse of lake, shimmering like silver in the gathering duskiness of late afternoon, and with the over-lake ranges shrouded in a haze that was almost violet.

Involuntarily Veronica exclaimed, 'It's like fairyland! If I lived up here long I'd never want to leave it.'

Again the derisive note crisped his voice. 'A very rash and ill-considered statement from a professional actress. It's not always like this. There are times when winter storms blot out even the shoreline below us, when you can't see a hill, just a curtain of rain or great swirls of mist. When the bleating of the sheep is as eerie as a foghorn, when the wind howls like a banshee round our chimney-stacks, when the power-plant fails or it can't carry the load and we're reduced to dimness. When the weight of snow cuts the telephone wires, and the streams rise and the river. Believe me, you'd be yearning for the footlights and the audiences then.'

She longed to tell him how wrong he was, but she must do nothing to undermine his and Lucy's confidence. Then something struck her.

She didn't even try to keep the edge out of her voice. 'Surely you didn't think for a moment I was entertaining Geoff's idea? You're quite safe, MacBride of Tordarroch ...

it's a beautiful place, but one can pay too high a price for beauty of surroundings.'

She could have struck him when he laughed. 'I get the point. I'm not that way inclined ... or as vain! I suppose dramatising every incident comes natural.'

Veronica didn't answer.

As they came to a stop he said, entirely without rancour, which in some way annoyed her further, 'See the small inlet off this one, on the left? That's Distaff Bay, humorously called that because ever since the first generation there seemed to be maiden aunts living there. Chattan House is tucked into there. It's named for Clan Chattan. My mother's aunts live there, Maudie and Adelaide. Theo will suppose you've already met them. I'll tip them off that your name is Veronica, not Victoria.'

She felt a little alarmed. They might give the show away, if Gus hadn't managed to warn them. Though he'd do his best, she was sure. She decided to put a doubt into Dermid's mind about the contented life he supposed his great-aunts lived up here. 'It's a wonder when they didn't marry that they wanted to stay up here. Some people would have decided to travel, to see the world. Or head for one of the cities where they could see concerts, operas, plays.'

'Well, that's supposing they'd want to live your sort of life. So at present they're staying at Chattan House.'

She looked at him curiously. 'At present? What do you mean?'

He said hurriedly, 'A slip of the tongue. Forget it.'

'Why?'

'Because we have plans for them. They think Mother and Dad are buying a place in Wanaka to retire to. But in reality we'll be sending the aunts there. But we don't want them to know yet.'

A surprising anger sprang up in Veronica. How autocratic! MacBride of Tordarroch was actually going to order their lives ... all unknowing that they had dreams of their own. Well, some day it might give her great pleasure to tell him they were quite capable of ordering their own lives, and, through her, realising that dream!

Dinnertime, she thought, would be less of an ordeal than if Theo had been present at the table. He insisted, however, that Lucy should sit with them, and added, 'But leave the door open, so I can hear your chatter. I shan't feel so much out of it that way. Thank goodness this is a hard unyielding divan. Dammit, I can't even lift my elbow without agony. I'll go screaming mad if I have to be fed—it would be most humiliating!'

So they couldn't even be themselves for the meal. Veronica subdued her dismay and said with a chuckle, 'You big he-men are all the same! My brother burned his hands once and performed just like that because his wife even had to hold a straw for him to drink from. He said he didn't wonder small children were devilishly hard to feed, because when people shoved food in your mouth, they let bits dribble down and then most ungently scraped it off again.'

Theo gave her a grin, said, 'You paint a charming picture ... I thought you were all for romance and men being articulate and showing lashings of affection ... my image is going to suffer if I'm to be treated like a baby!'

Veronica's eyes twinkled. 'For a supposedly inarticulate man you have quite a knack with words, dear Theo. Perhaps being laid aside so helplessly is going to sharpen your wits and tongue. I daresay you thought a physical show of affection enough ... that Lucy ought to understand you adored her ... but now you're completely incapacitated it'll do you the world of good. You'll have to rely completely on the power of your voice to woo her.'

Theo stared, then gave a great bark of laughter and yelped as he shook. 'I don't reckon anyone ever talked to me in my life the way your girl does, Dermid. And I did think being demonstrative was all that was necessary. Well, I'll give it a go. There's nothing else to do. Dermid, you've made a good choice. Here's a woman who won't let you have it all your own way. That ready tongue of yours will be more than matched!'

'Watch it,' warned Lucy. 'I could get jealous if you praise Veronica too much!'

Theo looked astounded, then gratified. 'Well, it's a new sensation for you, love. I've wished often, you *would* show a spark of jealousy about me. I'm a jealous hound myself, but you seemed so lacking in it I thought you couldn't love me—well, not enough, anyway.'

The pale lily was a rose again. 'You've a lot to learn about me. Better not try to make me jealous—I'm the type to rend the other woman limb from limb if necessary!'

Mrs Stephenson was helpless with laugher. 'This whole day has been an eye-opener for me! Veronica, set the table. Good job I prepared most of the dinner yesterday when I knew you were coming. Theo, I know from Algie that you're going to have to have yours lying down. Good job it's chicken casserole—it's easy to spoon it in to you. Lucy can do it now. We'll shut the door to spare your pride, then she can sit up with us. There's just jellies to follow.'

While Lucy was doing this Mrs Stephenson betook herself to the back porch to get over her mirth. Veronica joined her, then Dermid followed them out and tried not to succumb.

'Mind,' he said sternly, 'no giving way in front of Theo. I admit it has its hilarious side . . . poor Theo, he doesn't know if he's Arthur or Martha! Veronica, you and I must sit up late tonight and make ourselves familiar with each other's backgrounds and pasts in case we get tripped up. No, of course they won't think us unsociable, they'll think we we're going in for a spot of amorous solitude.'

The green eyes met the brown. Veronica looked down. 'Instead of which,' she said, 'I shall be taking down notes.'

'Spoilsport!' said MacBride of Tordarroch.

CHAPTER THREE

IMMEDIATELY after their meal Dermid raised his head to listen. 'I can hear the aunts coming. I'm not surprised—they've been unable to raise us on the phone, so they couldn't bear to stay away any longer to find out how Veronica is.' He added, looking through the archway at Theo, 'Veronica's by way of being a firm favourite with my aunts. Good thing too. Instead of doting on me they're now doting on her.'

Veronica thought: Doting! When in reality you're by way of being a tyrant, not approving of them selling their own things, poor darlings, and plotting to get rid of them down to Wanaka!

Aloud she said, 'Did you hear the clip-clop of hooves? What sharp ears you must have!'

'Hooves? What made you think they'd be on horseback *this time*?'

His look was a warning. She was supposed to know them and their ways. She was out of Theo's sight, though he wasn't. She whispered, 'Well, I couldn't hear anything but motorbikes coming. I thought it must be the men going somewhere, like down to the bay.'

He lost no time hustling her out through the back door and round the house. When they were well away he said, 'I ought to have briefed you. 'It's Addie and Maude on their bikes.'

She faltered, 'On motorbikes? I didn't think they were riding horses, I thought perhaps they were frail, white-haired old ladies driving around here in a gig.'

He gave a bark of laughter. 'Wait till you see them! Mother's aunts are bang up to the minute. They may live surrounded by antiques, but they're anything but antique themselves. As for white hair! Maude had three months in Christchurch just after the war, learning hairdressing. She keeps it up, too. All the latest hairdressing magazines come to

45

Distaff Bay in our private mail bag. And they love their motorbikes. We've got a crib at Wanaka and when they holiday down there, we have to put the bikes on the launch. Flaming nuisance!'

Veronica blinked, her preconceived ideas about the old ladies shattered. 'I could have given the show away that time. And what do you mean . . . a crib?'

'Of course you're from the north. In Otago and Southland we call our holiday cottages cribs. You call them baches. My dear fiancée, you have a lot to learn. I'd have thought you had been in Dunedin long enough to have heard that one.'

'That word just never cropped up. Oh, here they come, just scorching along. Wouldn't one bike have done them, one riding pillion?'

He shrugged. 'They like to race each other along the paddocks and tracks.'

'You'd better fill me in on any other eccentric foibles of the people here. Anything I do fall down on will have to be excused on the gounds of just one visit here prior to this.'

As the two figures neared Dermid said, 'I thought it best for you to meet them out here so I can warn them I made a mistake over the name. It would never do to have them call you Victoria. Theo would really think that odd.'

Veronica felt petrified. The aunts would give her away. At that moment the bikes drew to dead level stops in front of them and two incredibly elegant and slim figures dismounted. They came rushing forward, called loudly and joyously, 'Veronica, dear child! How lovely to see you again!' Veronica wanted to laugh at the look on Dermid's face. 'How could you possibly know she was Veronica?' he demanded. 'I told you Victoria—I know I did. It was a bad line and that's what I thought Anne said.'

The taller one, Adelaide, struck a pose, said, 'We're psychic, that's what. We felt in our bones she must be Veronica. Besides, you're very bad at names. Most men are. They're always getting mixed up. Like our dad—he always called Genevieve Faulkner Vivienne. It used to infuriate her!'

He said, 'You're sidetracking me. You couldn't possibly

have known she was Veronica. Oh, I get it—Gus's Mollie managed to get you on the phone. It must be only ours that's out.'

Adelaide relented. 'No, Gus called in to see us. He spent only a split second. He thought it important enough to warn us in case we put our great big feet in it in front of Theo. Good of him when he was so late. Isn't it the most gorgeous fun? We're going to enjoy ourselves up to the hilt! We can talk about the wedding, planning for it, all sorts of things. We've thought of some already. We'll say it's going to be a lake wedding at Belleknowes station at their Chapel-of-the-four-winds. How does that sound?' Her eyes, as green as Dermid's, gleamed with mischief.

Dermid looked really alarmed. 'Play it down, you two! You'll over-invent. You've had no practice at this sort of thing, not like Veronica who's used to acting a part. It's no job for amateurs, so don't get too involved. You'd better not come over too much while Theo's here.'

Maude gave an anguished cry like a child deprived of a treat, protesting, 'Dermid, how can you? Like Adelaide says, it's such fun. I'm sure we'd have a talent for it. The ideas we've got already!'

'That's just what I'm afraid of. The simpler this is kept, the better. You need a good memory to be successful at this game.'

Veronica cut in. 'To be a good liar,' she said meaningly. 'That's what you told me, wasn't it, Dermid MacBride?'

Maude and Adelaide both giggled. 'He won't be able to stop us.'

Dermid said, 'Lucy has more sense than you two, and she's not noted for it, as you know. She's leaving it to us to set the stage and make the statements, beyond saying Veronica was at the motel with us, that I called her out from her boarding-house when Lucy landed in on me. I won't deny you a little bit of fun, but don't overdo it. Theo isn't to have the slightest suspicion Veronica isn't my true fiancée. I'm prepared to go to any lengths to keep him believing that. So if I see any signs of you carrying it too far, I'll send you to the crib!'

(Fancy saying that to one's great-aunts. As if they were naughty children!)

Maude showed no resentment. 'Well, if you want to be really convincing, dear nevvy, you could always marry the girl. Or put a notice in the paper, announcing the engagement and saying: "And the marriage will shortly take place." That's an idea.'

Dermid sighed. 'Come on and see Theo and get your visit over. Don't worry, Veronica, they'll soon simmer down. They know damned well there's a lot at stake for Lucy and Theo.'

All of a sudden Veronica wanted to laugh, thinking of the dear old ladies she had envisaged. Adelaide's tresses were dyed a beautiful copper and styled in an upswept sort of way. She must have used a lot of hairspray to keep it in that order on her ride. Maude was a fairly convincing sandy blonde, and the skilful use of eye-shadow made her blue eyes look as youthful as an eighteen-year-old's. They wore jump-suits as suitable for riding motorbikes, but still contrived to look extremely feminine. Their complexions, though undoubtedly not natural, were exquisite. How incongruous, yet delightful, up here at the back of beyond!

They were sweet with Theo, bending to kiss him gently, saying softly, 'Dear boy, how ghastly for you,' and 'Dear Theo, you'll be in the best of hands, and how fortunate it wasn't over Hawea. Lucy would have been run off her feet there. Here she'll have nothing to do but wait on you. With dear Veronica to help Stephie, it won't be too much for her either. Though I hope you'll be able to spend some time with us, Veronica. We *were* looking forward to that.'

That was Adelaide. Maude came in, 'You mustn't be selfish about her, Dermid. We want to show her all the family treasures, and tell her their history.'

Dermid played up splendidly. He flung his hands out in a gesture that looked like sheer exasperation. 'I think I'd have done better to have got myself a girl you didn't like at all, then I might have got more of her company. They even wanted to go down to Dunedin when she went home after her first visit here—to get to know her better, they said, but I told them she'd be far too busy.'

That was a mistake, though, because Theo immediately said, 'I've been meaning to ask, Veronica, what do you do for a crust?'

She dared not hesitate. He wasn't to know she was an actress. 'I work for a firm of antique dealers. I have for the last four years or so. Then just before I got engaged to Dermid I landed an assignment which is just wonderful. I'm a freelance buyer for them now, working on commission. It means I travel all around the provinces, tracking down treasures that but for my hunting could remain mouldering in old barns and lofts. Things that often date ever so much farther back than pioneer days, stuff the early settlers brought out from England and Scotland, Ireland and Wales.'

It was a good job Theo was looking at Veronica and not at Dermid. His face was a picture. Theo said, interested, 'You must come over to our place when I'm better—Hunters' Peaks. It's so remote no buyers have ever found their way up there. There's a whole top floor over the ancient stables where a couple of eccentric bachelors lived in the early days. It's full of what were reckoned throw-outs when some younger members of the same family took on the homestead. So between that and what the old chaps brought out from Scotland, some of it ought to be valuable. We could do with whatever it could bring. Lucy looked it over and decided she'd rather have what's already in the homestead.'

Veronica said slowly, 'You don't want to keep it for sentiment's sake . . . because it belongs to the homestead? Heirlooms to add to your own possessions for the family you and Lucy will have?'

Theo's face darkened. His tone was short. 'No. I haven't that sort of background. No property was dropped into *my* lap.'

Veronica said, interest lighting up her eyes, 'But it's all yours. You don't owe it to lucky circumstances. You don't have the galling experience that some people have. Like an estate I stayed on once up Auckland way. This man's father and uncle were always breathing down his neck to continue running the farm as they'd done in their day and generation. You may have a mortgage that would choke an ox, I suppose, but it's still all your own as you want to work it. You and Lucy can create a new dynasty and make your own traditions.'

Theo's own eyes lit up. 'I've never thought of that before. I've realised a dream I once thought might never come true. *I'm a high-country man.* Oh, if only I hadn't slipped this disc! Especially now.'

Dermid said, 'Theo, you might think it easy for me to be philosophical about it, but just imagine how much worse it would have been if it had happened in your first year when you were running it with just one young fellow and cooking your own meals to boot. I thought it was such a challenge I envied you. My particular destiny was always mapped out for me. I couldn't strike out on my own, particularly when Gerald didn't want to continue, and went into veterinary practice. There was a time when I didn't think I could take it.'

Theo looked amazed. 'I never looked at it like that. Frankly I envied you. I was dead jealous, if you like, even when I was a kid. When you used to come down to the Wanaka School at times, I looked on you as one of the silver-spoon-in-the-mouth brigade. I thought you had it made—son of a big estate.'

Dermid laughed. 'How little we know of each other! I envied every scholar in the class. You all of you belonged, while I was the outsider. I had my schooling done at home by a governess. I had the choice of boarding-school for primary days, but couldn't bear to leave home. I did later, for High School. But I felt all of you who lived in Wanaka and could go home at the end of the school day, yet have all the fun of team sport and mates calling in after school, had the best of both worlds. Boarding-school and, later, Lincoln, rubbed the corners off me, of course, but it's hardly been all honey or silver spoons. Now, do you want Lucy to give you a session with the heat lamp to loosen your muscles? I'll help her turn you. It'll be painful but beneficial. Out, the rest of you!'

'It'll give us a chance of a yarn with Veronica,' said Maude happily. 'Let's go up to Mother's little sitting-room for it. Take all the time you like, Dermid.'

They heard Dermid say to Theo as they went out, 'See what I mean, Theo? At least you have Lucy to yourself!'

The little sitting-room was situated dead centre of the top storey, and looked out over the inlet and across the lake, just visible now. It was going to be a cold night, with crystal-white stars appearing in a blue velvet sky devoid of clouds. They stood at the window, drinking it in. A late bird twittered from the side plantation, there was the occasional cough of a sheep, the sound of a little owl beginning to hunt, and across the far shore, so distant, the occasional headlights of cars on the road that beyond Makarora led through the rain-forests of the Haast Pass to the magnificence of the glaciers on the West Coast. It was so remote, so far-off, mysterious. Could Theo's place be even more remote?

Maude said, 'Everything's going to be all right—I feel that in my bones. Theo is losing his jealousy of Dermid. It was evident, even at their wedding, and was there, deep-rooted from when they were schoolboys. Theo's family were so poor, so improvident, but he's risen above all that. He was the only one with any get-up-and-go. That sort of background can cripple a lad. But what life does to you doesn't have to maim you for all of it. We *know*.'

Veronica wondered what they knew, how they knew. There was such conviction in Maude's tone. They looked so self-assured and there appeared to be generations of security behind them, and they'd probably lived here all their lives apart from holidays, untouched by the events and tensions outside their world of lake and sheep and cattle. Or was she being too naïve, too superficially judging?

She turned and said, 'What a delightful room—homely. You said it was your mother's sitting-room, then I take it you once lived in this house on the estate?'

Adelaide said, 'Yes, and this was a special place. The big kitchen-living-room downstairs was the core of the home with its fires at each end. We were a big family then, and those who wanted to talk gathered at one end and those who wanted to read at the other. Our power-plant was feeble compared to the one we have now. It was very temperamental, so we often had to use just lamps, though we had good ones. When we wanted music we went into what Father always called the drawing-room. We all played some instrument and we had a wind-up gramophone. We could toss the mats back and dance—no wall-to-wall carpets then. But we loved the living-room best. I can still see Father leaning back in his big chair, the picture of comfort, reading bits aloud to Mother, who was always knitting or spinning.

'But this was Mother's special place where she could talk to each of us, as we needed it, alone. She said no matter how large your family, every child needed a parent to itself at times when no other member of the family could butt in, laugh or criticise. So many of our big moments took place here, with our joys or our sorrows enhanced or lessened by it.' Adelaide's eyes seemed as if they looked backwards into the remembered scenes of long ago. 'Some people may have thought Mother's life restricted up here with a boat only once a fortnight, but she was the wisest person we ever knew. And though she took us on our own as a rule, she knew instinctively the one time when Maude and I needed each other's company. Forty years ago it was. But that's a story for another day. My dear, we must make the most of this time when Dermid's busy with Theo. Isn't it hilarious that he thinks you're an actress? We just said vaguely that one of these days a young friend of our Christchurch friends would be coming for a holiday. He won't think a thing about it.'

Veronica couldn't help matching those impish grins, but she sobered almost immediately. 'It's also vital not to give ourselves away. It was rather marvellous of Dermid, when he thought Theo and Lucy's marriage was at risk, to invent a fiancée he'd dragged in to chaperone them, but he thought it would soon be over, never that Theo, even if he did chase Lucy over here, would have to stay. We've done well, so far, but it's going to be a strain keeping it up remembering what we've said. That's why I said I was an antique buyer. I can be more natural about that. The only thing is that evidently Anne said about this Victoria that she liked everything of the most modern. I forgot that when I had to answer Theo about my job.'

Maude beamed. 'That was as great an inspiration as Dermid's in the first place. Dermid will never suspect you're really a buyer, so he won't get all het-up too soon about us disposing of these things so we can go to Italy. He'll think you're very clever to have invented a career so different from acting. Theo really might have got suspicious if he'd known you were an actress.'

Veronica said unhappily, 'I'd rather Dermid knew, but Gus seemed to think he'd have no confidence in my ability to carry it through if he thought I'd come into it through sheer accident.'

Adelaide nodded, 'And you could have put us in rather in awkward position because we'd been so vague about this girl, a friend of Christchurch friends, who might come up for a few days' holiday. As it is, if you find our things worthless, or if they won't bring us enough for our fares, then there's no harm done, no rumpus, no kerfuffle at all.'

Veronica passed a hand over her brow. 'But couldn't an estate like this stand the fares for a trip to Europe? I know farming is dicey these days with chancy markets and stockpiles, but I guess you've pulled your weight up here for years, and if you had enough for your accommodation, surely the estate could stand your air tickets? I've got a brother in travel business. He could advise.'

Maude said slowly, 'We thought this too. We were just going to ask when Dermid happened to say money was tight just now. He's usually so open-handed, but he must be feeling the pinch of falling prices and rising costs. We top-dress here by plane. Those costs are astronomical now, and the price of fertiliser has gone sky-high. We dare not cut down on it, production would drop. But that's not all. Dermid said he's got some project going that he doesn't want to mention till it's certain. So if it's something that will take all his spare capital—if any of it can be called spare—we decided against asking. We wouldn't worry him.'

Veronica pursed her lips considering it. It would be a case of ploughing back all you could into the land. The land had a greedy mouth, she knew. Pity twisted her heart. Already she felt drawn to Adelaide and Maude. Why must it be the land that took all and two darling old dears like this relinquished a dream? No, she *wouldn't* tell Dermid who she was, and she *would* value the stuff, and as long as they were Maude and Adelaide's mother's things, it couldn't matter to Dermid. They wouldn't be Shaw or Macbride heirlooms.

Dermid came into the room just as she asked them would they teach her to ride a motorbike. The tawny brows came down, the mouth tightened. 'Not on your life! I don't want any broken limbs, thank you. It might seem fun to you, but I don't want two patients on our hands, and especially with the phone out. That would be the end. It looks easy when you see Maude and Addie at it, but they've been careering round here on bikes since they were in their harumscarum teens. You can drive the Rover if you want some mobility.'

Veronica pulled a face at him. 'It's not half so exciting.'

'Excitement! I've had more than enough of that in the last month. What with Lucy turning up at my motel in the early hours of the morning, then running away from her husband over here, plus being stuck with Theo for weeks ... I'd like a placid existence for a while, thanks. It's the Rover or Shanks's pony.'

She couldn't resist pulling a face at him. 'All right, MacBride of Tordarroch, I bow to the head of the clan.' She executed a sweeping obeisance.

He shrugged. 'Take no notice of her, aunts. It's just her stage mannerisms cropping out.' Then he added sharply, 'And what's so funny about that?'

'Nothing,' said Adelaide hastily. 'It's just that we have a different brand of humour from you, and it seems dear Veronica shares it.'

Maude, not to be outdone, said, 'So clever of you, dear boy, to bring such a kindred spirit into the family.'

The dear boy boggled. 'Well, I know you two are born

romantics, but for goodness' sake don't take all this play-acting for real!'

'You ought to be glad we do it on-stage and off-stage,' Maude countered shrewdly. 'I mean, if we do it all the time there's much less chance of slipping up when we're with Theo.'

There was tartness in Veronica's tone. 'Not to worry, MacBride. You won't wake up some morning to find yourself married to me. This is a job to me, nothing more. I'm a career woman, and it's not a career I could carry on, tied to an up-lake sheep and cattle station.'

Two disappointed faces confronted her, then one, Maude's brightened. 'That's what a lot of modern girls say till they fall in love. Then it dissolves like morning mist on Wanaka. Anyway, girls who make statements like that usually only do it because they've been crossed in love. At heart girls are the same as they were in our girlhood. There's nothing new under the sun except giving it a different slant.'

Dermid said quite sharply, 'Maudie, that sounds mighty like probing. You can't expect Veronica to tell you her life-story within an hour or two of meeting you. Leave the girl alone. Now off with you. Veronica and I have things to discuss.'

Obediently they made for the door. Adelaide looked back over her shoulder. 'If she really wants to learn to ride a motorbike, you could teach her on the three-wheeler. That's safe enough.'

He waved a dismissing hand and they disappeared.

He went across to the window and stared out. 'Phew! As if the situation isn't complicated enough without those two getting all romantic and matchmaking! They can't resist it.'

'Well, like I said, MacBride, you're quite safe. But tell me, how is it that with their romantic leanings, their looks and their figures, they never married? Such gay personalities too.'

In an instant his features became all planes and angles and the green eyes had a flash of real pain. 'Same reason for both of them—a common one, belonging to their day and generation. World War Two. Their father, possibly wisely, thought they were too young to marry in the highly emotional atmosphere of those times. They weren't out of their teens. Their fiancés went away together and were killed together on the same day, on the slopes of Cassino.' He added, reflectively, 'Their mother had to tell them. In this very room.'

Cassino! Italy! That was why those two wanted to go to Europe. It was to be a pilgrimage to the graves of their war dead. Didn't this man fathom that? Surely over the years he could have guessed, made it possible. He'd looked sad for them, yes, but that wasn't enough. Veronica vowed that if anything she could do would bring their dream to fruition, she'd do it. Good job this man thought she was an actress, that she had no interest in antiques.

MacBride, drumming his fingers on the windowsill, said, 'I expect my forebear, their father, thought that if the worst happened, they'd get over their loss more easily than if they lost husbands, that they'd probably marry when it healed. They had their chances, I believe, but didn't take them. Possibly it's a pity—I don't know.'

Oddly, he swung round on her. 'It might seem strange to you, but don't curl your lip about it. Today's values are different, I know. But I don't find Maude and Adelaide comical. I admire them, *They* didn't settle for anything second-best or shoddy.' And with that he went out.

Veronica was left staring after him, completely bewildered. Why the emphasis? What was he so savage about? Was he more upset about this business that involved Lucy and Theo and himself than it seemed? Had MacBride of Tordarroch, that tough high-country man, really loved the gentle Lucy? Had Theo beaten him to it? He was certainly prepared to go to great lengths for her happiness.

She looked out over the great lake, darkly purple below. It looked so peaceful, but was life up here more serene than life in the rat-race of the cities? Perhaps that was a sweeping thing to think. Mother and Dad had achieved together a life of great serenity, as nearly as ideal as any marriage could be. Surroundings had little to do with it. Veronica went downstairs. Lucy might have need of her.

She looked into the annexe. Theo, doped with pain-killers, was lying very flat, very still, deep in sleep. Lucy, on a little low nursing-chair, had her hand in Theo's. MacBride, from the kitchen, was watching them, an unopened book upon his lap, his face quite unreadable.

Later, without disturbing Theo, speaking only in whispers, they put up a folding bed for Lucy. They had a last snack themselves, bade Lucy goodnight with MacBride whispering for her to call him if she needed any assistance with Theo that night. Mrs Stephenson intervened. Her voice was soft but firm. 'Oh, no, you don't! I'm the one you must call, Lucy. Theo, naturally, will hate being helped by Dermid. He'll not mind me, whatever.'

Stephie came into the room they'd given Veronica. 'Men haven't the sense of a new-born baby. I can just see Lucy in those frilly nighties she wears . . . and Theo, dopey with pills, looking up and seeing them together. It's your job and mine to save Dermid from himself. Lucy chose Theo and it's up to her to make her marriage stick. I've no patience with all this shillyshallying, creating situations where they don't exist. Well, you're a game lass to take this on and we'll be eternally grateful to you once we get that pair back over the other side of Lake Hawea and Theo's not gunning for Dermid any more. Sleep well, lass. I'm glad you're here.'

It was a long time before Veronica slept. It was all so involved she felt like cutting and running, but she couldn't. She must see it through. She felt it most for Theo's sake, to give him peace of mind.

Maude and Adelaide were sweet. If it lay within her power to provide them with the wherewithal for their fares to visit those war graves, she was going to do it. It was like Rupert Brooke had written, of that earlier war, '. . . think only this of me: That there's some corner of a foreign field that is for ever England.'

For Maude and Adelaide, there would be a spot on some Italian hillside that was for ever New Zealand. Their mother, that wise, loving woman of the little confidential room across the passage, would want them to sell her treasures so they might keep a tryst with their short, sweet past.

CHAPTER FOUR

SPRING sunlight struck through the curtains the next morning and bathed the walls with pale light. That sun would have risen from the Pacific nearly two hundred miles east of this lake, but it was lighting the grey and lavender foothills across it and flinging rose and coral banners on the snows of the peaks behind them. Last night, in one of the more tranquil moments, the housekeeper had named some of them for her, and Veronica had thrilled to the loveliness of their names— Mount Alpha, Mount Aspiring, Mount Avalanche, Fog Peak, Black Peak, so-called because the rocks at the apex were too sheer to hold snow and peeped through.

The air was so bracing she dared not linger at the open window. She'd had a shower last night and there was a wash-basin in her room, so she washed, donned serviceable and warm brown trews, with a coral turtle-necked sweater and tied her hair back with a coral ribbon. Many of the fears and tremors she'd known last night had disappeared. She was conscious now of a certain exhilaration in the situation. It was helping save a marriage and she had her own secret purpose in it, not just a matter of earning commission but helping two delightful characters attain their heart's desire.

MacBride himself was rather a problem figure, enigmatic, probably overbearing, but that too constituted a challenge. A month ago, though pleased she could now freelance, Veronica had been conscious of a feeling of staleness, a niggling craving for adventure. Well, if that had been it, she was certainly having it!

Sounds of activity downstairs made her hurry, but they'd surely excuse her being late for breakfast on her first morning. As she ran downstairs a door at the foot opened and Dermid appeared. He saw her and bounded up, the very epitome of the eager lover, saying loudly, 'Oh, hullo, darling. Up so early? Good for you! And you've got my favourite colour on—I mean my favourite on you. Coral or rose-pink for a nutbrown maid.' He seized her face between strong brown hands and kissed her, full on the lips.

She must react . . . she patted his cheek affectionately, said, 'Good morning, love. I meant to be earlier still, I didn't want you going out without me. I've so much to learn about the life up here, I don't want to miss any of it. How is Theo this morning?'

'He was just waking up as I came out of the kitchen. I'm afraid he groaned as he tried to turn. Lucy's in the kitchen in her dressing-gown.' He grinned, dropped his voice. 'Stephie's been playing chaperone. Lucy had crept out very quietly. The longer Theo slept the better, the less hours of pain to endure. A really bad back can be devilishly painful—I know because of Algie. We had to have him up here and he's so self-sufficient he made a shocking patient.' They heard a groan of real pain and came down into the kitchen, and looked into the porch.

Theo seemed furious. 'Makes a chap look a real calf, this. I've seized up.' Veronica said swiftly, 'It's only because you've hardly turned all night. Normally everyone turns without waking, but even though you were drugged, you'd be so conscious of the pain you'd stay rigid mostly. You'll limber up once you get moving even a little. You'll have to get to the bathroom and it'll be horribly painful, but groan all you like, it'll relieve your feelings. Don't crack on too hardy,' she added. 'I once worked as a nurse-aide and I know it doesn't help a bit to be too stoical. That side-hall has that ledge along the panelling halfway up. It'll be a godsend to you. I think Lucy's too short for supporting you. What about Dermid and me? We won't help too much, that could hurt you. Just use us as props and make your own pace.' The agony was such that huge drops of perspiration stood out on his forehead, but they made it and at the bathroom door Veronica left him to Dermid's ministrations.

They came back, inching along. Theo said, 'I couldn't possibly sit up in bed to eat. I admit I'm hungry, but how the dickens . . .? This is much worse than last time.'

Mrs Stephenson said, 'I knew it! Algie was the same. You're going to have it standing at the kitchen dresser—it'll give you a rest from being flat on your back. It's too humilating to be fed in bed, isn't it?'

A reluctant grin mellowed Theo's grim countenance. 'I'll say . . . one sees oneself as a tough hero and it's deflating to the ego to be babied. But you folk seem to understand.'

'It can happen to anyone,' stated Dermid simply. 'Who should know better than I? At Lincoln I managed to damage both hands in some machinery, and they were swathed like an Egyptian mummy. My crowning humiliation was that one of the nurses in the ward was the very girl I'd been trying to impress most at the local hops. She belonged to Lincoln township. At twenty you're much more vulnerable than at our age, Theo. Talk about embarrassed! Now take it easy to that dresser. The porridge, Stephie, while I cut up his bacon and egg. Even the movement of your arms gets you, doesn't it?'

'Sure does, especially the right arm, but I can manage a fork or spoon with one hand. Thanks, MacBride.'

Definitely the tension was easing between them.

'Due solely to your presence here,' said Dermid later, as he manoeuvred Veronica outside, ostensibly to go round the sheep with · him. As they'd gone out she'd heard Mrs Stephenson giggle and say fondly, 'I've never seen him like this before over any girl. He can't bear her out of his sight! She's certainly the right one for here—loves the outside work and is very good in the house as well.'

'Are you?' asked Dermid now as they set off together in the Rover.

'Am I what?'

'Good in the house? If not you'll have to polish up your skills. Never do to let Stephie down.'

She said cautiously, 'I don't know about good, but I like keeping house. Mother saw to it that we all did our share, and though I hated some jobs to start with like cleaning the stove or doing windows, once you've mastered it and disciplined yourself not to dodge those chores, they lose half their sting.

Trouble was we all liked cooking, even my brother, but hated washing up after. We all liked vacuuming but not dusting, and nobody enjoyed dishes. But now for some reason I like clearing up, especially after the evening meal, when you know soon you can settle down in front of the fire.'

'Depends who you're settling down with, I suppose.' Then his brows twitched together as if the thought didn't please him. Why? Had there sometimes been people up here who caused discord? If you had extra help perhaps you had to endure having them in the bosom of the family whether they were kindred spirits or not. Then he said, 'Sounds as if, essentially, you're a home-maker. It's quite different from housekeeping. Some girls are like that, I believe—so keen on having a home, they settle for second-best.'

Veronica was surprised. 'Surely not these days? You can have a flat of your own, and make a home out of it, without marriage.'

His tone was dry. 'Yes, how true.' She couldn't fathom his inflections. Were they disapproving? Had it anything to do with Lucy?

She didn't know quite where to go from here in this dialogue. She said, 'I do hope Lucy makes a go of it this time. She's got the ball at her feet. She's doing it for a husband, the man she loves. She ought to be careful from now on, or Theo might turn for comfort to someone else.'

She was instantly aware of a withdrawal in him. 'I hardly think so. I know relationships are more easily broken these days, but high-country men have a habit of being faithful.'

She said slowly, 'That sounds rather smug—a holier-than-thou attitude. It's lumping people into categories ... the goodies live in the country, the baddies in the city. I don't like it.'

She didn't know if he shrugged, as if her opinion didn't matter, or if it was just the jolting due to the huge paddocks they were crossing. But presently he said, 'Sorry, I didn't mean to sound pompous. Just that ... oh, it seems easier in cities to find someone to take a deserting wife's place. Which can be a pity, because if replacements come so easily, it can cut out the chance of a reconciliation. I just thought that some girls so desire a home, even if they keep on with their careers, a home with a man as the centre of it, they're only too willing to take second-best.'

Veronica gave it thought and finally said, conscious he was waiting for a comment, 'I think you're making this almost a personal issue. It sounds to me as if you're thinking of some specific situation. One you don't like. So, as it seems to involve a third person, perhaps we should leave it alone. It doesn't matter to us, anyway. We're just acting a part. None of it's for real.'

'I suppose so. It's just that these peculiar circumstances have thrown us in very close involvement. I had the idea that a little discussion on our values, I mean the things we each value, might help.'

'I doubt it. Even at the longest it won't be for long. As far as I'm concerned, it'll be a pleasant fun-making interlude in my life. Though I promise you I'll never talk about it to anyone—it's too small a world. What's the drill, by the way? We get Theo better, ship him back to the other side of Lake Hawea; I take off again, then, when a suitable time has elapsed, we let it be known that after all, Mother was right and I'm not suited for the life of an up-lake, high-country sheep station.'

'How very prosaic! I think we could stage something more spectacular—some great misunderstanding.'

'Oh, no. Misunderstanding would be cleared up in all probability. That's no reason for a permanent rupture.'

'Not necessarily,' said Dermid drily. 'Some never get cleared up.'

'Do you mean they do in novels but not in real life? My mother would say time usually reveals the right.'

'No, I don't mean that. I'm not as cynical as all that. Besides, one estate up-lake is a living example of that. There's an ideal couple at Belleknowes Station—been married for years now and still in love. Fiona and Edward Campbell. Appearances at their first meeting in Scotland were dead against her. But here, in the solitudes, things sorted themselves out and Edward found out the truth.'

Veronica turned to him, eyes a-sparkle, 'How delightful! But with Theo we don't want him to find out the truth. This fabrication of ours seems to be the only thing that will save that marriage, otherwise he'd always have doubts about that night. As such we don't want to risk complicating it by staging some mythical and dramatic clash between us. He's probably so grateful to us, just now, that if we did he'd try to patch it up. Besides, I can't imagine what we'd have a dramatic clash about.' She looked mischievous and added, 'But then I haven't your imagination in the first place.'

'I don't know. I thought you did pretty well with your mother's aversion to our marriage and your supposed career as a buyer of antiques. We could think of all sorts of things to part us. Let me see . . .'

She said sarcastically, 'Well, for sure I won't be able to think you're double-dating me, up here leagues apart from any other woman bar Lucy. Unless, of course, I discover you have a woman tucked away in the dark fastnesses of Lochnagar!'

Dermid rattled over some cattle-stops leading to another great empty paddock. 'Lochnagar? Oh, you'd better make it nearer home . . . Lochnagar is even deeper in the ranges than Skipper's Canyon. Our station doesn't boast a helicopter like Minaret and Belleknowes do.'

'What can you mean? I didn't even know New Zealand *had* a Lochnagar. I've only met it in Byron's poem and Prince Charles's book for youngsters, *The Old Man of Lochnagar*.'

'I'll plead a matching ignorance. I didn't know about Byron's, though I know our Lochnagar is named after the one in Scotland. How come you know it?'

'My grandmother was a gay Gordon and Lord Byron was George Gordon. His . . . and our . . . ancestors suffered in the Stuart cause. The heartbreak of those times was handed down from generation to generation. My grandmother's grandfather handed those stories down and I loved the poem she taught me.

' "Ill-starred, though brave, did no visions foreboding
   Tell you that fate had forsaken your cause?
Ah! were you destined to die at Culloden,
   Victory crowned not your fall with applause:
Still were you happy in death's earthy slumber,
   You rest with your clan in the caves of Braemar;
The pibroch resounds to the piper's loud number,
   Your deeds on the echoes of dark Loch na Garr." '

She appreciated the short silence he gave that. Then he said, 'You must meet Fiona Campbell. To hear her play and sing the Skye Boat Song is to hear the echoes of that ancient tragedy.'

A strange tremor ran over Veronica. How many men would you meet these days, with a feeling for ancient griefs, even if in him too ran the blood of Scottish forebears? The next moment she was saying in a puzzled voice, 'Fiona *Campbell*? Lamenting the Bonnie Prince?'

He laughed. 'I should have said she was born a Macdonald. But ancient enmities dissolved when she fell in love with Edward—as they should. The aunts thought it most romantic. Fiona said she was reconciled to marrying a Campbell when she found that Edward's mother belonged to the other side too and had made up for it by calling her son Charles Edward. Though he was always known as Edward. You won't be able to turn *me* down because we were on opposing sides. The MacBrides belong to the Macdonald clan. I haven't a guilty secret tucked away at Lochnagar, so the breach will have to come through you. I'll discover something about *your* secret life and ditch *you*.'

'You'll do nothing of the sort!' Veronica retorted. 'We'll keep it simple. No modern girl would break an engagement because it didn't please her mother, but I could, after staying here longer, come to the conclusion that I missed the city lights too much.'

'The footlights,' he corrected.

'But you've wiped the footlights. Theo isn't to know about them. And I've set myself up as an antique buyer. Now, stop all this nonsense. This paddock we're coming to has a gate, not cattle-stops, and I know the golden rule, the passenger opens all gates. Right!'

She sprang out, tall, slender, curved, her nut-brown hair swinging away from her eyes, held back the gate, closed it, then sprang in again. The keen air, mountain-fresh, had whipped up the colour in her cheeks; what a life this was! She wondered if she should give up her search for a permanent flat in Dunedin and find a holiday house to rent in one of these glorious lakeside townships. Surely the whole area of the Lake County would be a happy hunting-ground for neglected treasures? 'Let's keep off the too-personal now and advise me on the size of the station and what you carry,' she said, 'I could be expected to take an interest in my prospects even if they think I'm marrying for love.'

'You mean not just for security?'

'I mean that we're creating the impression that we're rather bowled over, for Lucy's sake.'

'And Theo's,' added Dermid. 'That impression's got to be good, that it's going to last. Don't give any more ideas that your mother has doubts. I want Theo to think this is for keeps. He must believe I was genuinely terrified of losing you that night in Dunedin.'

'Might I remind you we were supposed to get off the too-personal? How large is Tordarroch? How many sheep do you run? How many cattle?'

'It's forty thousand acres, much of it mountain slopes with grassy plateaus and basins where the sheep feed in summer. At present, of course, with lambing so near, the ewes are farther down. We do some riding, not much. Our autumn muster, of course, bringing them down from the tops, has to be done on foot, in blocks. We lamb later up here than near the coast. We used to start on October the eighth, but now we do a pre-lamb shear early in October, and lamb later in the month. Wethers are shorn in early November so they can be put straight back to follow the receding snowline to their high summer grazing, the alpine basins. We run eight thousand merinos and about four or five hundred cattle, mainly to diversify our markets because world markets are so tricky. They're all Herefords here.

'Look, I'll show you something that'll give you an idea of it. You know about the men going out on different beats, I suppose? Going out from the top hut, each with their own dogs, then they start bringing them down, working their own blocks, till they begin to converge. It takes days, though I've got splendid men. It finally looks like a moving mass of white, like pouring rice down the gullies, then spreading out as the ground levels.'

All this time they were crossing the vast paddocks towards a track that turned the shoulder of the hill and the terrain sloped down. More gates here, then a stand of trees, mainly gums, with a more defined track through them, then, coming out into brilliant sun again, they headed towards a gully that cleft the ground far below them.

'There'll be a river down there, Dermid? I can't see for the bush.'

'Yes, the Chattan River. It's very shallow just now. The suns aren't strong enough yet to melt the snows back in. Its headwaters are away back. It cuts a mighty swathe across our land.'

'How do you get the sheep across for shearing and so on?'

'Good question. That's what I want to show you.' They came out on the verge of the cut, and ahead of them the track dipped steeply to a narrow swing bridge.

Veronica gasped. 'You have to get sizeable mobs . . . across there . . . with every chance of a jam if they panic. They could pile up and smother.'

'You've got it in one. It's very tricky. We brought seven thousand over last autumn muster. We timed them, and it took an hour and a half. Then we had a straggle muster after that. Don't want too many long-woolled sheep the following year—they have a double coat then. We always get some. These mountain sheep are cunning devils.'

'And how do you get your wool away?' she asked. 'I mean the number of bales you'll get from a flock your size will take some shifting. There's no steamer on this lake, like on Lake Wakatipu.'

Dermid looked at her with respect. 'You must have retained a lot of knowledge from those childhood farm holidays. I didn't expect an actress to make such a sensible remark.'

Her lips twitched. 'Actresses are made, not born. Could be they're interested in a few things other than their own careers. What about your sister Anne? What could be more different from her former life than her life now?'

'Touché! I cry pardon. That was stupid, enough to make you think I'm a hidebound horny-handed son of the soil.'

'I'm not as silly as all that. I've already appraised the books on your shelves—new and old. You don't keep up with only farming lore. You've got a fine variety—autobiographies, novels, world affairs.'

She thought he looked pleased. 'Once reading was pretty well all that kept Tordarroch in touch. In the early, pre-radio days, I mean. So it became an ingrained habit, from generation to generation. Nothing quite takes its place. All things come late to this remote spot. But now, even though we still haven't main power, we have television, though only the last few years and then only one channel. But what's happening in both Northern and Southern Hemispheres comes to our ears and eyes as it has happened—a great advantage when you're trying for labour up here, especially for women. We're very lucky with our married couple, Tom and Rena. They'll be back next week, complete with a new baby daughter and their four-and-a-half-year-old son. They timed the new arrival well, to be back here for lambing. I gave them two months off.

'Rena's parents live in Nelson, so she went home a month before the baby was due. They went up through the Haast Pass and the West Coast, and had an extra month to get the baby established.'

Veronica knew a feathering of alarm. 'Will that mean two more people to be let into our secret? Too many know now.'

'No. Since ours is supposed to have been a whirlwind affair, those two can just think it happened in Dunedin soon after they left.' He looked at her shrewdly. 'This situation really scares hell out of you, doesn't it? I think you're thinking of the gossiping in stage circles. I know, because of Anne. It's very different up here, Veronica. Stephie and my men are loyal to the core. They'll take no chance of a leak upsetting Theo's marriage.'

They were still leaning over the wooden rails that barricaded the approach to that frail bridge over the awesome gash of the gully. Veronica found Dermid surveying her, and inexplicably she felt warmth flow into her cheeks. His voice was kind. 'I expect it's all horribly strange to you. Makes you unsure of yourself, specially being involved in a charade like this. You've suddenly cut yourself off from all that's known and familiar and you're probably plain homesick. Is that it?'

Their eyes met. His seemed searchingly keen. Why?

She answered uncertainly. 'I don't know that I am, Dermid MacBride. I can go back to Dunedin any time I'm no longer needed here. I kept my flat on.'

The copper brows came down. 'Someone in it?'

'No. My flatmate moved out, went away, but there was no reason for me to move.'

'No, of course not. Unless . . . you wanted a complete break with—with your former life.'

She felt puzzled. 'Oh, I don't. This is just an interlude—a part to be played, then over and done with. Incidentally, I must be careful not to mention the flat. I said boarding-house to Theo.'

'Right. Now I'll take you to the aunts. It's just a couple of miles from the homestead, a bit longer from here. They may want us to stay for lunch.'

She said firmly, 'I'd like you to leave me there. I think I'll find it restful away from Theo.'

Distaff Bay she found utterly charming. It was a small inlet with a tiny jetty of its own. A dinghy was the only boat moored there.

This house looked much older than the homestead. 'Yes, it was the original home,' said Dermid, 'built here because it had a natural beach and they had no jetty at first. They could just beach the whaleboat on the lake shingle when they brought their first provisions up. There was enough native bush here for shelter from the tearing winds that used to whip down the lake from the mountains and they came in summer, so they lived under canvas a couple of months till they could turn the tussocky sods to make the first hut that sheltered them. You can see they used the natural resources from the beginning. The house itself is part stone. The first Shaw had been a stonemason in Scotland, but haste dictated that they had adequate shelter immediately, so it was sod. That part is just a storehouse now. The rest is part stone, part timber. If you go close you'll see the marks of the saws on the wood. The planks were sawn from trees placed across a pit, one man below, one above.'

It was a darling house, preserved through generations in a remarkable way, even to the wooden shingles on small dormers peeping through the roof. 'The rest of the roof explains the good state of the house. It was of Welsh slate. The first cottage had to be roofed with reed-thatch, but later Findlay Shaw managed to get a load of Welsh slate that had been ordered for a Dunedin merchant whose business had failed before it arrived. But I'll be boring you. Anne said you liked all things bang up to the minute.'

An irrepressible chuckle escaped Veronica. 'In answer to Theo, I've saddled myself with a career in antiques, so any gen I may seem to have could be valuable. Brief me on everything. I dare not ask too many questions at Tordarroch. So if your aunts have any treasures comparable with those over there, you'd better make me seem knowledgeable about such things, so I can impress Theo. But to save your time, the aunts could do it.'

They came running out all eagerness. No doubt visitors were an event. They kissed Veronica warmly, then drew them in. The rooms were small as pioneer homes were apt to be, with materials so scarce or hard-won from their environment, but they were also numerous, no doubt to accommodate the large families of those days. It was chock-full of treasures, as she saw at a glance. She only hoped Adelaide and Maude knew exactly which were Shaw and MacBride heirlooms, and which were their mother's. When this ploy of being engaged to MacBride was over, she'd have to tread very warily about the business. They took her up the narrow spindle-banistered stairs to the bedrooms. Beside Adelaide's bed, on a small table that was early Victorian, with a pouch beneath it in faded brocade, meant to hold embroidery silks, was a picture of a young man in uniform, a lieutenant's uniform of World War Two. In Maude's, on a three-quarter Scotch chest, was *her* lost love's photograph, in a private's garb. Suddenly Veronica's eyes blurred. These boys should have been here now, not have lost their lives in the horror and heroism of Monte Cassino. They should have been grandfathers, full of years, with golden memories behind them of life with Adelaide and Maude. It stiffened her resolve to see that these two women were able to visit the spot where they were laid. It would mean trouble, of course, with MacBride of Tordarroch, but clinging to possessions was no substitute for realising a dream.

The dining-room, long and narrow, with small-paned French windows that gave access to a small paved courtyard beyond its verandah, made her catch her breath. This furniture was pure Regency. There was a D-ended dining-table, probably made about 1800, in the middle, and in a recessed angle that jutted out at the far end was a Regency breakfast-table, small, exquisite. The chairs, too, were Regency, with sabre legs, beautifully curved.

Delight made her lower her guard. '*They* couldn't have been brought up here by dray and then whaleboat, surely? There isn't a scratch! They're pure Regency. And Dermid said the first folks had only a few treasures to bring!'

Adelaide began to say something, hurriedly, but Dermid cut in, 'Oh, no, they were brought here from Christchurch, much later, by my great-grandmother, Maude and Addie's mother. *Her* forebears brought them out from the family home in Wiltshire.'

Veronica was struck dumb with dismay. Of course . . . the aunts' mother was also a forebear of Dermid's. Why hadn't she thought of that? So, even though they'd been left to her daughters, Dermid could quite understandably regard them as belonging here. Besides, *these* should never leave Chattan House. They were so right here. This room would look bereft without this exquisite furniture. Let's hope other pieces, less beautiful, could be more easily spared.

Dermid too was struck, but not dumbly. His voice was bewildered. 'How on earth did you recognise it for Regency?'

Veronica saw alarm flicker over the aunts' faces, but Dermid didn't notice, his eyes were on her. She achieved a laugh, a shrug, and said with mock-pride, 'Didn't you see that last night I took that book on antiques from your shelves to bed with me? I swotted it up madly, in case Theo tripped me up asking what was what in the furniture at Tordarroch House. I thought I'd better display some gen about makers and periods occasionally. I've got a very retentive memory. It was Truus Daalder's book on New Zealand Antiques.'

Dermid said warmly, 'Good girl, keep a step ahead.'

This undeserved praise stabbed at Veronica with a sense of shame, hot and unwelcome. She had taken the book, but just to check up on a bureau she'd noticed in the homestead. But now this easy way of slipping into deceit was getting to her. Yet didn't these two darling women deserve something for the ungrudging years they'd spent serving this isolated property on the shores of Lake Wanaka?

The aunts wouldn't hear of Dermid returning for lunch to the homestead, so they had it in the kitchen of Chattan House. Outside the east and south windows was a never-ending chorus of birdsong. Maude put her head on one side. 'The blackbirds and thrushes are beginning their mating songs. They go from dawn to dusk. You have to go further from the house to get the *tuis* and bell-birds and the wood-pigeons, into the native bush up the gully at the back, but in summer they're thick round the flax-flowers, the red-hot pokers, the blue agapanthus, dipping their brushy tongues in the florets in search of the honey they love. Occasionally they come next month, when the *kowhai* and the flowering currant are out. In winter they come for jam and water that we put in bowls on the bird-tables.'

'It's not just jam and water,' said Dermid sternly, attacking a delicious plateful of land-locked salmon with potato cakes. 'Last month when the stores came up I was bamboozled to find a dozen bottles of raspberry cordial in with the soft drinks. Even young Timothy prefers lime and orange to raspberry. These two spun me some ridiculous yarn about liking variety. The fact is, I copped them later, adding it to the birds' sugar and water—said the birds had got so used to the elderberry jelly and water they'd been putting out, they weren't drinking it when it was colourless!'

Adelaide looked sheepish. 'Well, it was practically an economy to give them that elderberry jelly. The apples we'd put with it weren't green enough and it didn't set, so we used it up that way. We were brought up not to waste. The birds just love the raspberry. But I promise you, Dermid, next year we'll preserve elderberries just for the birds.'

Dermid grinned. 'Okay ... but you know darned well you can twist me round your little fingers ... you'll mesmerise me into putting more cordial on the next order. I know!'

Could they twist him round their little fingers? How did that tie up with a selfish nephew? An autocrat? When the time came to reveal all, Veronica had an idea that she was going to to be torn with longings to make their dream come true, and her conviction that these pieces belonged here.

She felt more natural when Dermid left. The aunts had persuaded him it would make their day if she could stay a couple of hours. 'We can bring her back pillion on one of the motorbikes. We've got a spare helmet.'

'Right, but no larking. No whizzing down hill paddocks just for the fun of it. No need to go round any of the sheep— the men are seeing to that. And no showing her how to ride one!'

He took off. Adelaide said, 'Now we can relax. Isn't this fun? We nearly died when Gus said he'd kidnapped the wrong girl! But I'm sure it's meant to be. This Victoria couldn't possibly have done it as well as you. For a start, she's probably not the sort Dermid would be likely to fancy, and she may never have had a farm holiday in her life and would have been bored to tears and shown it.'

'Oh, hardly,' objected Veronica. 'She's a qualified actress. I'm certainly not.'

'You ring true. Besides, I've an idea she was only going to be able to stay a couple of weeks at the outside. Of course then we thought Theo would come raring over here, yank Lucy off on the lake, stupid girl that she is, and Victoria would stay a week or two just in case Theo rang up from his place. Then later, they'd break the engagement. I wonder what's happened to her? Maddening not having the phone working. Perhaps poor Mollie, Gus's wife, will offer to give her a holiday there, to compensate. Trust Gus, he was always a prankster, he was enjoying this up to the hilt. He'd taken a great fancy to you.'

'Mollie must be a sport,' said Veronica, bringing up her left hand to study her ring, 'to actually lend her engagement ring! Stephie suggested I take it off to do the dishes last night. I said fondly, as if I couldn't bear to, "I've never taken it off since Dermid put it on," but what I meant was I was plain terrified I might lose it. And when we've done these dishes, I'd love to browse in your cabinets. What I see there makes my mouth water! Neither of you must part with a thing unless you get it valued by someone else too. I can just imagine some of these freelance buyers—the untrustworthy ones—who travel round the country picking up things for a song, scooping the pool here.'

'We aren't likely to do so. We weren't born yesterday.' Maude looked too virtuous for anything. Something made Veronica suspicious. She asked, 'Have you ever been diddled by one?'

Guilt registered on both faces instantly. 'Yes, but long ago. We wanted new motorbikes. We could have asked Dermid's father, but he'd just sent all three children off to boarding-school. Everyone was off to a field day in the Cardrona Valley, and we were here on our own, when a private launch called. A red-faced man in a brown suit was on it. He looked like a film character—you know, bookmaker type. We should have known, but we got carried away. The prices seemed so good for such small pieces. And as I told Gregor, Dermid's father, we did stop when we got the price of the bikes; he ought to have been glad of that. But he wasn't.'

'What sort of small pieces?'

'Oh, just a bit of Spode and Worcester, one or two Chelsea figures—we've never really been fond of Chelsea—some ruby glass, and one or two silver serving spoons. Really, you could hardly see where the pieces had been. The cabinets are far too crowded even now.'

That was true, but it had been a sin to let the stuff go for what would have bought a couple of motorbikes all those years ago. This transaction was going to be horribly complicated. Especially when she herself had got so involved with the family. 'Adelaide, you said this girl was *only* to be here a couple of weeks. For the love of Pete, how long do you think I'll have to stay?'

Adelaide was maddeningly matter-of-fact. 'When Algie put his back out the doctor wouldn't manipulate for the same reason, and it took seven weeks. Or was it nine?'

Veronica's eyes bulged. 'Oh, no! Seven—or nine! I can't keep this up that long! Yet I wouldn't dare leave right away even then in case he got to know.'

Maude backed Adelaide up. 'Algie was in severe pain for a month. Even the next three weeks he was bad enough. Though of course he was an older man. I'm afraid you're stuck here, dear. You aren't the sort to let us down.'

Veronica said limply, 'I suppose not. But I've a living to earn, on commission.'

Maude waved an uncaring hand. 'Write to your firm from here. I'll give it to Gus instead of you having to put it in the mail-bag where Dermid might see it. He'd not only have less confidence in your being able to act it out so long, if you weren't an actress, but he'd be livid if he knew you were interested in Mother's antiques. Better he doesn't know till the very last. Better let your folk know too. Just that you've been invited to take a break here.'

None of this was making Veronica feel any better, but she couldn't help loving the aunts. She got completely fascinated with the contents of the cabinets.

She said soberly, though, 'You'll have to be extremely sure of which are your mother's. There must be no mistake about that.'

She didn't feel like saying, yet, that in a sense they also belonged to Dermid, as their mother's great-grandson. But if they had been legally gifted to the two girls, perhaps they had a right to sell them. Oh dear!

Adelaide said, 'Nothing there to worry about, I mean which were our mother's. She itemised everything. There were no flies on Mother. Our father was a bit rigid on inheritance— you know, all goes from eldest son to eldest son, *ad infinitum.* But Mother was a lass of spirit, said those things were hers to do what she wished with them, and we would value them whereas a wife of a son might not, and her girls were to have them whether or not they ever had homes of their own. We have copies of the lists and the family lawyers in Alexandra have the originals.'

Veronica knew some relief. 'I wouldn't dare cause any kerfuffle in a family. The firm who buys from me is very careful about that, as it's known for its integrity. Now . . . you say you'll need just the few thousand dollars necessary for your fares, that you've enough for spending money and accommodation? Have you any idea of the exact amount?'

'We have. We want to fly to Italy first, then see Vienna, Salzburg, Luxembourg . . . we used to do the Luxembourg Waltz. Then go to England, to see the Wiltshire village where Mother's people came from.'

'Yes, you must see that. Well, you've got such treasures here that only a few of these need to be sacrificed to raise the money. No furniture at all, mostly silver and china and that bric-à-brac which, surprisingly, fetches good prices. I'll slip over from time to time, to value them, then I'll send a list up to my firm for confirmation. I'll be vague about my length of time here—I'll say there are such exciting prospects in the district I'm making this my headquarters.'

The aunts produced some travel brochures from under a pile of ancient table-linen—a good hidey-hole. Veronica checked the fares offering, allowed a good margin for they were bound to want to visit the places their Scots forebears came from too, and was satisfied it could be done, if MacBride of Tordarroch permitted it. It seemed as if a few of Great-grandfather's ideas had rubbed off on him. This was such an isolated pocket of civilisation, it was still very much a man's kingdom.

By the time Veronica arrived back on the pillion of Maude's bike, the keen air had whipped up the colour in her cheeks to match her coral sweater. She'd tied back her hair with a piece of black velvet ribbon Addie had produced, to keep the hair from whipping across her eyes if they went at speed. They did.

Dermid was in Theo's porch, talking to him, and once again Veronica had to admire his reactions and his natural flair for playing a part. He said, 'Why, love, you look glowing with health. It suits you up here.' He caught her hands and kissed her. Over her shoulder she saw Lucy's eyes narrow a little. Did that mean Lucy didn't—quite—like it? Was it possible Theo was justified in his jealousy? Was Lucy dog-in-the-mangerish, being fascinated by Theo, but still wanting to rely on Dermid's undoubted chivalry?

Dermid said, 'I've just been telling Theo the phone's restored. I heard the testing tinkle. They had a bit of trouble at first, it kept fading out, so in case we lost the link again, I rang the doctor, and though he can't come today or tomorrow, as he's got a couple of pregnancies on his hands, due any time, he'll probably make it this week. He practically confirmed our diagnosis, though, and approved our treatment. He's very doubtful about manipulation, says he'll try for a helicopter trip. I told you Minaret and Belleknowes have their own 'copters, didn't I? Both piloted by the wives. Have you ever thought of taking up flying, my love? You could enjoy it. He was glad to know we still had some muscle relaxants from Algie's bout, and that I've given Theo some. We're to keep up the pain-killers—and no wonder! It's devilish, isn't it, Theo?'

Theo's face was very drawn and his tan appeared to be receding. 'I can't even hold a book for long. Incredible to think that even turning a page jabs at me. I'm sure Lucy's voice will give out.'

Veronica said, 'Could I take over? Lucy could go out for some fresh air. Very fresh!'

Dermid said, 'Good idea. I'll saddle up Brownie for you, Lucy. As long as neither of our respective partners gets the wrong idea and the green-eyed monster raises its ugly head again. But I tell you what, Veronica darling, I draw the line at you holding Theo's hand. You can leave that to Lucy!' They all laughed, though Theo's laugh was cut in half by a groan.

Veronica envied them as she saw the two riders trotting away shortly. She hadn't yet told Dermid she could ride after a fashion.

Unfortunately Theo wanted to talk. She would have felt safer reading. 'You look a nice, uncomplicated sort of girl. I'd like to say I think Dermid is extremely lucky.'

She felt anything but uncomplicated. She said quickly, 'I'm lucky too. Dermid's a straightforward sort of guy and he'd help anybody. In fact from schooldays on he's got himself into pickles through dashing to rescue people, so the aunts told me. Very like his mother. She positively mothered all the students who came up here on holiday jobs, men and girls alike. So Dermid was big brother to them too. Mrs MacBride was particularly sorry for Lucy who was so unsettled, first with one parent, then another, so she always ran to them when in trouble. She was always a nervous little thing, they said, but given security, she could become a strong character.'

He nodded, then wished he hadn't. He shifted carefully so he could look at Veronica. 'I'm afraid I made her more nervous. I look a great hulking brute anyway, but despite that, I kind of wanted someone to lean on to. I wanted my wife to be strong. I think we're going to need each other in a very special way. I must remember not to shout at her. How would you take to your husband shouting at you, Veronica? Would it make you act like Lucy and run for cover to someone else?'

She considered that, then the dimples flashed out. 'I'm trying to be analytical . . . and Theo, I've got to confess I'd probably shout back! That might be the wrong thing to do, too. It's awfully hard to know, at the time. But your Lucy has it in her. Look how she reacted when you fell! She just took over. You needed her, so she responded. Let her see more that you need her. Not that I'm in any position to advise—I'm not even married yet!'

'But you soon will be. You and Dermid must come over and stay some time,' Theo added. 'I think most of the fault was mine. If I'm unhappy I get morose and sulk. I've had a chip on my shoulder ever since I was a kid, and for some reason, mainly because his people were so much better off than mine, I resented Dermid. I feel no end of a heel now, knowing he was so lonely when he spent his odd weeks at Wanaka School. So I was jealous of Lucy looking on Tordarroch as a second home. But not any more. They made me feel quite welcome when this happened. And knowing Lucy wasn't at all welcome when she turned up in Dunedin, that she scared the hell out of Dermid in case you got the wrong idea, has put the whole thing in the right perspective. It was darned sensible yanking you out of your lodgings, so you were in no danger of behaving the way I did. But perhaps you aren't the jealous type. Are you?'

Veronica found herself replying, 'I don't know. I'm not jealous or envious by nature, but I *could* be where Dermid is concerned.'

A disconcerting thought flashed across her ... she hadn't liked the idea that possibly Lucy had a tendresse for Dermid! She picked up the book. 'Oh, good. It's one of James Heriot's vet books. I love them. How far had she got?'

She read for three-quarters of an hour before Theo's lids drooped and the sedative had its way with him. She was glad—the longer spells he had without pain, the quicker would the healing be.

She saw the riders come back, silhouetted against the skyline, and unaccountably her spirits rose. Lucy and Dermid came in the back door and through the kitchen where Stephie put a finger to her lips. They looked in on the sleeping man. Veronica rose and tiptoed out, gently closing the door behind her.

Dermid said quietly, 'Good ... sleep will do him more good than anything. He can't worry about lambing or being beholden to us, or anything else, when he's asleep.'

Veronica said, 'What's that saying? "Blessings light on him who first invented sleep! It covers a man all over, thoughts and all, like a cloak." I haven't the faintest idea who said that, but isn't it funny how such things just pop into one's mind?'

Dermid said, 'I'm going to be smug. I happen to know who it was. Cervantes, who wrote *Don Quixote*. Isn't it fascinating to think that the words of a Spaniard who helped provision the ships of the Armada can mean something to us today, four centuries on.'

'I'm most impressed,' admired Veronica. 'I remember quotations but rarely who said them.'

'Except, I imagine, the authors of the plays whose lines you have to learn.'

Oh dear ... she'd trip up yet! She wasn't cast for all this pretence. There were hazards at every turn. She managed a laugh, said, 'That's true, and I recall all my lines perfectly, even the very first play I was ever in.'

Lucy said interestedly, 'Which play was that, Veronica? And could you say some of the lines for us, right now?'

Mischief leapt into the brown eyes, 'I could. They're engraved on my heart, like Bloody Mary said of Calais.' She put back her head, opened her lips over her slightly crooked teeth, white and sparkling, twirled imaginary whiskers each side of her cheeks, and emitted: 'Miaow! Miaow!'

Stephie and Lucy stared but Dermid slapped his leg delightedly, 'Dick Whittington's cat!' he announced. 'Oh, Veronica, I do wish you had your long black tail and the device that switched it!'

When their quiet laughter had died down she said, 'I must go on upstairs and get this oil off my trousers. Next time I'll wear jeans on their bikes.'

Lucy said, 'I'll come up with you. While Theo's asleep I'll wash my hair.'

As they went in the bathroom in search of cleaning fluid, Lucy said impulsively, 'You and Dermid are so right for each other. You both quote things—they all do in this family. Comes from all their years without television, when they just read. You suit.'

Veronica gazed at her. Nothing less jealous could be imagined. She had been wrong. Then she said uneasily, 'This is a false situation. I hope nobody else gets that idea—it would make for embarrassment. I'm here today and gone tomorrow.'

But back in her room, she found herself staring at her mirrored face. In her eyes she read the truth. That she wished it wasn't false.

CHAPTER FIVE

VERONICA hadn't got to twenty-four without having known more than one attraction, but none had lasted. A sudden anger at her own foolishness shook her. There was no future for her here in this isolated pocket of one of New Zealand's beauty spots. She'd come up here to deceive, in the first place, before being swept into this charade. How lighthearted it had been, just an impulse to make two dear old ladies realise a dream which had seemed in danger of being thwarted by some cross-grained old bachelor she'd supposed to be in his fifties.

She wished she could confess right now, because having got this far in pretending she was his fiancée, he might not be so nervous of her ability to carry it through to the bitter end, but he'd certainly be furious to think she'd sneaked up to spy out the antiques. The previous time the aunts had been diddled would accentuate that, of course. And if a row did flare up, Dermid might not be able to carry on as well as till now, as the adoring swain! She grimaced at her reflection and said sternly, 'So don't complicate things still further, Veronica Rose Blakeney, by falling in love with the wretched dictatorial man! This is a self-contained world and he's very much king of the castle. He'd react more strongly than most men about deceit like this. Oh, how I wish Addie and Maude had told him straight out what they were going to do, that the treasures were theirs, and they were selling them to go to Italy to visit those graves—and then had sent for me. There'd be no false colours then.' She felt a most unusual sense of depression.

'Oh, snap out of it!' As a typically feminine antidote to such feelings, she showered, decided against trews tonight, and slipped into a light-weight angora dress in a soft rose with a plaited black leather girdle, and a black filigree brooch in the form of a rose at one shoulder.

81

She brushed the slightly longer than shoulder-length hair till it shone like a polished nut in the lights and curled round her jawline like hyacinth petals tippped with gold. She took out a black velvet Alice-band and slid it over her head. She hated the feel of her hair swinging over her face, though she didn't feel like tying it back tonight, it was too severe. She sprayed white rose perfume behind her ears and on her wrists, and feeling less down, came out of the door just as Lucy came out of the room she was using.

She was in pale blue and looked like a little girl dressed up. 'I'm having mine with Theo. I've discovered that the bookshelf in the porch is the same height as that dresser. He'll feel less selfconscious than out in the kitchen.'

Veronica put an arm round Lucy's shoulders. 'Good girl! Much better than him hearing us talk and laugh at the table about the day's doings. He's at a great disadvantage, poor darling, just when he's sure of you ... and hardly able to move! But as long as he thinks you find him the centre of his universe, and dressing up for him too, it'll be all right.'

Lucy's blue eyes looked mischievous. 'I know ... it ought to have been the time for a grand passionate reconciliation ... a second honeymoon. And the poor soul slipped his disc and is practically immobile! Well, it'll keep, but I've got to make it up to him somehow!'

A door opened behind them. Dermid's. He cocked a mock-reproving eye at them. 'I thought I'd better let you know I'm here—goodness knows what you girls might say next! But I agree. It's too bad. But you're doing fine, Lucy.' He looked at Veronica and whistled.

'I certainly did well out of this affair, didn't I? You look just like a rose, my love.' He dropped a kiss on the cheek nearest.

Knowing what she'd just discovered about herself, Veronica instinctively drew back. 'You idiot!' she hissed. 'You only have to play up when Theo's around.'

He looked at Lucy, shook his head as if ruefully. 'Isn't she a proper spoilsport? And how do you know it isn't because inwardly I'm so scared I fluff my lines when he's there that I keep on practising? It's okay for you, you're a professional.'

Lucy giggled. 'Well, that's as good an excuse as I've ever heard, but I'm glad you're getting some reward out of the situation, Derry. It makes me feel heaps better. I landed you in so much, made a complete mess of things. But now, for the first time in my life, I seem to know what I'm doing.'

Veronica had recovered from her recoil, her dread of showing how she was feeling about this man. She turned to Lucy with shining eyes. 'Good for you, Lucy! I feel it's a new start altogether for you and Theo. It seems he had a tough childhood, but you've got a great chance of making that up to him, to say nothing of the challenge of creating a fine high-country estate out of something that was run down and neglected.'

Lucy was no lily-pale creature now; she had a lovely colour. 'I'm going to tell Theo what you said—that ought to help him get rid of his inferiority complex! That's evidently what made him such a bear at times. I didn't help, nagging at him to be paying me compliments all the time, wanting him to tell me how marvellous he thought I was to sacrifice so much. I expect I wanted reassuring because of my own unwanted childhood. We're two different people now.' She whirled away down the stairs.

The other two were left looking at each other. Dermid was freshly tubbed too. The chestnut hair was still damp and he wore rust-coloured cords and a brown shirt with a dark green cravat tied loosely beneath it. It accentuated the coppery whipcord thoughness of the man. The green eyes even looked a little tender. 'I'd never have believed it,' he said.

A line appeared between Veronica's golden-brown brows. 'Never have believed what?'

'That one of Anne's stage friends could come up here and be so darned sensible. That any one of them could fit so well into a situation like this and make it seem right. Definitely right.'

She turned her head away to look out of the landing window at the darkening lake below. It still had a shimmer from the fading sunset. She didn't want him looking at her too closely. 'You sound as if you haven't a high opinion of Anne's friends. Of actresses in general.'

'I'm not as bigoted as that, Veronica. Some of them are fine people and work damned hard, but some she's had up here at times for a break couldn't seem to stop acting. But there's a sincerity about you. You've identified with the situation. I like it. You care—you care about those two people and their future.'

Veronica turned back to him. 'Thanks, Dermid. I do care. At first I thought Lucy was going to be one of those annoying clinging vines who are always getting other people into awkward situations; now I see her more as the victim of circumstances but capable of rising to a situation and admitting herself to be wrong, which isn't easy. We all do things we regret deeply, but can't undo, but if we see they were wrong and start again, it's something, isn't it?'

Without knowing, she made an appealing gesture towards him with both hands, and he caught them between both his, clasping them together. She could feel the callouses on his palms against the back of hers. That one small touch stirred her as she had never been stirred before. Those green eyes were very intent on hers.

'It's more than just something, Veronica. It can be a big thing. It can mean a whole new start, no matter what. Remember that.'

She was struck by the sheer intensity of his tone, and puzzled. Did it mean so much to him ... that Lucy should find herself and her happiness? A strange man this, with probably a hard streak in him, inherited from that autocratic great-grandfather who hadn't let Adelaide and Maude wed their young lovers, yet a chivalrous sort of man, wanting the best for a girl who had spent some of her lonely, less happy times up here. To understand Dermid MacBride you had to know he was primarily a man of these immense lake solitudes.

He seemed to be waiting for her to comment. Instead she said lightly, freeing her hands, 'We're getting too serious. Time we went downstairs.'

Stephie had felt the need of dressing up a little too. She was out of her overall and looked more the chatelaine of Tordarroch House in a not too fussy yet elegant dress of patterned blues and lilacs that brought up the glints in her silvering hair that had once been fair, and her soft rose complexion.

Veronica said, 'Oh, Stephie, how you suit pastels! It must be this gloriously pure lake air—you've a complexion like a young girl!'

Dermid laughed because Stephie blushed. 'But Veronica has something there. Our roses up here hardly get a spot on their leaves. No petrol fumes to speak of, no industries, only good country smells and the expanse of the lake to keep it sweet. Incidentally, what perfume is that, Veronica?'

Her turn to blush. She felt annoyed with herself. She shrugged. 'Very ordinary. Nobody ever gives me anything else because of my name.'

Dermid looked staggered. 'But veronica bushes have no perfume to speak of. I know, because they grow on the opposite side of the lake where we moor if we happen to go across. Though we usually call them by their native name, *koromiko*.'

'I meant my second name. I'm Veronica Rose.'

Stephie said, 'I like that. It's euphonious.'

'So I usually get rose perfume given me. Sometimes white rose, sometimes black rose, but both lovely. Stephie, let me help dish out.'

They carried the dishes in for Lucy and Theo and Dermid helped Theo out of bed. How patient and gentle he was in this! When, to the accompaniment of gasps and grunts from the sufferer, they'd got him in a good position for eating from the top of the bookcase, Dermid said, 'This reminds me of the time I brought a girl here from Lincoln College—not the one who nursed me, another one. I was very enamoured, and I thought she was too, but her enchantment with the lake setting died within a week. Dad insisted on teaching her to ride. He thought I'd met my fate and she'd be no use here if she couldn't. You know all the old jokes about eating off the mantelpiece? Poor Judy. No, come to think of it she was Julie. She had no sense of humour, so she wouldn't have done for here. She literally couldn't sit down, but neither would she submit to the indignity of eating from the dresser-top. Dad thought it hilarious and teased her, and she tore strips off him. What a temper!' He chuckled.

'I made the most awful blunder—I laughed. She swung round on me and said, "It wouldn't matter if the woolclip brought in millions ... I wouldn't live in this god-forsaken place if you asked me on your bended knees!" To which I replied, unforgivably, I realise now, that I had no intention of asking her even if I'd been seated on the throne of England, much less on my bended.'

Theo gave a great guffaw, then yelped and groaned, 'Dermid, I'll kill you if you keep making me laugh! Give me warning first.'

Dermid said, 'Whereas your luck held. Lucy never hesitated about going right up river with you, across Hawea.'

Theo looked astounded. 'Neither she did. I never thought of that. Lucy ... you were wonderful, doing just that. I took it for granted.'

Lucy caught Veronica's eye, and both laughed and wouldn't say why. Dermid said, 'You must have something I haven't got, Theo. She never set her sights on me, and with two helicopters this side of the lake, plus that launch, it's like living in Piccadilly Circus compared to yours. Well, come on, Veronica Rose, I'm starving! At least my girl this time round has got what it takes. I'm incredibly lucky.'

Veronica, as they came into the kitchen, drew the door shut. Dermid raised a brow. 'Giving them privacy?'

She fixed him with eyes that had lost their pansy-softness. 'The idea is that if Theo can't hear you, you don't have to play up this nonsense. You're laying it on with a trowel. I've come to the conclusion that wherever Anne got her flair for acting from, it's starting to come out in you. It's all that could account for it.'

The green eyes narrowed. 'You must be the least conceited girl I've ever met. It could be I'm enjoying it.'

Stephie put down a bowl of steaming beef Stroganoff on the table and laughed. 'I agree with that last remark. You *are* enjoying it. But what man wouldn't? But you've hit the nail on the head, girl, the very first Shaw to come out here was the great-nephew of a talented actor in Edinburgh. It crops out now and then, most of all in Anne. It would have been a shame to deny that girl her chance. Her parents were too sensible, and loving, to do so. After this season in Australia, she's off to London. She'll say goodbye to her parents in Queensland, at Gerald's place.'

Veronica said slowly, 'Then your father, Dermid, wasn't as autocratic as the aunts' father was.'

He paused with a forkful halfway to his mouth. 'Meaning?'

'Not allowing them to marry their young men before they left for the Middle East.'

He considered it. 'Gone all romantic on it with you, have they? I wonder if by now they do consider themselves frustrated? But my mother told me once that her grandfather had always regretted he'd advised them not to marry. But they were very young, neither of them twenty, and he did think that if the worst happened, his lovely young daughters would surely marry other men. As the years went on and they didn't, it got to be almost an obsession with him. He even sent them off once on a very expensive Pacific cruise hoping that away from this restricted setting they might fall in love again, but they seemed interested in places more than people. I'd like to have known him. Stephie here did.'

Stephie nodded. 'I wish you had, you're so like him in every way.'

In every way. Making decisions for the women of the family came easily to him, putting practical things and possessions before the intangible things of the spirit. It would be a mistake to fall in love with such a man. Veronica's sympathies had always inclined to run away with her.

Dermid took her at her word and kept the heavy door closed between the two rooms and kept the conversation to such ordinary topics she realised with a sinking and wayward heart that it was deadly tame. Lucy and Theo stayed in the sun-porch. Dermid had fixed up a radio for them. Theo couldn't raise his head for long to watch television. Dermid turned their own on, and the three of them settled to watch.

Veronica found she was watching but not listening, that nothing was registering, her thoughts were so concerned with the situation up here. Presently she slipped quietly out of a door behind her and upstairs. She took a fleecy white coat down, because there was a hint of late frost, then changed her elegant shoes for flat walking ones and let herself out.

Immediately she felt calmed. Who wouldn't be soothed by the beauty of such a night? The sheer magic of the lake took hold of her. Till now she'd always lived within reach of the sea. The inland areas had never appealed, but this had a charm all its own. That deep mysterious hollow of the violet-dark lake, rimmed by the even darker shadows of the foothills that in lesser countries would have been called mountains themselves, and there was the eerie fascination of knowing that this side of the lake was unroaded, that farther in, and west, were alpine range upon alpine range and all Fiordland farther south, till it levelled out to that narrow strip of rich earth that was Westland, edged by the wild Tasman Sea that stretched between the shore and Australia. A world of its own. Deep in those ranges must be some undesecrated stretch of ground where no human foot had ever trod, some miniature Eden, sweet with birdsong, fragrant with mountain wildflowers, valleys rich with rain-forest, where waterfalls spilled their music and the little creatures of the earth went about their daily and nocturnal lives secretly.

Presently there would be a moon, but just now only the stars gave light. Not a lamp-post, no traffic, no house-windows lit to speak of human habitation. Her restlessness disappeared before the therapy of silence. Oh, a light had appeared on the far side of those dark waters, coming towards her. It must be coming through the Neck. When you took the Haast Road from Wanaka township, you couldn't skirt the lake all the way. You went to Hawea, came through the Neck, and picked up a road by the far shore of Wanaka again. The white beams turned, cut twin swathes through that far darkness, then vanished. A late bird, disturbed by her passing, twittered. It looked as if this tiny path through the garden took a loop here and joined the track that led to the jetty. A short cut. Veronica took to it, caught her foot in a gnarled root, fell and rolled. She gave an involuntary cry, not loud, and rolled right over a small bush, but caught it in passing. It was pungent. Oh, creeping rosemary, planted here to cover the rocks. She scrambled up, brushed herself down, laughed.

She ought to have brought a torch. To step outside in a well-lit city was one thing, quite another to find oneself in country darkness with only stars to guide. Fancy if she'd sprained her ankle! Dermid would think there was a hoodoo on Tordarroch. She managed to join the track, and at that moment the moon freed itself from the clouds and shone a shaft of light directly on the rough metalled way. It made all the difference.

In the sharp crisp air her footsteps rang out. She came to the bend where she'd sat down and laughed when first she'd embarked on this imposture. The hill had been gouged away here for the road. She stopped, one hand on the rough chipped rock of the bank to look down on the scene below. By the jetty was the white gleam of the pleasure launch, *MacBride's Lass*. A dark shadow, larger, was the roll-on, roll-off steel barge with the dropped front that these days took the station's stock, vehicles, wool bales, hay, and themselves down to Wanaka. The goods were then consigned for sale for either domestic or export use. To the left was the break in the bush-rimmed shore line where Distaff Bay, small and exquisite, indented the half-circle.

Into the silence fell the sound of footsteps. Male footsteps. Veronica didn't know how she knew they were Dermid's. She had known him so short a time . . . and yet. . . .

He called, 'Are you there, Veronica? Veronica?'

She turned, the movement making her white coat visible. 'Yes, here, by the bend in the track.'

He'd probably tear a strip off her for venturing out in the starlight in unknown and rough territory. Well, just let him! She'd say she'd found the restricted area of the family too cramping all of a sudden. She'd had to get away from it all.

He moved with a litheness that suggested complete physical fitness. A man very sure of himself, this. There was that faint hint of leashed strength, there to be called upon, a ruggedness that wasn't arrogance, more a touch of the inborn right of command. It attracted her yet put her back up. She found her fingers had curled into fists. She would *not* be ordered about by this man!

He came out of the shadows of the pines on his left and the moonlight struck right on him. No sound of reproof roughened his voice. He came straight to her, reached for her hands which instinctively uncurled themselves and allowed him to grasp them.

'Were you restless? Or bored? You should have said, and we'd have done something about it. We're so used to life lived up here at our own possibly slow tempo we forget what it must seem like to someone used to the city.'

Against her will Veronica burst out laughing. 'Slow tempo? You must be joking! I've hardly been able to catch my breath since I arrived, rushed willy-nilly into an engagement with someone I'd never seen before ... the life almost crushed out of me in a passionate embrace as I leapt off the launch, pitchforked into a personality to fit the image, endowed with a past and a profession, and terrified out of my wits at times in case I don't remember who and what I am. And you say "slow tempo"! Oh, Dermid!'

She liked that deep chuckle of his. 'Put like that my remark was off-beam, wan't it? I was contrasting the life you must live in town among your stage friends with this existence up here, and thought you might be feeling appalled at the thought of weeks of it. I wondered what we could do to liven things up for you. It's too near lambing to get up a party. Oh, we often get them going, bigger affairs than most town ones, possibly, with most people coming by boat, some by helicopter and all of them staying till next day. They bring their dancing shoes and their bedrolls. But not at this time of year.'

She shook her head. 'Preconceived ideas can err. Stage people need their sleep more than most ... rehearsals in mornings, matinees and evening performances. So most of them live quiet lives, and still have a bit of home-life.'

Dermid picked her up immediately. 'They don't have many matinees in Dunedin.'

That had been a mistake. 'I was thinking of other centres farther north, and Australia.'

'But you've been in Dunedin the last six months, haven't you?'

She'd better agree. 'It suited me. But I'm quite free now.'

There was a pause. He was still gripping her hands. She thought he was searching for words. Then he said, rather diffidently for Dermid, 'Yes, you're free now. At first I was against Anne sending you, but now——'

She interrupted him. 'Against it? What can you mean? I thought I was an answer to prayer, saving Lucy from the wrath of Theo in the most compromising circumstances. Why didn't you want me?'

The next moment she was wondering if she should have asked just that. But he said, quite gently, 'I shouldn't have told you that. Just I didn't know if you sounded right for this affair. But you were the only one free. However, you've been everything we needed and more.' Then he said a surprising thing. 'Look, I know I'm an intolerant sort of guy, and don't always like the things that pass for freedom in this present-day world of ours. Could be I'm a bit out of touch. I've got to remember we almost live a charmed existence up here, insulated from certain influences. We forget others have to live in this so-called liberated world, and some of it's bound to rub off. Perhaps we fail to make allowances for that.' He stopped. 'I think I'm sounding pompous.'

Somehow Veronica didn't want him to stop. She said, 'I find I rather like it. Especially as I did suspect you of being rather cocooned by the life up here. I—well, perhaps I find it more refreshing. Go on, Dermid MacBride.'

He shook his head. 'No, I'll say too much. Not yet, anyway.'

He saw the coral lips curve up at the corners. 'All right. I've not taken offence at what you said, so better not risk any more. I think you worry about your sister, away in a very different atmosphere, but I guess her years up here will have given her a sense of values that will stand her in good stead. Is that what it adds up to?'

'Partly,' he said, and there was a strange glint in the eyes looking into hers. 'But the real reason was much more personal. But I'll leave it for some time yet.'

She had a sudden horrible thought. Her hands slipped out of his and she gripped his upper arms quite vigorously. 'Dermid MacBride, you aren't going to tell me you were afraid this actress friend of Anne's might presume on the situation, that she mightn't make it easy for you to break off this phoney engagement? Why, why, you——'

Her fury was unmistakable. He brought his hands up and freed himself, laughing. There was a hint of deviltry in that laughter. It was provocative, challenging. 'Heavens, no! What do you take me for? Look, forget my woolly conversation. Imagine wasting time like this, when that moon rose specially for us a few moments ago. Should I say it was just waiting in the wings? Don't you realise, girl, that this is just the perfect setting for an opera? I should be singing to you, you should be singing back to me. But I can think of better things to do with my mouth!'

He slipped his hands inside the loose white coat, linked his fingers together at the back of her waist, imprisoning her. Veronica felt powerless to resist him. He put his cheek against her cheek first. It was cool from the faint hint of frost on the still air. Dermid held her that way for a long minute, a delightful preliminary to the kiss that was surely to come. He turned his face then so that his lips touched her cheek gently, trailed his mouth across her cheek till it found hers.

Never before had any kiss made her feel like this. How could one kiss, and a first kiss at that, mean such utter commitment? How could any touch of lips waken you to a blend of feeling that was tumultuous, yet carried within it that passion of feeling, the sense of coming home to safe harbourage? An impish remembrance came to her of herself at seventeen saying to her father, 'I think kissing is very overrated, Dad,' and her father laughing and saying, 'You won't always think that, my naïve young daughter!' And tonight, that had come true. What a stupid thing to think back like that, in a moment of sheer delight like this! She gave herself up to the rapture of the present.

Just one kiss, but it seemed to last and last. Dermid's clasp loosened a little, and he drew in a deep breath, a steadying one. He smiled a little. What a strong mouth he had! Then a touch of whimsy crept into his voice. He put a finger under her chin, tilted it, so his eyes could look into hers. 'Not too stodgy, is it, life at Tordarroch? We have our moments.'

Veronica strove to keep it light too, so answered, 'I can only surmise you think this the way to keep me from being bored.'

He laughed. 'Can you think of a nicer way? For sheer delight?'

All the tension went out of her. Her answering chuckle held real mirth. 'No, I can't, and I feel much better now.'

He seized on that immediately. 'Then there was something. You weren't feeling very happy, so you came out here to walk it off. Would I be probing if I asked were you missing someone from your former life? Missing them very much?'

Her reaction was immediate. 'No, it wasn't. Just that—oh, how can I explain it? I could so easily embarrass you because you began it, though in a sense you had to. I mean it was inspired and done from the best of motives. I mean——'

He shook her a little. 'Come on, girl, out with it!'

Her eyes went grave. 'It's just that this . . .' she waved at the vastness of the scene about them, 'that this gets to me. It's so big, so beautiful and serene. It makes one's values . . . well, some values, seem tawdry. Makes you wish——'

'Makes you wish what? Do you mean you're wishing some things you've done undone?'

'I wish I didn't have to keep on fibbing. It has to be done to bolster this imposture up, but it leaves a nasty taste behind. Yet it would be unthinkable that Theo could have any real doubts about that night you gave Lucy somewhere to sleep.'

He said slowly, 'I thought you were going to tell me

something different. But I realise we've not really known each other long yet, though it seems a long time. We've been flung together so closely. I thought you might be frank—no, I won't say what about. It would have to come spontaneously. I know how you feel. One bit of me thinks it great fun, the other regrets the necessity. But I don't care about any of it so long as Theo doesn't get hurt.' There was quite a pause, then he added, 'Veronica, you do know it was all on the square, don't you? That there was never anything between Lucy and me that night, or ever?'

In the moonlight, as she lifted her face to him, the look on it was believing. 'I never had a moment's doubt of that, MacBride.'

'Thank you. I hoped you'd feel that. If you hadn't there was nothing a chap could do to prove it. If it comes to the bit, apart from a chaste salute on the cheek on her arrivals and departings all these years, I've never even kissed Lucy. Not like I kissed my fiancée just now. That was really something, wasn't it?'

Veronica said hastily, 'I came out for a walk. I don't want you to think I was after dalliance under a moon. Understood?'

'Understood, pal. It's tough but wise. Let's walk.'

They walked for an hour, during which time they had a shoes and ships and sealing-wax and cabbages and kings conversation. Some things they agreed on, some not. Dermid took her elbow when the going was rough, relinquished it when it wasn't. Most of the talk was on books.

At last they came up the terraced garden to the homestead. The porch light was out and upstairs only Stephie's showed. Dermid laughed. 'Theo will certainly look on this as roaming in the gloaming and envy me the amorous opportunity!'

They paused on the top step of the verandah and as one turned to look on the sleeping lake below. 'Almost a crime to leave such beauty,' Veronica said dreamily.

'Mm, makes me think of a line I read somewhere—I've no idea where. Half a line really.'

'Then share it, Dermid MacBride.'

'It was: "... and leave the world to silence and to God." '

Veronica thought as she drifted off to sleep that some day she could tell a man like this of her own deception.

If he stayed that way.

CHAPTER SIX

Two days later the unmistakable whirring of a helicopter brought all except Theo out to scan the sky, but by the time they did, it was already hovering to settle. The doctor, for sure.

Veronica let a small gasp escape her, though she tried to stifle it. Dermid's ears caught it and she looked up to find his piercing glance coming her way. 'What is it?'

Even if she hadn't been ashamed of the instinctive and selfish feeling that had swept over her, she couldn't have told him it had brought her the realisation that on this visit depended her length of stay here. What if the doctor whisked him away?

When she didn't answer, Dermid repeated his question. She said, and she was confessing her second thought, 'I know it's nothing to you, because it's a commonplace, but to see one land at such close quarters makes me nervous in case something happens.'

To her surprise he didn't think that feeble or alarmist. He crossed to her, took her hand, said, 'She's very experienced. But I understand. I never get the top-dressing planes in without wondering how the day will end. It's a risky job.'

She seized on one word. 'She? Oh, now I remember, you said there were two women pilots up here. Which one is this?'

'The one that belongs to Belleknowes. Come on and meet everyone.'

Three figures got out as the whirly-bird stilled. It turned out that Fiona Campbell had gone down to Wanaka to pick up the television man. Their set was on the blink. It sounded so casual. So the doctor had taken the chance of a quick visit.

Lucy wanted a word with the doctor before he saw Theo. The doctor nodded, eyes twinkling in his brown face. 'I ken fine what you're anxious about. I remember last time he did too much too soon. He thought as soon as I manipulated, that he could be out and about again. He'd never be able to resist it back on his own place. Even at Wanaka I'd not trust him. He'd take the first chance of a hitch-hike by 'copter with deer-hunters or top-dressers and would try to kid you it was for supervision only. It's not now when he can't move that's the trouble, it's the half-pi convalescent stage that's bothering me.' He turned to Dermid. 'Any trouble about coping here? I know your lady mother's across the Tasman, but it looks as if you've got help apart from Lucy.'

Dermid drew Veronica forward, 'Yes, we're in luck as far as the house is concerned. Lucy is nurse and my fiancée's up here for a few weeks, so can give Stephie a hand. This is Veronica Blakeney, Doc.'

Veronica was surveyed by a pair of shrewd eyes. 'No doubt I'll see quite a bit of you when you're wed. It's about time this tough hombre settled down. High-country men need wives even more than most of us.'

'Hey, Doc,' protested Dermid most naturally, 'it's not a marriage of convenience! I mean . . . look at her!'

'I am looking, and I find the scenery grand. Welcome to my round, Veronica. I'm not going to call you Miss Blakeney. I guess it'll be Veronica MacBride before too long.'

She found herself responding just as naturally, 'You're probably right. I'm so fascinated with this place I can't wait till I come back for good. You'll all come in while the Doctor does his examination, I suppose? Stephie slipped back, I know, to bring the kettle to the boil. Her guardian angel led her to bake a huge batch of scones not half an hour ago.'

Fiona Campbell said, 'No, we're going on to our place to save time on the TV repair. Another crowd will be taking the doctor back. It so happens a television crew for a series called *The High-country Men* have been over at Tarras doing some preliminary work and they were in the TV shop when I arrived. So they decided it was an opportunity not to be missed. Poor Theo. They began talking about "Intrepid farmer's wife thinks nothing of flipping down lake in her own helicopter to pick up a repair man for her TV though it has been used for far more dramatic things like rescuing stranded climbers, a shepherd with a broken leg and so on." They're portraying me as a toughie. I didn't dare tell them that when I first came up here as a governess I was terrified to death of even a horse. I thought it might take the heat off me if I told them there was a minor emergency on today, that the doctor was coming to Tordarroch to attend another high-countryman who'd injured his back. Veronica, I'll drop in some day and get you and Stephie over for a visit to Belleknowes. Lovely to have another woman neighbour so near. Dermid, you secretive hound, you must tell me all about your romance next time. How you met and so on.' And she and the repair man made their way back to the chopper leaving all but the doctor with a sense of dismay. The engagement mightn't have been announced in the local paper, but it looked as if before long it would be flashed over every screen in New Zealand!

When the doctor went in with Lucy to make his examination, Stephie and Veronica and Dermid dropped into chairs at the kitchen table and gazed at each other. Finally Veronica said, 'Dermid, you must play it down. You could just say, 'This is Veronica, who's having a lakeside holiday.'

Stephie said, 'You've got a hope! Belleknowes was featured in a programme once before, years ago. Poor Fiona, it was not long before Elspeth, their second child, was born. She thought this would mean she could stay in the background, but no, this was great human interest, a woman expecting up here, with no road coming to her door, facing all the hazards of a possible premature birth ... Fiona has always said she'd love to appear in another, slim and graceful ... so if they took a few shots at Wanaka when she took off with the doctor, she'll have achieved just that. Veronica, I can't see much chance of keeping this engagement under wraps.'

She gave a slight moan. 'Just imagine it! That goes out on the main network. I've an extremely large circle of friends in Dunedin and Christchurch, and I can just imagine the mail. They'll all rush out and buy engagement cards. You too,

Dermid, you're taking it very calmly. Don't you feel in a flap? Don't you feel trapped?'

'Why? Do you? Trapped, I mean?'

She didn't answer. He shrugged, maddeningly. 'I'm sorry for your sake; you've been such a sport, but we couldn't have foreseen this. Sorry I landed it in your lap. But what's the use of turning turtle over something we can't hope to circumvent? We can still stage our parting when the dust of the programme settles. Jove, I've just thought ... these programmes are made almost months ahead. Theo and Lucy will be back across Hawea long before it comes out, so if we have parted by then, they'll know. It'll just mean that the programme, in that small particular, will be out of date.'

Veronica frowned. 'Dermid, it doesn't alter the fact that umpteen of my one-time friends will write. They wouldn't know the engagement was off—I mean, girls do; men don't so much. Stephie, I have an idea you'd be more helpful than Dermid. He's making me mad!'

He lifted an eyebrow at her. 'Why? I can't just pluck ideas out of thin air for blocking it.'

Her tone was sour. 'You plucked the idea of a mock fiancée out of it, why shouldn't you put the great brain to work on saving *me* pain and embarrassment?'

He scowled. 'Have you someone particularly in mind who might be hurt by it? Some man? Might it throw a spanner into your private life? Is that why it's so important?'

'No, it isn't! I just hate the idea that's all! I wish——' she came to a sudden stop.

He had been bending over the scrubbed kitchen table, tracing a line of little dents where Stephie had been using a pastry wheel, but he shot a glance up from under his brows. 'You wish ... what?'

She hesitated, then said, but with much less vigor than she'd started, 'I wish I'd never come.'

'Do you really, Veronica Blakeney? Do you wish you'd never seen Lake Wanaka like two nights ago, in the starlight? Do you really?'

She evaded his eyes. 'It was a big price to pay ... a tangle like this. For one beautiful scene. There are other beauty spots.' Even as she said it her unreasoning heart said to her logical mind, but none so dear, so dear.

He looked sceptical. No other word for it. She said crossly, 'Why go on like this? Why not spend the time thinking how to dodge saying who I am to those cameramen?'

'I don't think the cameramen have anything to do with the script.'

'That's quibbling. I'm sure Stephie is longing to say: "Oh, what a tangled web we weave when first we practise to deceive." And oh, how true it is!'

Stephie chuckled. 'I did think just that a moment ago, but to be quite candid, Veronica, Dermid acted from the best of motives, to save a marriage. To dispel doubts that might have remained in poor Theo's mind year after year. He might never have quite trusted his Lucy again. A lot was at stake.'

Veronica bit her lip. 'I feel rebuked, and rightly so, because that *is* all that matters. But please, please, unless a question is asked, and you can't avoid saying I'm your fiancée, please don't mention it.'

'Fair enough, pal,' said Dermid MacBride. Pal—she liked that. She knew why. Because it linked up with that tender but poignant moment when her father had said goodbye to her mother. Her mind flew back to it. Because the mists were gathering for him, Dad hadn't realised that his youngest daughter was sharing that watch with her mother. Veronica had been sitting in a big wing-chair, unseen. Her mother was by the bed, holding her husband's hand, giving it a little pressure now and then to let him know she was with him.

He'd opened his eyes, smiled, said to her, 'I wish we'd had longer, Marian, but I hope the memories will be sweet for you. It's been so good. I've been a lucky man. We've been not only lovers, but pals.'

That had said it all, and the young Veronica had taken it for her own ideal of marriage and treasured the memory. Not that she thought her parents' marriage had been all harmony . . . no, at times they had quarrelled, of course, but the core of it was trust and true love. They'd known the big moments.

Now, to her consternation, a tear fell on the back of her hand as it lay on the table.

Dermid looked horrified. He stretched out a hand to her, 'Oh, Veronica, I've upset you! It's my fault for not seeing this means more to you than to me. I find it hard to take seriously. Look, my dear, it may not be mentioned at all.'

She dashed at her eyes impatiently. 'Sorry . . . don't either of you feel upset, please. I'm being stupid. It's nothing to do with this—this publicity, or the dread of it. It's—it's only that you called me pal, and I had a rush of memory. My dad used that word when he was dying, when he said goodbye to Mother. He didn't even know I was there. Stupid of me to spill. It's a lovely memory. I'm just being awkward.'

Stephie said quickly, 'No, you aren't. Thanks for sharing that memory with us. It's sweet of you not to mind telling us.'

'Why, I think so too,' said MacBride. 'Right . . . we'll play it by ear and take everything as it comes. I think Doc's coming.'

He was, and chuckling. 'I've got him right where I want him. Last time he spoiled my good work by getting up too soon. This time he can't. It'll be six weeks at the earliest before he can move without any pain. The longer he rests the better. I'm leaving plenty of pills that will loosen up the muscles and more pain-killers. He's going to need them. A nerve is badly affected.'

'I thought he'd blow up when he heard about the television team, but he's tickled pink. It'll take his mind off it. Fiona sketched in the background of Theo's property and they're dead keen to go over to Hunters' Peak and photograph the way Theo's bringing that once derelict land into production. Pity he's not there, but they'll bring him into it here, as the reason for the doctor's call. Now, let me have that tea before that mobile studio drops down on us.' He grinned. 'When I came up here after doing my post-graduate stuff in Edinburgh, someone told me I'd stagnate. As if this could ever be boring! I never have two days the same.'

In no time the sound of another helicopter was heard, a much larger one. As all the gear was piled out, Veronica said to Stephie, 'I've an awful feeling that we've got visitors for lunch, and the longer they're here, the greater the chance my supposed identity will have to crop up.'

Stephie twinkled. 'Then to take your mind off it, you'd better help me rustle up what we can give them to eat. Fortunately I've plenty of loaves and some rolls defrosted and there are those bacon-and-egg pies you made and put in the deep-freeze. Whisk them out and put them in the bottom of the coal oven. Say we serve bottled tomatoes with them? It could have been worse. I might have been in the middle of cleaning the flues! This easy access is all right, but at least in the years when there was a fortnightly boat, we never got caught on the hop.'

It was all less fearsome than expected. There was a free-and-easy air about these experts, and their delight in having, as they said, a flying doctor dropped into their programme's lap, was rather endearing. Photos were taken inside and out and with Maude and Adelaide on their motorbikes. They'd arrived over, having heard the first 'chopper', to find out what the doctor had said. Dermid and Veronica knew great apprehension when they saw them arrive, but they behaved most circumspectly. Dermid was taken on horseback, with his men and dogs, supposedly setting off for the far huts, and they were going to fly back in, when the pre-lamb shearing was on, for a few shots of that.

Theo came up trumps and was quite humorous about being leg-roped like a reluctant steer, and he managed to look lugubrious enough to satisfy the director at the prospect of being immobile here at the approach of lambing time when his own station was even more remote. They got through with no reference to Veronica's status and she was beginning to breathe more easily when suddenly the director said, 'Now of course, some more about the women of the family. That's always good viewing, and so far we've only got Adelaide and Maude on their bikes.'

Dermid said quickly, 'I'm only sorry my mother, with my father, is visiting my vet brother in Australia, but Mrs Stephenson here has been our housekeeper and guardian angel for as long as I can remember. She and her husband had the married couple's house when I was born. She's the one who came through all the tough, more isolated times.'

'Indeed yes,' said Stephie, playing her part admirably. 'In fact my husband was here in our courting days—and some courting that was, with our only means of communication the radio-telephone link, which meant it had to go through a third person. It had the effect on us of shortening our engagement!'

This was well received, but unfortunately also where Theo put his oar in. 'I believe you like contrasts. You ought to do a bit about the modern girl not shrinking from the isolation either . . . which can still be grim, because though we appear to have undreamed-of luxuries now, we're still at the mercy of gale and storm, snow and flood, when we can be completely cut off from the outside world and be minus telephone, power, and access to stock. Sometimes the weather's too bad for flying, even. Yet our women still follow us. Take my wife, Lucy, for instance. If ever there's a place at the back of beyond, Hunters' Peak is. Wait till you see it! And now Dermid here has got himself a girl of the right sort. The good-looker with the brown hair, Veronica, is his fiancée. Giving up a good job as an antique buyer to live in the backblocks!'

There . . . it was out!

It was all jotted down. 'We'll play this up,' said one. 'Sort of renouncing the world for love, eh? What antique firm do you work for, Veronica? Who knows, we might get a shot of their showrooms for contrast.'

This time even Dermid flinched. They were bowled out. Veronica didn't hesitate. 'No firm in particular. Like Theo said, I'm a buyer. Perhaps a little unusual but I'm a freelance in that line. I sell to many firms, as far away as Auckland, and I live on commission.'

She sensed rather than saw Stephie, Lucy and Dermid sag with relief. All unknowing, the script-writer introduced a topic that took the heat off Veronica. 'Doctor, you must have had some hair-raising experiences up here . . . mountain rescues of stranded trampers, women about to give birth when cut off by flooded rivers, perhaps having to be winched out . . . and I daresay you've had some hilarious experiences too?'

The doctor obliged, with the dramatic incidents first, then began to laugh. 'Hilarious? Well, Fiona Campbell, your pilot and star of your programme, once gave me my biggest laugh. Mind you, she'll kill me for repeating it, but it's too good to keep out of an occasion like this. Fiona's not one for getting in a flap, as you can see. She worked in an orphanage in Edinburgh before coming to New Zealand and can cope with most things, but when her Elspeth was rising two, she'd seemed off colour all day.' He gave a guffaw. 'Off colour just about describes it! The child had gripey pains. Fiona thought it was no more than a teething upset till she went to change her nappy, and she found blood. Edward and his men were away up one of the gullies. She hadn't learned to pilot their small launch then, but she saw the tourist launch from farther up heading back to Wanaka. She grabbed a rifle and fired a quick volley to attract their attention, and they came in.

'She managed to leave a note for Edward and was down at the jetty with the children by the time the launch got in. Young Robert was about four. It was a rough trip down, Elspeth was sick, and everyone on board most concerned. It's a long trip when you're anxious about a child, three hours and more.

'Fortunately I was in. It sounded serious. Fiona was just producing the nappy when all of a sudden young Robert said consideringly, "Of course, Mummy, it could have been that lipstick she ate yesterday." Blister me, it was! Fiona was completely humiliated. But oh, boy, I've told it at every medical get-together since. Edward arrived two hours after her, mad with anxiety as she had been, and they went off to their Wanaka crib for the night. I reckon that had as much to do with Fiona taking her helicopter licence as the time the head shepherd broke his leg.'

Veronica hoped they now had enough human interest. She even hoped that when it was edited, the bit about her would be cut. She faded out of the limelight to make sure the pies weren't drying out. Everyone else seemed to enjoy it except her. She felt resentful that Dermid seemed to have dismissed it from his mind and entered into all he was asked to do with great gusto, mock-ups of drenching, drafting, tagging. Sheep were hurriedly penned, the dogs behaved perfectly, and Theo was delighted when they took some glamorous shots of Lucy as: 'The girl who can take the life.' Her ethereal beauty was in such contrast to the ruggedness of her surroundings.

Then, after much stowing of gear with great care, they departed, soaring like a bird against the lake skies and heading down to Wanaka. 'Well, do you ever know?' asked Theo contentedly, 'I can't think of anything better to take an immobile shepherd's mind off his slipped disc. Stephie's cousin, my head man, is going to get a shock when that bird drops out of the skies. Lucy, I'm glad we got that front verandah repaired. It will show things are happening even in our little old neck of the woods!'

'And it's all yours,' said Dermid, 'not handed to you on a platter, as Tordarroch was to me. You're far more of a pioneer than I'll ever be.'

There was a satisfied flash in Theo's dark grey eyes. Veronica went out, Dermid following. In the passage he looked at her closely and said, 'I detect signs of strain. It's been too much for you. Come in here.' He indicated his office. He shut his door, turned to her and said, 'Don't worry too much. Ten to one a lot will be edited out and it'll be so long before it's shown, from what they said, you'll have time to warn your people this was just a mock-up for the best of all possible reasons. They'll think you were a sport. Now, don't get all weepy. It's not as bad as appears.'

Veronica shook her head, fishing for a handkerchief. 'It's not that. I realise we've got time. I——'

He patted her shoulder. 'Then what's got into you?'

To his astonishment she blushed. 'You'll think me an emotional twit.'

'Well, you'd better risk that, because I mean to find out. I don't like to see you like this. You've been a good scout.'

'It—it's Theo. I thought he was going to be like that man at the garage said, a mean sort of bloke, and at first sight he looked so thundery, with rage making those steely grey eyes of his almost black under that thatch of fair hair. But though he looked positively murderous, underneath he's so vulnerable. Yes, he's had a chip on his shoulder, but there have been reasons, back in childhood.'

Dermid seized her chin, made her look up. 'And that dewiness was for Theo? Lucky Theo to get you as his champion. Have you a thing about underdogs? If anyone's lonely or misunderstood you want to comfort him. Is that what led you to——?'

'What are you breaking off for? Led me to what?'

There was a pause, then he added lamely, 'Led you into this situation?'

'Hardly, it was thrust upon me before I had time to think.'

'Then that makes two of us. Perhaps three. Anne's that way too. If course, she'd forgotten for the moment that she was supposed to be up here at Anne's instigation. Dermid added, 'Though in this case, it was kindness on Anne's part for you too. She thought you'd get over—over your loss away from— away from old associations.'

Veronica dared not ask what he meant. This was no time. Neither was it time for confession. She wanted to value those antiques and to try to persuade him they were the price of a dream. It mustn't be done suddenly, and certainly not when they were stuck with Theo for some time yet.

He still had his hands on her shoulders. 'Sometimes we have to discipline our sympathies, Veronica. Or they run away with us. Don't get too fond of Theo.'

She looked astounded. 'That's just ridiculous!'

'It isn't. How can it be when you've been touched to the point of tears about him?'

'It wasn't just him.' She bit her lip. What was she saying?

'Not just him? Then what?'

She could think of no othr excuse, so it had to be the truth. She flushed. 'Now you *will* think me a twit.'

'Go on. I like twits. People who can admit they're twittish at times. I'm waiting, Veronica. Foe heaven's sake, be natural.'

'Well, just that I thought you were a toughie too, very much king of this particular castle. I thought this isolated existence here had even made you arrogant. And you turned all my ideas upside down. Especially in being so understanding of what Theo needs. He needs friendship. He needs *your* friendship. He's had this massive inferiority complex and it's made him prickly. In especial, it seems, he envied you, your security, your fifth or sixth generation property. But you've applied exactly the right treatment. You've even let him see you had yearnings too, that you'd like to have had a place you'd bought yourself, carved out of the wilderness, like he's doing. That sort of understanding got to me. I liked it. And it affected my tear-ducts.'

Dermid drew her a little nearer him. 'I like your liking it. I like you telling me you did. I feel I've only just got to know Theo. Things are going to be better for him from now on. For Lucy too. She's quite different. She needed to be. Veronica, in a very short time you've got so close to all of us.' He looked extremely serious for a moment. 'Is it perhaps the experience of your own life that makes you more tolerant than some of us?'

'I expect that happens to all of us, our experiences shaping and making us. Even the ones we wish hadn't happened.' She was wishing passionately she had nothing to confess. That she wasn't here falsely, as Anne's supposed friend.

'Yes, that's true,' he said heavily. Then, as if he shrugged off an unwelcome thought, 'But don't give me credit for realising Theo needed someone to envy him. I wasn't acting a part. I did. I was the younger son. Gerald should have had Tordarroch. Dad was magnificent the way he took that blow on the chin. I just couldn't tell him I wanted to make my own way. He couldn't have taken it twice. I didn't even know what made me want my very own place.'

Veronica's eyes were wide, they searched his. 'Don't you, Dermid MacBride? Don't you think it would be because in your veins runs the blood of Findlay Shaw? Pioneer blood. I read once that no man is free in whose veins runs the blood of a thousand ancestors. True to type, I can't remember who said it.'

He said absently, 'And I don't know either, this time. I like that. It explains myself to me. I felt such a heel when I didn't want this property dropped in my lap.'

She said softly, 'But you didn't refuse it. You took it out of your love for your father. So in a way that makes it truly yours. It will never go into alien, less caring hands. And in time your son may be glad to inherit it.' This had taken that heavy, rueful look from his face. She was glad of that. 'Dermid, I meant to tell you this. It was rather sweet in a way. I got mud on my shoes from the sheep-pens and sat down on the porch steps to scrape it off. Theo and Lucy didn't know I was there. Theo suddenly said to Lucy, "*I* gave *you* a much more expensive ring than Dermid gave Veronica, didn't I?" and there was the greatest satisfaction in his tone. He went on to say, "It's a very modest one, isn't it? I'd have thought, being the family they are, it'd have been an heirloom one."

'Lucy took it well—she said, "Well, it could be Dermid's mother had still got the heirloom one, if one exists, and as they only got engaged after his parents went to Australia, this might be just a stopgap." I thought that pretty smart thinking.'

Dermid lifted her left hand, gazed at the ring and said, 'It *is* modest, but it suits your brown hand somehow. You really are a nut-brown lass, aren't you? Brown skin, brown eyes and lashes, brown hair with golden ends.' He released her shoulders, put his hands under the petalled strands on her shoulders, fluffed them out and up, then let them fall softly back against her cheeks, where the colour had heightened at his compliment. He put his hands about those cheeks, bent and softly kissed her lips. Then suddenly he took his hands away and seized her, gathering her closely to him, so that she was arched against him. She felt him tremble against her and knew an exultant thrill at the knowledge of the intensity of his feelings. His kiss became more demanding. She knew that perhaps it was merely a male reaction to their proximity, the piquancy of this situation they were caught in, but what did it matter? She was filled with a wild longing such as she had not before known.

Then she relaxed against him, returning his kiss. There was sheer magic in it. Gladness filled her ... if there was this rapport between them, when time came for confession, it might not be so terrible. Dermid lifted his mouth from hers, but laid his cheek against her hair, still holding her. The door opened and in came Stephie.

She checked her brisk walk, hesitated for a moment that seemed too long by far, then giggled and said, 'Well, nothing like a bit of practice! You can do with all of it if your luck's going to hold. Six weeks, the doctor said!'

The other two laughed. It seemed to be the only thing to do and covered up their real feelings at the interruption. Veronica took advantage of Dermid's slackened hold to slip away, following Stephie out after she'd laid some housekeeping notes on Dermid's desk.

Stephie, wisely, said nothing more. Veronica, also wisely, did the same.

Theo seemed more resigned to this long period of rest from then on, oddly enough. Lucy said quite candidly in front of him, 'I thought Theo would have been like an enraged lion, crippled up in his den.'

Veronica laughed, as she went out with Dermid, 'Men are so surprising. I think he likes being spoiled.'

Theo narrowed his eyes and said to Lucy, 'You'd have been afraid to say that to me once.'

Lucy dimpled. 'Yes, but not any more. You're all roar and no bite. It wasn't altogether your fault. I'd been so timid I made you that way. I felt so inadequate, always needing a shoulder to weep on ... so I ran to the first one available and very nearly messed up our lives, and also Dermid's and Veronica's.' She blinked, and turned away. Heavens, she was getting so into the spirit of this, she'd forgotten that *that* was make-believe! She turned back, gave Theo a saucy look, and said, 'So though I'm afraid it's meant a lot of suffering for you, I'm not sorry it happened. There are great compensations, Theo my darling.'

He scowled at her, but it didn't mean a thing. 'Of all the

unfeeling remarks. I've ever heard that's it! You'd never have dared make it if I could move an inch without a groan. But don't count on it too long. I'm much less stiff than even a few days ago. Those muscle relaxants must be starting to work. I can flex my muscles a little while lying now. So watch yourself, my girl!' They both laughed. Lucy came across, kissed him gently but lingeringly. 'Life's going to be very lovely, now, for both of us. Oh, how I want to go home!'

Stephie and Veronica spent a lot of time over at the cottage in preparation for the married couple coming home with Timothy and the baby daughter. Veronica said, 'The MacBrides house their men well. So often married quarters are nothing compared to the main house. But this is lovely— spacious, which is what they need, I guess, when their family is young, and everything's in good taste.'

'Yes, when it was redecorated Dermid's father let Rena choose her own colours and the furnishings. The furniture belongs to the place, because transport up to here is devilishly expensive, and it hampers a young couple if they feel they want to move to another position or set up their own property, if it means they must pay their own removal expenses. However, Tom and Rena love it here so much they could stay for years. Dermid, like his father before him, works on a bonus system for his men. Oh, that sounds like Addie and Maude arriving.'

In they came, all eagerness, with boxes taken from the pillions. One held cake-tins generously filled, the other examples of the most exquisite baby-wear in knitting and crochet, and a large bundle proved to be extra napkins. 'Nobody ever has too many,' quoth Maude sagely. 'It'll be marvellous having a baby at the station again. It seems so long since Timothy was an infant. Rena used to let us bath him. I hope we haven't lost our touch. We've missed Timothy horribly. I hope he doesn't find our kindergarten mornings too boring after two moths in Nelson with other children.'

Stephie said, 'He's bound to miss his playmates, but Rena

said on the phone one night that child's such a high-country man in the making, all his talk is of getting back to the dogs and horses. And the sheep. Veronica, we've had so many children up here on correspondence lessons, with Maude and Addie providing the oversight, they're expert governesses for all ages really.'

Maude said, 'We were so much younger than the rest of the family that we were aunts before we grew up, so we got pressed into service in the schoolroom. Now if only Dermid would get married soon we'd be back in that sphere of service in no time, not just filling in time at Chattan House.'

Again scalding pity touched Veronica. These two women had filled in their empty lives for so long. She mustn't lose sight of her original quest in the role she'd been pitchforked into. There was just a month to go of Theo's convalescence. So the next day she told Dermid she'd been invited over to Chattan House for lunch and dinner.

'Oh, good, my aunts will enjoy that. Tell them I'll come for dinner. Make the place seem more civilised to you if you get asked out once in a while.'

Without thinking Veronica replied, 'Who wants civilisation?'

They were up in the Little Sitting-room, with Stephie placidly darning farm socks. Dermid looked at Veronica sharply. 'Coming from one who's got greasepaint in her blood and the applause of the crowds in her ears, that sounds like rank heresy!'

She found her cheeks growing hot, and bent down to poke the fire to disguise that. It was so hard to remember. She said lightly, 'I don't see why actresses can't love the solitudes too. I might not be in the Hollywood class, but they often own ranches so they can get away from it all, don't they?'

He sounded sceptical. 'Mm. Perhaps. I guess it soon palls, though.'

Stephie took him up sharply. 'Not necessarily. Some girls just drift into the theatre. With some it's their whole life, like with Anne, but with others it can be just the same as any other job before marriage, and they aren't dedicated to it.

Some careers continue, some don't. Others are taken up again when they've got their children to the independent stage.'

The MacBride eyebrows came down. 'Not up here they don't. Any girl who takes on a high-country, up-lake, water-access owner takes it on for the rest of her life. No commuting to business from here. In that respect, any wife of Tordarroch is as tied to the station as Euphemia Shaw was from the time she stepped ashore here from the whaleboat.'

There was an awkward silence, then he asked, changing the subject, 'How are you going across to Chattan House?'

'I'm getting quite proficient on Blondie. I'll ride her over.'

'You can have the Land Rover. Then if you feel like dressing up, which will delight the aunts, you'll be suitably attired. They might even give you the meal off that Regency table you're so keen on. What a versatile creature you are, when I think how Anne described you!'

Her voice had an edge to it. 'Again, as you remarked just now, it could be just novelty. But thanks for the transport, though I'll go over in jeans. I'm to help them springclean the attic.' That was in case he caught them at it.

'You don't know what you're letting yourself in for. It's jammed with junk, with Victorian hideosities that ought to have been dumped long ago, even bottle-green plush curtains with bobbles.'

Veronica's spirits rose. There could be saleable stuff there that the lordly MacBride despised. So he'd have no objection to turning it into cash. That could lessen his anger at her deceit.

CHAPTER SEVEN

VERONICA decided that if the aunts would be pleased if she dressed up, then dress up she would. At least she told herself that was the reason. What she chose might have seemed a bit out of place here at Tordarroch House, with Theo still awkwardly eating his meals off the bookcase, but at Chattan House, in that small exquisite dining-room, it wouldn't.

The aunts were enchanted when she arrived and announced that Dermid had invited himself and had told her to dress up. Maude said, eyes astar, 'We so nearly rang up to suggest just that, but we decided it might look a little too contrived.' Adelaide gave her sister a quelling look. Veronica pretended not to notice.

She said crisply, 'I'd like to get straight at this attic. How about it?'

Adelaide nodded, 'Maude will go up with you. I'd better make apple pie. We had decided on a lemon soufflé, but like all men, Dermid thinks you can't better apple pie.'

From the front of the house, Veronica had seen only dormers, but the attic was an odd projection from the back roof, jutting over the original sod cottage.

Maude shut the windows against the cool spring breeze coming straight off the mountains inland. 'I left them open all morning because it smelled so fusty, dear. Goodness, there is a conglomeration of stuff here! Mostly junk, I'm afraid.'

Veronica's trained eye was already picking out one or two pieces that were anything but junk, but yes, she agreed, some of this was only fit for burning. By the time Adelaide came up they had cleared a corner and arranged on an old washstand, past repair, some china that was neither elegant nor coveted by dealers, but which would still fetch prices not to be sneezed at. The colours were sombre but had come back into favour again, jardinières in heavily embossed mustards and olive green, cake-stands in oak, china figures that were only passable, inkstands and ornate trays.

'They're also ours, from our mother, but given to her by an old aunt, who'd had no taste at all. Those beaded hassocks are hers, and those hideously fat pincushions. Purely ornamental, you'd buckle any pin you tried to stick in them. When this old aunt saw Mother taking down that Regency stuff, she decided she was the one with feeling for old things and bestowed them on her. Poor Mother, she was so embarrassed when her new husband was faced by twice as much stuff as he'd expected, and it took two trips in the Government launch. Our father was much relieved when he found Mother wasn't attached to it, so most of its time was spent in the loft over the stables. When our brothers took a fancy to making the loft into quarters for themselves, this was all shoved up here.'

'Where are those brothers now? Didn't they carry on here?'

'They were a lot older than us, but one died quite young. They were pre-penicillin days, of course, and pneumonia often proved fatal. The other one was Dermid's mother's sire. He had only Rhoda. He sent her off on a visit to Scotland, and it was a great joy to him when she married a very distant MacBride connection. He thought the wheel had turned full cycle. The first woman here, Euphemia, was a MacBride.'

The green plush curtains Dermid had despised turned out to be mantel drapes and as such, in demand for lovers of Victoriana. They were wrapped round some bulky items which almost bounced off the stand as she undid them. They were blackened with years of tarnish and neglect, but the very elegance of their shape filled Veronica with delight. She was almost sure they were Georgian silver. She picked up some cleaning fluid and rubbed vigorously at the bottom of them. The first one turned out to be a fruit basket, definitely Georgian, exquisitely scrolled and pierced. The next, an épergne, all fluted edges and silver chains. There were silver candelabra, matching, and a silver teapot and stand, that surely would have a cream jug and sugar basin to complete the set. Her pulses quickened and she swung round on

Maude. 'We'd have to be sure these were your mother's and not Shaw or MacBride possessions. They're valuable. Whose were they?'

Maude, for some reason, looked guilty, and Veronica wondered if she was going to become involved in a family squabble, but the explanation was laughable. 'We were very naughty, Veronica. Cleaning these darned things was our most hated Saturday morning task when we were small. Even when we were older we hated it. And this house and Tordarroch house were just full of these things. Each bride seemed to bring more—if not heirlooms, wedding gifts. So——' a gleam of mischief peeked through, 'when we had Chattan House to ourselves, we took one look at the things Dermid's mother didn't want there, plus these, and we stowed them up in the attic! We'd heard you should store silver in green baize and we didn't have any, so we just wrapped them up in these frightful old mantel drapes.'

Veronica couldn't help it. She burst out laughing. 'I feel I ought to reprimand you as your grandmother might possibly have done, you wicked things, but I'll forgive you if you can tell me who they belonged to in your family.'

'I'm afraid except for that fruit basket, we've no idea. There was a mention of it in Euphemia's diary she started on board the sailing-ship. She said it hadn't got as much as a dent on arrival, rolled up in blankets with feather pillows all round in the sea-chest, despite the rough journey, the shifting by dray to the lakeside and the fact that when they beached the whaleboat in this bay, the chest fell into the shallows! That épergne and the candelabra could have been there too, we just don't know. So we can't sell those, but if you can get rid of those other monstrosities, Dermid couldn't possibly object.'

Veronica said, 'In fact, he ought to be glad you got me up here whether he sells this silver or keeps it. But they must be on show, Maude. Oh, there you are, Adelaide. These are really valuable and we can have great fun cleaning them up. They should go in those glass-fronted cabinets downstairs, or over at Tordarroch in theirs. Would Stephie find it a great chore to look after them?'

'She would have once, when Dermid and Gerald and Anne were small, but there's more time now. Rhoda, his mother, has often said she must get these things out again. She'd love them now.'

Veronica's voice held real regret. 'But that would mean they'd be banished from this place where Euphemia brought them. His parents are retiring in Wanaka, aren't they?'

'If they ever do. Gregor is going to break his heart leaving here and Rhoda knows it. She feels Dermid must have a chance to run this place on his own, but Gregor would need an interest. She has a vague idea that Tordarroch House could be turned into one of those farm holiday homes that overseas tourists are so keen on, where they can ride, watch shearing and dipping, get away from it all. One that has access only by water, would be a bigger draw than any. So show-pieces like this would be of great interest. We could do out cards for them, the story of their origin . . . the ones we know, anyway.'

Veronica was shining-eyed. 'It sounds ideal. They wouldn't want this other stuff. It's nowhere near as valuable, but it would give you a jolly good sum towards your trip to Italy and we've got a lot to uncover yet. Let's get at it, girls!'

Suddenly they did seem girls to her. At the light in their eyes she could suddenly see those young girls who went to Wellington in the nineteen-forties, and waved goodbye to the troopship taking their young men out of their lives for ever. She hoped passionately to find more valuable stuff still among their own mother's possessions without having to rob downstairs of any of those gracious treasures that enhanced the rooms. Any hint of that would surely put the cat among the pigeons as far as Dermid was concerned.

Hours later Veronica knew that if, when Theo and Lucy were gone, Dermid gave his consent, Adelaide and Maude could book their flights to Rome without any doubts. 'Now, let's get the dust off ourselves, and change. Mind, not a word to Dermid about any of this. He thinks that anything I sound knowledgeable about to Theo is what I've swotted up from that book over at the homestead. I don't want him to know yet that this is my own trade. Not till I can present to him a true picture of the value of this stuff, and itemise, from your lists, from whom it came.'

Maude and Addie loved dressing up. They might not often leave the sheep station for Dunedin or Christchurch, but when they did they certainly knew how to shop, and both were splendid amateur hairdressers. Adelaide was in a rich russetty colour which suited her so well, and Maude in turquoise blue. They came into the spare room to watch Veronica dress just as if she had been a loved granddaughter, the granddaughter they might have had now, had it not been for the wastefulness of war. They said so.

Maude was determined to style Veronica's hair. 'You can do so much with hair this length.' They loved the brown skirt she produced, softly flared, with a scarlet and green striped inset running diagonally from waistband to hem. Over it she slipped a long loose blouse of richest cream silk whose bishop sleeves fell in heavy graceful folds to her wrists. It had a narrow plunging neckline, and against it her brown skin glowed.

Addie clasped her hands in delight. 'That's perfect! You have just the right sort of bosom for that blouse . . . don't you think so, Maudie? Bosom is a much nicer word than "bust", don't you think? When ever I go in to be measured for a new bra and they say: "What bust?" I always feel like saying, "I didn't hear anything." A very ugly word.'

Veronica giggled. 'Oh, I do love you two! I hate being with people I can't giggle with. You're quite mad, you know, but it's such an endearing sort of craziness.'

Maude, her head on one side, said, 'The ivory necklace and the earrings to go with it—the very thing! She's ideal for them. Addie, you hunt them out while I fix her hair.'

In vain Veronica protested, then said, 'Well, just for tonight. I won't wear them back to Tordarroch House. I'd be terrified I'd lose them. It's enough responsibility having Guy's wife's ring!'

Adelaide said slowly, 'We've no one to leave them to. We've given Anne what she wanted. Well, dear child, wear them tonight to please two romantic old things, and if you can bear to part with them, you can leave them here meanwhile. And you never know——' she stopped dead, changed it to, 'But we'll leave them to you in our wills. You can't do a thing about it then.'

Veronica flung out a hand. 'Oh, don't! You're so vital . . . so much part of here. Don't say it!'

'Isn't she sweet?' said Addie fondly.

Maude placed her on a stool in front of the triple-mirrored dressing-table that had featured whole generations of Shaw and MacBride wives and daughters, brought in two tortoiseshell combs that had belonged to Phemie, brushed the nut-coloured hair till it shone, took a wing from each temple, secured it with the combs, sweeping it upward, then caught the two ends together and tied them over the fall of her back with a long cream ribbon in satin, a style she'd never thought of trying before. 'Oh, I like it,' she said, bending forward to examine it. 'Maude, you're an artist!'

'Why, I think so,' said a voice from the doorway. Dermid, in knife-edged brown trousers, so different from his casual farm attire, and with a putty-coloured pullover on top of an immaculate cream silk shirt, with a brown tie. The chestnut hair was damp from his shower, he looked elegant, at ease, suiting this darling house.

He had something in his hand and now came forward with it, grinning. 'When you take a girl to dinner in town you often buy her flowers—it can't be done here, but with a name like Blakeney, I thought this was fitting, and could almost be called your plant-badge.' Laughing, he held out a tiny spray of scarlet pimpernel, taken from the Tordarroch pastures.

They all laughed at the sheer absurdity of it, but Veronica took it. 'I like it. Of course that was the name of the Scarlet Pimpernel, Sir Percy and Marguerite Blakeney. Now, where shall I pin it?'

He came across, picked up a pearl pin from the dressing-table. 'I'll put it in place for you.'

Adelaide said, 'Maude, you left those sheep-shanks on the bench, didn't you? I've just heard Patches jump in the window. Come on, you know what he is,' and they disappeared.

Veronica wished the aunts weren't so obvious. She found her cheeks growing hot and sighed.

Dermid cocked his head in their direction. 'Don't let them bother you. You can't do a thing about it. They're very romantic at heart and it certainly doesn't worry me.'

He surveyed her. She was acutely conscious of his eyes travelling over her. Conscious too that she liked it, liked the little smile playing around his mouth. He said, 'I think it would be perfect in the V of that neckline.'

His fingers were cool against her flesh. She held herself rather rigid, not wanting him to know the effect his touch had upon her. He fastened it in, neither hurrying nor taking too long about it, stepped back and said, 'Perfect. The splash of scarlet in your skirt and the tiny touch there.'

Veronica rose from the stool, touched her hair a little selfconsciously and said, 'I couldn't stop them. They said they hadn't a granddaughter to dress up.'

He took her elbow. 'Poor Veronica ... a product of a different age, even of a permissive age, having to submit to the idealism and sentimentality of Maude and Adelaide! But you're putting up with it very well.'

She immediately felt defensive. 'I didn't say I didn't like it, MacBride. I know I'm a product of my own age. So are you, except you were a little more insulated from change, up here in this kingdom. But it's not to say that underneath it all, girls like me are so very different from Maude and Adelaide.'

He then regarded her very consideringly—why, she didn't know. Finally he said, 'I wonder. I just wonder. Well, come along, Lady Blakeney. Dinner awaits. I'm sure I can smell apple pie—with cloves.'

She took his arm. 'You can. We were to have lemon soufflé, but when they heard you were coming, apple pie it had to be.'

Well, the aunts might have treated that old Georgian silver shamefully, but this, on that beautiful table with the lace place mats, was well looked after. Another fruit basket sat there, filled with tawny pears and rosy apples, each fruit polished as brightly as the silver. The cruet set, with its blue glass insets, bore no evidence of neglect, nor did the cutlery and the napkin rings. The china looked at first glance like Willow Pattern, but proved to be blue and white Asian pheasant and rose design. The big ashet in the centre, carried in as they came down, was the same, and was piled with a delectable mound of saffron rice, and in the centre, in the shape of a wheel, were beautifully browned mutton shanks, surrounded with a ring of parsley and topped with a barbecue sauce that appeared to be compounded of Worcester sauce, chopped bacon and onion, all delicately spiced. Jacket potatoes were wrapped in foil, and dishes of their own beans and peas, frozen months ago, flanked the main one.

Dermid surveyed it, said, 'Just as well I was out on the hill on Desdemona all afternoon. I've worked up a rare appetite. Otherwise after all this, and that delectable soup, I'd never manage the apple pie. But I'll try to do full justice to it.'

He was in good form ... the loved great-nephew ... MacBride of Tordarroch ... the king of the castle. All these things went racing through Veronica's mind. Talk turned on former times.

It could be said Maude and Adelaide glowed. They had an audience. They were reliving other days. 'Perhaps best of all was the prosperity that followed Word War One in the early twenties. The false prosperity. We were tiny children,' said Adelaide, 'but we can remember how generous our father became, generous to a fault. The property was not so mechanised then, so there was a larger staff and at shearing and mustering huge gangs arrived. Tordarroch was often visited by politicians, V.I.P.s, even Governors-General. There was a great attraction for them about a sheep station where all the mutton and wool went out by water transport. There was always a permanent cook for the men—well, permanent is possibly the wrong word to describe them. They were in the main eccentric characters, robust, colourful, but they often had their reasons for getting away from it all, and sometimes they disappeared as suddenly as they came. But Mother and Father coped. She just loved the entertaining. It brought the world to her lonely door, and compensated greatly for all she gave up when she married Father.'

Veronica took a sip of the ruby-red wine from her goblet, a goblet that had been in use for well over a hundred years. She said, 'I take it that your father was a robust character too. Very much king of the castle?'

Adelaide and Maude stared at each other, went into a peal of laughter. 'Father? Oh, how priceless! Well ... he was a curious mixture. He had all the rugged qualities needed to run a place like this at the back of beyond, but he had a heart of butter. Mother could twist him round her little finger. And if we were ill, his touch was as tender as hers was.'

Maude said, 'I once had scarlet fever. We were so susceptible to infection when we went to town. In those days you used to be sent away to fever hospitals and it meant six weeks away. They shaved your head. No, I'm wrong, they cut your hair very short—they thought your strength went into it. No antibiotics. Fortunately, mine didn't develop till we got home. I'll never forget the fever, the nightmares that went with the raging temperature. I came out of delirium one night to hear Father say, 'Josie, you canna keep up night after night. Go to bed, lass. Of *course* I won't fall asleep. Do you think I could, with our bairn needing me?' And all that night as I surfaced at odd intervals, he was sponging me, turning me, getting fresh, dry pillowslips, spooning magnesia and cool water between my dry lips, murmuring all sorts of endearments.'

Adelaide nodded, 'And though they worked like Trojans on the estate, both of them, they played as hard as they worked when they took a spell off. Father, when he took us to Christchurch for occasional holidays, would buy Mother the most frivolous, rather unsuitable things. And he brought some secret parcels home always, to produce for times when he thought she needed cheering up. It was a real love match. There's been a great history of love matches at Tordarroch.'

All three of them stared at Veronica. She was blinking rapidly. Her cheeks crimsoned. 'Don't mind me. I've got over-active tear-ducts ... it's almost an affliction! It makes me feel so silly, to cry at films, or sometimes listening to music. And that wasn't sad, so that makes it more stupid still.'

Dermid said, 'Don't apologise. There's too little of that nowadays.'

Veronica said, dabbing, 'That makes you sound of another generation.' Then she caught his eye and for a moment it seemed as if no one else was present. 'But I like it,' she added.

He accepted that, as of right, with a brief nod.

She then said, 'Anyway, I stand abashed. Somehow I imagined this to always have been a sort of one-man kingdom—I thought of Findlay Shaw as a dour, determined man bringing a young inexperienced girl here as a bride, to a remote, harsh existence. A place of incredible beauty, yes, but meaning hardships such as we can only guess at now. I felt that in many of these tough pioneers there had to be a ruthless streak, a sort of greed for the land that would trample over the lives of their women.'

Across the table Dermid's eyes met hers. She could have sworn they held a challenge. He said slowly, 'We must catch you up on the family history. Some of the old pioneer types were just that, but not all, and don't forget they'd be products of their day and age, just as we are. Theirs now seems to have held incredible hardships, but perhaps they didn't seem that way to them. The conditions in the Old Country they left were often far from ideal. Some young wives didn't know what it was to have a home of their own. They had to live with in-laws, and that's never easy.

'Oddly enough, it was Euphemia who wanted to emigrate. Findlay's family, the Shaws, had had quite a fine family tradition, but like so many Highlanders, lost possession of much of their land. Ours was a very minor branch, though a few heirlooms remain.' He touched the goblet in front of him briefly. 'So we hadn't the urgent need to emigrate that some crofters had when they were driven off their land by greedy landowners wanting to run more sheep. But Findlay was a seventh son and the holding wasn't large. Phemy thought his potential for hard work would never be given scope there. She it was who was the motive power behind that embarking on a three-months' voyage under sail. Then coming up here where, provided they stocked this land within a certain time, they were granted it.'

Veronica's eyes were shining. 'Then this has always been a happy house. I felt it in my bones, but told myself not to be too fanciful. That there could have been great sorrows here, hardships, domestic tyranny.'

Dermid looked at his aunts. 'Some day she must read Euphemia's diaries. She wielded a nifty pen, Veronica. If she'd had the chance she'd probably have become a writer. Some entries are terse for want of time. Once she said, "I must put down these things for my children in case I forget. I must record these sunrises and sunsets. I'd like to think our descendants could look on these same scenes and think because they'd read what I've written of them, 'Why, our grandmother, or great-grandmother, saw a sunset like this in 1869.' I'd like to think they didn't just know my children by names on tombstones in a lakeside cemetery, but that because they read these pages, they would think of my Matthew as the three-year-old who brought me a bunch of buttercups on my birthday, and Esther as the little girl who laboriously worked me that sampler on the dining-room wall." Have I got those entries about right, aunts?'

'You have,' said Adelaide softly. 'We're very lucky indeed, in this day and age, to have a nephew like you who cares for these things. That's what Phemy hoped for. And there, Veronica, is the sampler, on the wall behind you.'

Dermid rose, took it off the wall, blew the dust off it and handed it to Veronica. Perhaps small Esther's mother, mindful of how weary little fingers get, had chosen the smallest possible text. 'God is Love.' She turned it over and there, in what was presumably Euphemia's writing, was written: 'Worked by Esther Shaw, aged eight years, ten months.'

Veronica was starry-eyed. 'I can just see her, bent laboriously over her sewing, longing to be out with her brothers and sisters, damning up creeks, playing with kittens and puppies, but determined to finish this in time for the birthday, because there weren't any shops where she could buy her a present.'

Dermid laughed. 'What a change has come over our Miss Blakeney, the girl our Anne said liked everything slick and modern! "You should just see the with-it décor of her flat," was what she said, so who knows? Veronica, you could become so changed, you might give up the stage entirely and become an assistant in an antique shop like that yarn you spun Theo!'

Veronica bent her head so he couldn't see her face. 'It's quite an idea. Other people suddenly take on new interests ... like Churchill taking up painting at forty ... why not me? It's always possible to make an entirely new start, I suppose. So why not antiques?'

Adelaide, suppressing a cough, rose and said, 'I must get that coffee.' Maude scuttled out after her.

Dermid said, 'What's come over them? Pretty sudden, aren't they? We're not exactly dying of thirst.'

'I suppose they want to wash up and settle down soon. They want to watch something at eight o'clock.'

'That thing on pot-plants? Then we'll go for a walk then.'

Veronica dimpled, 'Now you can see why I thought all your ancestors were petty tyrants, Dermid! You just announce that you're taking a girl for a walk. She doesn't get asked. It might be too cold for me. I might be too tired. I might yearn to see that thing on pot-plants.'

'*Are* you too tired?'

'Well, no, but——'

'And it couldn't be cold. It's so warm tonight it fills me with alarm. The false spring always does. It's too warm, too soon. It sometimes means something is brewing among the mountains. It's perilously near lambing. As you know, we've got the pre-lamb shearing over.'

'Is it very tough, coping then?'

'Very. Oh, we do cope, but it means losses, of course, and dozens of lambs cluttering up both houses and needing constant attention. But I'm really thinking of Theo. You don't feel so bad if you're on deck on your own place, but if we get a season like we had five or so years ago, it'd be the very devil for Theo, cooped up here. That year we were delivering lambs and hopelessly looking round for a dry place to put them down on. In fact, for anything less than a puddle! Those born during the night, unnoticed, hadn't much of a chance. Theo needs a good season. He's got good men, but it's not quite the same as being there yourself. And they can't stand too many extra pressures on that marriage of theirs.'

She leaned her chin on her hands. 'I don't know. Isn't adversity bringing out the best in Lucy?'

'Seems to be. But I'm frightened if Theo gets morose again, it will dishearten her. Stands to reason a chap'd be morose if faced with heavy losses.'

She said, 'Didn't Euphemia and Findlay, and Matthew and his wife, and the aunts' parents all face severe losses at times? Stephie has told me quite a bit about life up here. The disastrous snows of 1867, the floods of 1878, the terrible frosts of 1922 when the hens froze to their perches. That's what brought them close together, Stephie said.' She added, 'So Lucy and Theo could be okay.'

Dermid said simply, 'The ones you were talking of were Shaws. Their motto is "By fidelity and fortitude." And times were different.'

There was an edge to her tone. 'The Shaws haven't the monopoly of fortitude and fidelity. I think Lucy's got more in her than you give her credit for. I think all of you up here petted her, because she seemed so pathetic, so lonely. You encouraged her to cling. But she married Theo who didn't want a clinger, and because she so nearly lost him, she's got some stiffening in her backbone now. There's so often a turning point, a time when one turns one's back on the past and launches out into a new life. As I did myself recently. I'm on my own now, and I like it. I feel a different person from the one I was six months ago, even.' She stopped there because she suddenly realised she didn't want to explain that, about her job. His hand reached out across the table to her but couldn't reach hers because it was too wide. Also because she didn't stretch hers out towards him.

He said, 'Do you, Veronica? A different person? Good for you! Will you tell me about it some time? Some time soon?'

Her brown eyes looked steadily into the intent green ones. What meaning lay behind that look? She said quietly, and her tone was grave, 'I will—that I promise you, Dermid. I do have something to tell you, but it must wait till Theo has gone home. It's something you won't like, Dermid, but it will have to be told.'

His eyes narrowed. 'Then I'll wait till you want to tell me. But don't be afraid, Veronica. I'll do my level best to understand. If I can.'

At that moment the aunts came back with the coffee. Veronica was glad to have the conversation end right there. For two reasons—one that she wanted to value all the stuff first, two that they needed to preserve this mock engagement as it appeared right now, all sweetness and light. If she and Dermid quarrelled, it might show. Lambing had to be got over first, too, and Lucy and Theo must be over that other lake before she told him.

The aunts, fortunately, didn't twitter about it being foolish to stroll outside at this time, when there was still snow on the tops despite the unseasonable warmth of air at the lake-edge. Maude simply brought a cloak for Veronica to slip on. 'It's quite old, made from the shepherd's tartan of the clan. Sent out from Scotland during the fifties. You're so tall you'll suit it.'

She clipped it about Veronica's neck and the black-and-white checked folds fell softly about her. Dermid pulled on a brown suede jacket, lined with lambswool. 'First the flagged paths in the garden,' he said. 'Put your left hand through the slit on that side and hang on to me. The crazy paving is really crazy, but you can't comfortably put your arm round a girl in a cloak.'

Veronica lifted the clear line of her jaw to the faint breeze coming off the lake. 'I'm sure it's got all the tang of the rain-forests of the Haast in it, and as it gets into Maude and Addie's lovely garden, the scent of daffodils and narcissi. I love the way they bloom under the silver birches. By moonlight the silver birches are loveliest of all trees.'

'And in the autumn sunsets, the liquid ambers and Lombardy poplars. It's a dream then.'

Veronica had a sudden pang. She would never see them in autumn. Dermid would expect her to be back in Dunedin then. By then, too, she would have had to tell him she'd come up here to buy antiques. The other day he'd asked her, brusquely, if she intended to go on with a stage career. She'd had to say yes. Half the time she didn't know if she was Veronica or Victoria. Where was that wretched girl, anyway? Gus had never rung to say. He'd be afraid to do so in case he gave anything away or that her answers did. If he rang and got Dermid, it was ten to one Dermid would ask why he wanted to speak to Veronica.

Bluebells were peeping from under the rhododendron leaves. They'd been sent out from Scotland Dermid told her and were the true Scottish bluebells, not wild hyacinths. 'We go down here, through the shrubbery. Watch your step. It leads right to the shore. Chattan is so much nearer the lake than Tordarroch. They had to build the first rough cottage in the lee of the hill to shelter it from the sou'westers coming up from the bottom of the world. Then they found out they had sizzling summers and that the dry nor'westers could sweep up the lake and hit the front of the house, so they planted saplings for their lives . . . obliging little trees that conditioned themselves in amazing fashion to a change of season . . . when the cold frosts of autumn came, they obligingly turned colour. It must have seemed a long time before they grew tall enough, though. It finally made the Chattan garden a sheltered haven. Even now things grow here we can't grow at Tordarroch.'

'I've noticed that, and of course the aunts love this garden so much and spend such a lot of time in it. It has a history in every tree, every flower-bed.'

Veronica could sense his studying her in the light of that moon. His laugh had a note of exultancy in it. 'I think this place has worked a charm on you!' She knew he meant because she was so different from the girl Anne had described, who liked ultra-modern stuff.

She said, warily, 'Well, no wonder. There's such a continuity about it. I'm so glad Addie and Maude told me about their parents' love match. And the first Shaws. It fits this place. And though the aunts had their time of heartbreak, I suppose they were happy in the succeeding years that they had this security. They never had to leave it.'

Dermid guided her down some rough rock steps on to the path that led to the tiny jetty here. Then he answered her. 'I don't know, Veronica—circumstances kept them here too long for them to strike out, to make a new life. They stayed to see their parents through their last years. They've had, for a long time, I know, a yen to do something different.'

She caught her breath. Then he did know they wanted to visit those graves on foreign soil. Was this the time to tell him?

But he continued: 'Maude and Adelaide would like, after all these years, to have a home with a road running right by its door, in the middle of Wanaka. To join in with all the activities they love so much when they have their brief spells down there. That's why, when Mother and Father began talking of turning Tordarroch into a farm holiday place, I made it plain to them that they must, in that case, get hired help in addition to Stephie. I wasn't going to have Addie and Maude tied again to Tordarroch by their over-developed sense of duty.'

For once what she'd deemed the arrogance and dominance of MacBride of Tordarroch didn't irritate her. He was right in this. He hadn't hesitated to spring to the defence of these two women who had given their lives to this estate.

She said warmly, 'Oh, Dermid, I'm glad you feel that way. Some families take such things for granted, let one member do all the sacrificing. Only those two would be so in the way of helping, I daresay every time they thought your mother and Stephie were getting overworked, they'd pitch in.'

'Exactly—that's why I'm cooking up a surprise for them. If we get down to Wanaka before lambing I'll show you, but you'll be sworn to secrecy. I don't want any hint of it to get to the aunts yet. We've had that crib at Wanaka for years.

Mother used to take us down to it for our week or two off school, and her parents did so with her. It's as old-fashioned as Tordarroch House really. I've put it on the market for sale as a holiday house, the section's quite valuable and could sell as a motel site. I've put a deposit on a newly-built place on the hillside above Eely Point. The aunts have always drawn an income from the estate, of course, so they would have enough to furnish it. They could take things from here, but they've always said how they'd love to start with things of their own, if ever they lived in Wanaka. Modern things. They wouldn't have let me do it if they'd known, and I had to make a snap decision. There were others in the running.'

'Why wouldn't they have let you?'

'Because they'd realise I'd have to postpone the building of the new woolshed. This one is adequate in size, but the new woolsheds are dreams, with every facility for speed and comfort. Gangs are easier to book if they know they can work in such surroundings. The signing up is to be done soon now, but I didn't want to tell them till I can parcel up the deed, and put it into their hands. They'd never let me otherwise. It's even got a granny flat attached, so when Tom and Rena's children need their school spells there'll still be accommodation. And for my own children perhaps, in years to come.'

Veronica couldn't speak for a moment. Her mind flew back to the first impression she'd had from Adelaide's letter, that they had a tough, selfish nephew who was too mean to let his aunts travel as they desired. Later she'd detested him even more, because their travel plans were a pilgrimage to see the graves of the young men they had lost in war. Words almost sprang to her lips, telling him all, but she checked them. Because if he knew they were planning to spend the money he thought would go on furnishing the house he'd bought them, it would shadow that gift. What a dilemma! She choked back the confidence, the confession.

But she couldn't keep back the gladness in her voice as she cried out, 'Why, Dermid, that's the loveliest thing! I can imagine what a thrill they'll get. Wanaka . . . much better than retiring to a city from here. If they get homesick at all, they'd only have to get on Gus's launch when he takes tourists on a cruise, to see you all.' She gave a laugh of sheer mirth. 'I can just see those intrepid souls scooting all round Wanaka on their bikes!'

Dermid laughed too, but added ruefully, 'That scares hell out of me. I wouldn't put it past them to attempt the Crown Range if they took it into their heads to go to Queenstown. Or for that matter to follow on to Te Anau and Milford Sound! We'll have to try to sell the bikes and get them a second-hand car. I think Dad would come in on that. I'll have to keep the brakes on the aunts in the first flush of their enthusiasm for furnishing it, though. I expect it's to do with being so rarely in cities, but when they have their trips to Dunedin and Christchurch, they're big spenders. Now, let's stop talking family and just be two people getting to know each other. After all, we're supposed to be engaged.'

They had come to the little jetty and walked on to it by now. The dark waters mirrored the moon. There was only the sound of the gentle lap-lap of waters against the shingle lake-shore.

As he turned to her Veronica said breathlessly, '*Supposed* is the operative word, MacBride.'

He laughed down on her, his face was very near, the warmth of his breath against her cheek. 'Whenever you call me MacBride, I can feel the barriers going up. Do they have to stay up? Why not get some fun out of the situation, Veronica Blakeney. A man and a girl and a night like this . . .'

She drew back a little, well aware of the tumultous feelings surging within her. It could be just fun to him, meaning nothing.

He sensed her withdrawal and his voice was a little sharp. 'What's the matter? Find the idea repugnant?'

If only he knew . . . anything but!

She stumbled over her answer. 'No . . . at least . . . oh, Dermid, don't you realise some situations are difficult for a girl?'

His voice was strangely harsh. 'I rather thought they weren't so difficult these days.'

She considered that. 'I'm not sure what you mean, but what *I* mean, if I've got the courage to say it, is that even today, some of us like to set the pace. And—and—you mightn't like it if I appeared too—oh, aren't words clumsy, inadequate?'

The tone softened a little. 'Are you trying to say you don't want to appear too ready? Correct me if I'm wrong.'

She said gratefully, 'No, you're right. Only I thought it sounded pompous, priggish. But I don't want this situation to get out of hand in any way. I think we get so used to acting the part, it . . . it's inclined to go to our heads rather.'

His laugh sounded genuine this time. 'Veronica, aren't we being too analytical? Let's forget about this supposed engagement. Imagine I've just met you, say in Dunedin. Anne's introduced us and I've asked you to go for a ramble. Dunedin has some wonderful Lovers' Lanes. Say along that leafy road behind Otago Boys' High and into Maori Road? There won't be a lake, but below us we'll see the harbour lights reflected in the water and the moon. The same moon as here. Don't you think that even without that ring on your finger, I might kiss you, hold you?'

He tipped her chin up, kissed her lingeringly. He put his arms beneath the cloak and pulled her against him. She hoped that beneath that thin silk blouse he couldn't feel just how her heart was racing. What a giveaway! Then he took her to the seat on the jetty, kept his arm about her, said teasingly, 'Admit it, Veronica, that when you're, say, eighty you'll be glad we shared that kiss tonight?'

She laughed back. 'I'll have to be honest and say yes, but I've never been one to fall into a man's arms at the first approach.'

She thought he checked a quick reply to that, then he said slowly, 'I'm glad of that, it compensates for other things.' She wouldn't ask what he meant. Then in a tone she'd never heard from him before, a husky tone, as if he was suppressing some emotion, 'Does it always have to be the man to approach? Who kisses? Why don't you kiss me?'

For some reason that moved her. MacBride of Tordarroch

asking, not taking. There was also a hint of leashed longing. She felt him tremble. Was this moment for him, as well as for her, something real and vital, not pretence?

She couldn't, quite, trust herself to speak. She smiled instead, knowing he would see the smile because the moonlight was now almost as bright as day. She put her arms up, linked her hands behind his head, drew his face down and kissed him full on the lips. Then she was gathered close, kissed passionately. At last, a little shyly, she let her hands slide down as far as his shoulders, where he put his hands up to cover hers and held them there. He said, with a whimsical lilt in his voice, 'Thank you, Veronica Rose,' and as one they rose up to walk back to the house. Suddenly he stopped, swung her round and said, with a laugh in his voice, 'I think I'll remove that telltale scarlet pimpernel.'

'Telltale? What——'

'The aunts have such sharp eyes. It's crushed to nothing.' Again she felt his fingers cool against her flesh. He slipped out the pearl pin, took the withered spray, and, to her surprise, dropped it into the pocket of his suede jacket.

They were rogues, those two aunts. Dermid and Veronica came into the Chattan sitting-room to find soft music playing ... haunting, sweet. Beethoven. The lights were low, the glowing firelight supplemented only by two old-fashioned wall-lights each side of the mantelpiece.

Dermid's eyes gleamed with fun. 'A truly romantic setting! I hand it to you, my dear aunts, you're great organisers. By now, Veronica ought to realise that Tordarroch Bay isn't all isolation and crude living. We can turn it on, can't we? Moonlight Sonatas and all. Complete with genuine moons!'

They didn't disclaim they'd arranged it, which would have made a farce of it. Adelaide said calmly, 'Well, for a long time we've enjoyed our romances vicariously, in books, so we've every intention of making the most of this.'

Veronica felt a blush rising, but Dermid made it easy for her by giving one of his great guffaws. Adelaide shrugged, 'Well, it's such a delightful situation. We've enjoyed assisting in the deception of Theo enormously. And it's in such a good cause. We haven't had so much fun for years. And you, dear boy, might as well make the most it.'

The green eyes under the copper brows gleamed with fun. 'Exactly what I was trying to tell Veronica down on the jetty.'

She sparked up. 'Dermid, don't try your luck too far. You're a mad family. I don't know how to take any of you.'

'Take us as we come,' advised Maude. 'And dear, do give us a treat just as you did the other afternoon. Play to us. I guarantee Dermid hasn't heard you play yet. It took us back to our girlhood when we depended upon music of our own making.'

Dermid said, 'Don't tell me a girl in this day and age can play *Moonlight and Roses* and *Weeping Willow Lane*?'

Adelaide's tone was chilling. 'She can also play all the classical music—Schubert, Brahms, Mozart. Also, she can make up little tunes to favourite pieces of poetry that are just delightful. She vows she hasn't much of a voice, but we thought it very true and sweet, and she certainly has a knack of fitting words to music.'

'Then she must oblige. The things I *don't* know that I *should* know about this fiancée of mine! I'll put this lamp on the piano, Veronica—now, don't go all coy on me, I know I sounded cynical just now, but forget that.'

Veronica went across to the lovely old instrument and sat down. She did it very simply, announcing the pieces as she began. As she played, she grew less selfconscious till the music began to feel part of her, and in this she was herself, not that impostor she hated. To finish she played Dvorak's *Humoresque* with verve and spirit, and Mendelssohn's *Spring Song* with a magic that made her hearers see the dew on the grass and petals falling. Then she laid her hands in her lap and said, 'Enough's enough.'

'But you haven't sung for me,' said Dermid, and Maude added, 'Neither have you played those delightful little tunes you composed yourself. Now what would be suitable? The other day you sang us——'

Veronica swung round, a mischievous glint in her eyes. 'I

know what would just fit tonight. I found the verses in an old magazine about the joys of home, by different poets. This was by Joan Pomfret. I liked it because—well, it had a lot of meaning for me at the time. Do you know how I composed it? I was cooking dinner when a tune for the verse I'd read earlier began to run through my mind. I couldn't go to the piano, so I tried it out in a way my grandmother taught me. She couldn't read a note of music, but it was born in her. Look, I'll give you the first bars of my tinkling little tune, in the way I composed it.' She crossed to a cabinet, took out a silver cake-fork, and six glasses which she set up on the piano-top, and with the fork flicked each in turn, bringing out of them a sound that seemed to have been imprisoned in the glass till she brought it to life. They were enchanted.

Her eyes met Dermid's and she felt a tremor of gladness pass over her. He'd liked that. It gave her the confidence to sit at the piano again and say, 'Something about this appealed to me and it suits tonight.' It was jaunty, tuneful, tender, and her voice was low.

'My man likes an apple pie, flaky-crisp and sweet,
Joy for any woman's heart, just to see him eat;
Just to go and shop for him, planning meals for two,
Tasty bits to boil and bake, things to grill and stew;
My man likes an apple pie, apple it shall be
When his ship is signalled home after months at sea.'

It finished on a triumphant trill. All the gladness of the homecoming of a loved one was in it. She swung round, laughing, for once confident about her small gift. The aunts clapped. So did Dermid, but she couldn't see his face, his eyes. He was sunk in the depths of a big wing chair and his face was in shadow. For some reason she felt absurdly disappointed. When he spoke there was that hint of dryness in his tone she detested. 'How very suitable, in fact clever, to be able to bring out a song like that every time you serve an apple pie.'

To cover her feelings, her irrational feelings, she said

lightly, 'But the pie was Adelaide's . . . and don't some recipe books say, on their first pages,

"We can live without love, what is passion but pining,
But show me the man who can live without dining!"

'Dermid, we must get back to the big house. It's all right injecting romantic danders in the moonlight into life up-country to give it some zip, but lambing is nearly upon you, and shorter rations of sleep.'

They drove home in a silence that was a stiff one. Dermid thanked her formally for a very pleasant evening, and let her go upstairs by herself. He seemed to stay downstairs a long time, reading.

Veronica didn't fall asleep till she heard him come up. She felt restless, disturbed. She hated moody men.

CHAPTER EIGHT

FROM then on things were different. Outwardly the same, in front of Stephie, Theo, Lucy, but no more audacious follow-ups, no tender moments. Why did it have to happen this way? Why had she fallen so completely for a man as moody as this? Especially when, till now, she'd seemed so well armoured against sudden infatuations.

She'd longed to feel utterly committed to one person, someone whose voice, touch, build, features, awoke in you a response that was that exciting blend of spirit and body that poets extolled and singers interpreted in deathless music. Now it had happened within the compass of this situation that had a piquancy all its own. She'd dared to hope Dermid had found it irresistible too. She thought of the other men she'd met, liked, but had never felt here was the one to spend the rest of her life with, men who had been kind, pleasant to have as partners, even mildly attractive, but basically prosaic.

Her attitude had worried Mother sometimes. She'd said once, when Veronica had stopped seeing one of them, 'Veronica, you could be looking for the moon. In a way I feel it's our fault, mine and your father's. Ours was a wonderful marriage, and with his long absences from home, you used to see our glad reunions. We never had enough time together to take each other for granted as some do. Besides, your dad was unusual. I think you're looking for someone like him, and maybe they don't come in your generation. How many young men can quote poetry like your father did? Or love classical music? Stop crying for the moon, love.'

Twenty-two-year-old Veronica had cried passionately, 'I won't settle for less. I'd feel if he didn't love poetry and music and trees and animals that we lived in two separate worlds.'

Her mother had said shrewdly, 'Well, don't forget two people mightn't start off exactly kindred, but as the years go

136

by, each fits into the other's pattern. Look at me ... I was completely a non-sport when I married your father. I became knowledgeable about it and interested, quite painlessly. I'd have missed a good deal of shared interests with you children if I hadn't, and he was away so often when you were in school sports, I had to be there. Don't be so idealistic, Veronica, that life passes you by and you miss out on a whole chunk of experience because you want it perfect from the word go.'

Veronica had shrugged. 'Don't agonise over me, Mother. I'm quite happy with my career. I'm tremendously lucky to be in a job where all my working hours I handle things of beauty and antiquity. Who knows, some day I might meet someone *out* of his generation, if you like, who can quote poetry at the drop of a hat. But if I don't, marriage isn't the be-all and end-all of existence.'

Her mother had had the last word. 'But there are joys in marriage that enhance life beyond belief. I hope you find your ideal some day ... and recognise it.'

Now she had. She recognised MacBride of Tordarroch as what she wanted in a man. That night at Distaff Bay she had read a whole future into the closeness between them. What had gone wrong? Had he suddenly felt pressured by his romantically-minded aunts? That could be. Yet there on the jetty he had demanded response from her ... had asked her to make the next overture. Recollection of that enchantment swept back on her, then, succeeding it like the seventh wave that swamps all others, came the memory of his succeeding coldness, his withdrawal when she had finished singing that homely little song. The music had been hers, but not the words, the sentiments. But when she had sung 'My man likes an apple pie' had he suddenly felt hunted? Had he thought she was thinking of him as *her* man? At the thought her face burned. She would rebuff any softening he might show towards her. The slightest hint of intimacy and affection apart from their necessary exchanges in front of Theo she would nip in the bud!

Fortunately there was little time to brood. Things certainly hotted up. Rena and Tom came home with Timothy and the

new baby, and the aunts were so enraptured they weren't at
Tordarroch House so much to embarrass Veronica with their
fond and meaning glances. The lambs began coming and the
shepherds were out at the crack of dawn, often working long
after dinner. No more leisurely meals, long chats, watching
television.

The weather was superb, golden October days when the
daffodils withered and the laburnums and lilacs hung golden
cascades and purple plumes everywhere. Azaleas glowed from
all the terraces and the rhododendron buds were bursting
rosily. Stephie and Veronica, to spare the men, spent hours
with the electric mower keeping the fantastic growth of the
huge lawns down.

Even with days like these, there were lambs, weak and
helpless, to be coaxed back to life, on the big verandah where
boxes with sheepskin linings were ranged, with warming
lamps above them, or, when the numbers were too great, hot
water bottles. Some were even in the big kitchen huddled up
against the warmth of the ever-hot electric stoves. There were
two of these, the greatest boons except for the micro-wave
oven that was such a saving on power because the power
plant could support only a certain load. They had to be
careful, when they switched on the vacuum cleaner, to switch
off one of the stoves, and there were times, when they
overloaded, that the lights dimmed to a glimmer ... that
could have been romantic, but at the moment romance was
furthest from their thoughts.

The big house didn't get as much attention as usual. Dust
lay on the banisters, only the essentials were attended to. The
basic cleanliness, the bedmaking, the meals, the washing were
done and not much else besides.

It was a good year, with a larger percentage of twins, some
triplets. The men all used trail-bikes. Dermid had the only
three-wheeler. It was so safe, roaring up and down the
undulating paddocks. Veronica forgot one morning that she
was avoiding Dermid as much as possible. She said, 'You
promised me a ride on the back of that. I could open all the
gates for you.'

He looked away from her, said, 'Geoff, I'll take your bike, you take mine, Veronica wants a pillion ride on this.'

Geoff grinned. 'No fear! Apart from the fact that I'd enjoy her arms around my waist, I prefer my own. That one's great for the gullies, but when you're trying to corner a reluctant ewe it's not so mobile, and they're the very devil to catch when they've been pre-lamb shorn.'

Veronica said quickly, 'No matter. It was just a thought.' She turned away.

Dermid's voice was curt. 'It could be a help. I'm on the paddocks without cattle-stops. Hop on—sorry there's no cushion, but I don't want to spend the time. You'll have to put up with the bars.'

She went to throw a leg over the wide machine. He said impatiently, 'That'll be a fat lot of use. You'll take longer getting on and off than I would. You'll have to just perch with both legs on the left side and hang on for dear life. Be ready to get off as soon as I stop.' He called out to his men, 'I'm for the far paddocks.' She suspicioned he wanted to give her as long and rough a ride as possible. Right, MacBride, you'll see I won't complain! Off they roared.

Was it really necessary to zoom through these muddy entrances as she stood holding the gates, with mire spraying up in all directions? Or make for the boggiest patches unfailingly? He tossed a few words back over his shoulder. 'Great fun, isn't it?' in a tone she felt wasn't matey, but sarcastic. She managed a carefree laugh. 'Glorious . . . most exhilarating!' He went through a patch of thistles that she felt clean through her thick clothing and it was nothing but pure devilment. Right, MacBride, a Blakeney won't complain. After all, my grandmother was a gay Gordon and took everything in her stride! She yelled into his ear, 'Stop, you've not noticed that one! On the right—in trouble.'

It certainly was in trouble. One little lamb lay beside her and was quite all right, but its twin was coming the wrong way round and there wasn't room for it. It had probably been too long coming, anyway. Veronica couldn't fault MacBride now. His brother had passed on much veterinary skill, and of course in any case Dermid had grown up dealing with situations like this.

It wasn't easy; the ewe gave up the unproductive heaving, and seemed to realise he was trying to help, but his hand was so cramped between her pelvic bones. Finally he got it turned, said, 'If only it doesn't slip back again,' but the tiny forefeet and the little nose on top of them appeared, and the relieved ewe did what nature intended her to do and expelled it with very little help from Dermid. Veronica was crouched beside Dermid; she was becoming quite used to these situations, and she'd spoken soothingly to the ewe, who now struggled rockily to her feet and began taking an interest in these yellowish slimy creatures.

Dermid took a hunk of mutton-cloth from his belt, wiped his hand, and flexed it vigorously to relieve the cramp, while Veronica was clearing mucus from the tiny nostrils. Hard to believe that in two or three days these twins could be fleecy white and gambolling all over the turf with the sheer joy of living. Veronica's spirits lifted. 'I can understand now why men want to be high-country shepherds. It might be messy, but it's still got that incomparable feeling of ... well, gathering in the sheaves, helping with the increase of the earth.'

He looked at her, the strands of hair blowing back from her ears. The sun touched the brown with gold. She had on a plaid shirt that was far too big for her, one of his, but which still revealed her more feminine curves. She had some old three-quarter socks of his on too, with tartan trews tucked into them, rough boots on her feet. The trews were covered with slime and mucus and wool, but she was still every inch a woman. He said rather abruptly, 'Well, this one will do now. Let's get on. That one by the fence has no more mothering instinct than one of the rams. Look at her poor lamb trying to get a drink! She trots on every time. We'll catch her and teach her a lesson or two. She'll have sore udders if she doesn't let her milk go. Stupid creature!'

Certainly the three-wheeler wasn't as mobile as the trail-bikes for this, but Veronica saved the day by slipping neatly off at the crucial moment when it looked as if she'd head out of the corner, and got her fingers tightly hooked in the fine merino wool, short as it was. The lamb came trotting up eagerly. Dermid made a few skilful milking strokes with his fingers, then squirted the warm milk into the lamb's instantly open mouth, then it fastened on. The pressure on the udders instantly eased for the ewe, and in the end it was standing quite docilely and regarding its offspring with mild approval.

They had quite a lively morning, so had the others. Births were coming thick and fast, to their relief, for it was always on the cards that the weather could change treacherously. Algie was giving them a hand too, so all the men were eating back at Tordarroch. They washed up at the tubs on the back verandah and came in with ravening appetites. They were greeted by the sight of Theo, not up to the dresser, but perched gingerly on the edge of a high stool.

'Now I can believe that rest without manipulation can work wonders,' he announced. 'Couldn't believe it this morning when I found that though it had been agony when Lucy manoeuvred me under the shower, getting back over the lip of it with care wasn't. The hot water had loosened me up. I know I'll have to go easy, but it's a start, and I rang Hunter's Peak and got Stephie's cousin, and the lambing's coming along fine. Began a day or two before yours, but good percentages and ideal weather.'

They were just finishing their dessert when a sound made them all raise their heads to listen. 'That's the launch hooter,' said Dermid, 'must be coming in and wants us down at the jetty. I wonder what's up. Probably not much, just some mail that seemed urgent, perhaps. Gus is a good chap. Where are the glasses? Oh, here.'

He picked them up and went quickly to the front verandah, the others following. They could see the launch without glasses but no details. Then Dermid said, 'Ah, he's heading into Distaff Bay. I get it . . . it will be that young friend of the aunts' Christchurch friend here at last. I believe she rang them earlier to say her leave was cancelled. But I wonder why she didn't ring to say she was arriving today. If that's it.'

They stood watching it. Dermid reported that someone had indeed disembarked. A woman. Veronica's stomach did a somersault. Bound to be Victoria. Now what? The launch hooted a farewell. Behind them the phone rang. Bound to be the aunts. Veronica flew to it.

Adelaide's voice was a thin thread of sound. 'Veronica, thank goodness it's you! Are you in the kitchen? Go round to the phone in the hall, and say nothing that can give anything away.'

She turned and said to Dermid, who was naturally expecting it to be for him, 'It's for me—rather private, so I'll take it in the hall.' They all looked cheated, wanting it to be an explanation of the launch call, but Dermid scowled horribly. 'I see. Well, I guess you're entitled to some private life,' and he strode off and they heard the door bang.

At the hall phone Veronica said, 'Addie, just wait till I replace that other receiver. The men are in the kitchen and it resounds like nobody's business.' She was back in a breathless moment.

'Dear girl, we want you over here right away. Come in the Rover. You've got a visitor and we dare not bring her over till we decide what to do. I mean, not in front of Theo. And—not yet—in front of Dermid. Very definitely not in front of him. Hurry!'

'Adelaide, who is it? Tell me immediately . . . oh, you won't. Right, I'll get there pronto. No, I won't change, but I warn you I'm in the state one often is during lambing. I'm on my way.'

As she descended the verandah steps, Dermid barred her way. 'Well?'

She said, 'I need the Rover to go over to Chattan House. A vistor for me is there. Adelaide wouldn't tell me who.'

Dermid set his coppery jaw. 'Right. I'm coming with you.'

'No, you aren't to. I'm to go alone. Adelaide didn't want us to meet here. And in particular I wasn't to bring you.'

'Wasn't to bring me? What utter nonsense! Oh, I get it. That wasn't a woman in slacks, it was a man I'm not sure I like men I don't know coming on to my property *and staying*. What bee has Adelaide got in her bonnet now?'

He looked really taken aback when she said, 'It wasn't a man, she said *her*. Now, Dermid, I've got to do what Adelaide says. She wouldn't have gone on like that unless she had a very good reason. You must let me go alone exactly as she says.'

He said reluctantly, 'All right, but I'm staying here till you get back with whoever it is. If it's got to be so hush-hush, there's something wrong. If you want me, ring. I'll send the men out and stay in the kitchen.'

'Thanks. It's something to do with Theo. So we'll risk nothing.'

She lost no time. It was almost certain to be Victoria. They'd have to persuade this girl to pretend she was the one the aunts had invited here. But what on earth yarn could they concoct to satisfy Dermid for their not wanting him across at Chattan? Veronica gave up. If they couldn't think of anything, she herself would be revealed as a crafty buyer of antiques who'd gulled two elderly ladies into secretly trading their antiques. Oh, if only Gus had never persuaded her to pretend she was that actress friend of Anne's! What had delayed her all this time? Perhaps Gus hadn't found out who she was till she got on board. Oh, Veronica, *how* are you going to get out of this one? She pulled up with a screech of brakes and hurried down the rocky path to the back door. Maude came out, visibly agitated.

Veronica clutched her. 'It'll be Victoria! What's she like? Will she understand and just fade away after a few days' visit? Can we get the launch back then?'

'Oh, no, not Victoria. Just come in. She waiting for an explanation of your engagement.'

In a trance Veronica followed her. Could it be some girl-friend of Dermid's who's heard about this?

Maude went right through to the sitting-room where Veronica had played and sung and where Dermid had so inexplicably changed.

And there, sitting squarely in the middle of the couch, with a glass of what looked like brandy in her hand, and which undoubtedly she was in dire need of, was Veronica's mother!

Veronica cast her eyes heavenwards and dropped down on to a low green velvet chair that certainly deserved better treatment.

'This is all it needed,' she said most unfilially.

Marian Blakeney put the glass down on a small table beside her and said calmly, producing a clipping that looked as if it had come from a magazine, 'I want to know the meaning of this. Bring that chair nearer. Right in front of me.'

As if she'd been one of Mother's own nurses, being put on the carpet, Veronica did so. She held out her hand for the clipping with the feeling she was seizing a rattlesnake. She turned it round. It was obviously from a TV news-sheet announcing the coming showing, weeks ahead, of *The High-country Doctor Calls In*, and it had a sub-title, *Visiting Patients By Helicopter*. They were all there bar Theo, and named. Veronica was singled out specially as 'The antique buyer whose ways till now have been city ways. The girl who is throwing it all overboard to become a High-country wife.'

And they had thought they were so safe for so long! The sound Veronica made could only be described as a bleat. Marian Blakeney took up her glass again and sipped. Over the rim her eyes surveyed her daughter.

Veronica said, 'It'll take some explaining. It's a long story.'

Her mother said sarcastically, 'I imagine so. But then I've got a long time for listening. It couldn't be explained in just a word or two why any girl would get engaged to someone she's not known five minutes and keep it secret from her mother. It's beyond me. Have I ever been a possessive mother? All I wanted always was for your sisters and brother to be happy in their life-partners and the same for you. Why all this secrecy? You wrote saying you were coming up to a remote station on the lake to do some valuing. So what's all this? And what's the hurry?'

Veronica had managed to swallow so her throat was no longer dry. Her chaotic thoughts were assembling. 'It's not what you think, Mother, a sudden infatuation. Dermid, that's the man I'm supposed to have got engaged to, got himself into——'

'*Supposed*? What do you mean, supposed?'

Mother, I'm trying to tell you. It's a tangle. Please let me get it out.'

To the aunts' surprise, Mrs Blakeney fell silent.

'The aunts here ... well, really they're Dermid's great-aunts, and they wanted to sell some heirlooms of their mother's. Not Shaw or MacBride heirlooms, of course, because they want to—to make a trip to Italy. They thought their nephew would forbid it as they got diddled once before. So I was to come up here as a young friend of friends in Christchurch. Then if the things were practically valueless, there'd have been no ructions.'

'He sounds a very mean and unpleasant young man.'

Veronica found herself flying to his defence. 'He's not—far from it. Anything but!'

Her mother's lips tightened. 'Oh, I forgot. You're fancying yourself in love with him.'

'No, I'm not. Please, Mother! It's a *fake* engagement.'

This time it was her mother who bleated. Veronica continued, 'I was to get a certain boat, leaving my car at a garage opposite the jetty, at Wanaka. I arrived far too early, and got hustled on board as if all the hounds of hell were after us. Well, in a way they were. At least one hound. Theo.'

'You've lost me,' said her mother. 'A dog called Theo. What's a dog to do with anything?'

'He's Lucy's husband, not a dog, you see.' (Marian didn't see anything but decided it was no use interrupting, better let it all spill out and ask questions at the end.)

'Lucy is a lily—I mean she was pale and clinging, sort of timorous. This has been a second home to her, so when she and Theo got at cross-purposes she fled to Dermid. Only he was in Dunedin at a motel, and she turned up in the middle of the night. He had to put her up. Theo got to know later and blew up.'

'I'm not surprised. Go on.'

'Mother! Nothing happened. Nothing whatever. He simply bunged Lucy into the bedroom and slept on the lounge divan.'

'How do you know? You weren't there. Neither was Theo. I——'

'Mother, I do know. Dermid would never take advantage of anyone. And he looks on Lucy as a sister. Now listen. Dermid was back here when Theo found out. There was a real barney and she fled here. It was Dermid who had persuaded Lucy to return to Theo anyway. They're in an even more remote place than this. A helicopter came down there to pick up some deer-stalkers and Lucy hitched a ride—left a note for Theo. He was furious!'

'I'm not surprised. Go on.' Marian paused. 'In fact I'm past being surprised at anything. I have a feeling that sooner or later you'll explain how *you* came to be involved in it and how you got engaged to this man. It's like one of those Georgette Heyer period romances where everybody chases the wrong people in coaches and fights duels and things, yet everything comes out right in the end.'

'So it does,' said Maude fervently, 'and this one will too. You'll see. We saw it coming from the start. Dermid and Veronica are *so* suited to each other!'

This time it was Veronica's mother who cast up her eyes.

Veronica said feebly, 'Mother, take no notice of them. They're born romantics and are dying to get Dermid married. It's not like that at all. We're just pretending. I'd got to telling you I was rushed on to the launch. Gus, the pilot, was talking to me whenever he could. He had tourists on board, so it was all spasmodic. I didn't know what he was talking about. They thought I was an actress friend of Dermid's sister. You see, Dermid thought if one of them could come up here and pretend that she was Dermid's fiancée and that when Lucy had turned up at the motel he'd rung her and got her to stay the night too, with them, all Theo's doubts would be set at rest. Actually, Mother, you've got to admit that was sheer inspiration. Brilliant.'

Mrs Blakeney said faintly, 'I think you'd have to be young to think that.'

'Well, not till we were nearly here did I manage to get Gus to understand I wasn't this Victoria. I was Veronica and I was coming up here secretly for Maude and Adelaide. But by this time, Theo was racing his launch across the lake to get Lucy. He's sailed it across Lake Hawea, transported it across the Neck, then across Wanaka.'

'The Neck? This is all as clear as mud,' sighed Marian.

'A narrow neck of land between the two lakes. He'd got a friend from Hawea township to bring his boat trailer to where he beached his boat, if you want to know how it was done, but I'd like to finish. I'm terrified in case Dermid gets impatient and arrives. He was burned up with curiosity.'

'Well, that makes two of us. I get the picture. Boats, not coaches, and the villain in hot pursuit. When is the duel taking place? And why are *you* engaged to Dermid?'

'Because nobody knew where Victoria was . . . she hasn't turned up yet. I was better than nobody. They hustled me off the launch, as Theo was catching up fast, and Dermid and I went into a terrific clinch . . . and when Theo sprang out like an avenging Viking, I was introduced as Dermid's fiancée. All Gus had time to hiss at Dermid was that I was Veronica, not Victoria. Dermid thought he'd mistaken the name. By this time he was in a rare tizzy.'

'I'm not surprised. I'm in a rare tizzy myself. And——?'

'Well, for once Lucy stopped being a clinging vine and said all the right things and then they went into a terrific clinch too. We started up the track leaving them to it, and I was just going to tell Dermid I wasn't Anne's friend, only a stopgap, when Gus stopped me. He whispered if Dermid knew I wasn't an actress, he'd think I'd never be able to carry it through. I thought it couldn't matter much because it was only going to have to be till Lucy packed and took off with her husband, so the ordeal would soon be over.

'Suddenly everyone got matey, with the relief, and we decided to have lunch, then Lucy would pack. Theo was really convinced by now that Lucy did love him and Dermid put on a fabulous show of being scared to death she'd been going to sabotage his own engagement when she turned up in Dunedin. So all looked like being well, only——'

She paused for breath and her mother said, 'You fill me

with apprehension. So why are you still here? Oh, I suppose for safety's sake you had to stay on for a while. But of course by now Dermid will know you aren't an actress. Anyway, if this Theo's seen this article, he'll find it very convincing. And how's the poor man who hurt his back? That only referred to him very briefly.'

Veronica said hollowly, 'That was Theo. He's *still* here! He'll be here at least another three weeks. So we couldn't break our engagement off. We're in the middle of lambing. So is Theo's property, so that doctor won't let him go anywhere near—lambing's hard on your back. You should have seen the effort it took Dermid to bring a second twin into the world this morning.' She looked down on her indescribable trews and exclaimed, 'Oh, dear!'

Her mother said sharply, 'Get off that beautiful chair immediately!'

'Oh, it doesn't matter,' said Adelaide fondly. 'It's only an old chair.'

Suddenly Marian began to laugh chokingly. 'Only an old chair! I thought my darling daughter had more respect for antiques than that! Now tell me, what does Dermid think now about his aunts selling heirlooms?'

Veronica looked scared. 'That's it—he still doesn't know. We can't risk an explosion while Theo's here. He's been marvellous with Theo, who really had a man-sized inferiority complex. Mother, how *are* we going to explain you coming up here unheralded and unannounced?'

Mrs Blakeney gazed at her daughter and at Maude and Adelaide, who were almost beaming and looking most unrepentant, and suddenly gave way to laughter. She was helpless. The two aunts, much relieved, joined in. Belatedly, so did Veronica.

Maude and Adelaide, as they so often did, spoke in alternate sentences. 'It's been such fun pretending, and it's just as well it was Veronica and not this Victoria.' . . . 'Yes, she'd never have fitted in as well as your daughter and Dermid would have hated carrying on the deception so long. As it is . . . well, he hasn't found it irksome at all.'

Veronica said hastily, 'It was just that he so wanted things to stay right for Lucy and Theo, that's all.'

Marian said, 'Well, I can hardly walk in waving this clipping and demanding to know what it was all about, can I, with Theo and Lucy still in the house? Let me see ... I can just say I got the chance of a ride to Wanaka and thought how ideal to come to see where my daughter would be living. That I hadn't seen Dermid since the engagement party in Christchurch. How would that be?'

Veronica looked at her parent with great respect. 'Mum, you are a sport! You might be all that's needed to set the final seal of authenticity on this engagement.' Then her face changed, remembering. 'Oh, horrors, I got sort of carried away at first. I embroidered more than was necessary. I said you disapproved of Dermid, that I dare not let you know Lucy had spent a night with Dermid. I said you didn't like the idea of your darling daughter marrying someone on a sheep station that doesn't even have a road coming to its door, so if you heard any scandal about him spending the night with a married woman, that would put the lid on.' She put a hand to her mouth. '*And* I said you lived a life that was a positive round of bridge parties and social engagements, theatres and parties! Oh, darling, I'm so sorry. What a character I've endowed my mama with!'

Suddenly Marian looked very like her madcap daughter, brown eyes and all alight with mischief. 'What makes you think you've got all the acting ability in the family? I won't stay long, it would be too risky. You'll have to get Gus back here in a day or two, but if you've cast me as a flibbertigibbet, I'll flibbert and gibbet all I can for the rest of the time.'

'Bravo!' said a voice from the doorway. Dermid's. They all yelped, looking guilty. Veronica said quickly, 'Dermid! You weren't supposed to come. How—how long have you been there?'

He looked surprised. 'Does it matter? About sixty seconds. Your mother said she'd say she wanted to come up to see where her daughter was going to live, as I paused in the door. I knew it couldn't be anyone but your mother, she's so like you, Veronica. And a sport to boot. Perhaps before long you could take the line that now you're relieved. You think that after all she'll have far more security here than living on chancy commissions.'

So he hadn't heard them mention Victoria!

Dermid took Veronica back to Tordarroch House in the Rover, leaving his mare in the home paddock at Chattan. There was not so much constraint between them. Her mother's arrival had constituted another threat to Theo's peace of mind and to the new and very real friendship that had developed between him and Dermid, so for the time being it united Dermid and Veronica in a common determination to keep Theo happily ignorant.

'You seem good pals with your mother, Veronica,' he remarked.

'Yes, we always have been. She plays the mother's part when we need it, of course, doesn't hesitate to tell us when she thinks we're going wrong. Of course she was mother and father to us for so long, with Dad being away so much. She was strict, but we never resented that. 'It made us feel cared for.'

'M'm, it does do that. And as a nursing Sister she'll be with girls of your age and younger all the time. Could be a rather hairy job in the present age, I suppose.'

'It brings its worries, but she copes magnificently. Even the wayward ones love her and respect her the more for not bending over backwards to appear one of them. She fishes them out of trouble when they need rescuing and is far-seeing enough to admit that our world is a tougher one to grow up in than hers was.'

Dermid said, 'Sounds sensible. I daresay it's not easy. She'll grieve over some aspects of the permissive age. I suppose. In her oversight of nurses and of her own family. Sometimes parents have to go along with things they don't really countenance.'

Veronica glanced at him curiously, he sounded so intense. 'I don't think she has too many worries about us. The rest are married, and happily.'

'Perhaps her worries are confined to you, then.'

Veronica laughed. 'At the moment, yes. It must have given the poor darling a conniption when she saw that picture!'

'That was a good idea the aunts asking her to stay at Chattan House, it keeps her away from Theo a good deal of the time. Naturally, though, Theo will expect her to be with us for the evening meal. Sorry I had to squash your kind invitation to the aunts too, but they're so high-spirited and enjoying this so much, drat them, that I thought they'd go too far and let the cat out of the bag.'

'You're probably right. It was just I thought they'd feel a bit flat.'

'Well, it's all in a good cause. I dare not risk it.' He added, 'To make this whole thing authentic, about your mother looking the place over, you'd better dress up tonight. Oh, nothing flash, but go all feminine. Theo'll think I've got problems too! That though Lucy seemed to regard me as a dependable sort of fellow and he got it into his head she wished she'd married me, not everyone regards me as an eligible male for their daughters.'

Veronica's heart lifted. He was thawing out from whatever mood had possessed him lately. 'You sound like something from Jane Austen, Dermid! From the days when women didn't have careers; when they had to make good marriages or live the unenviable life of a maiden aunt.'

He nodded. 'How galling it must have been to have been regarded as second-class citizens instead of people, personalities in their own right. Incidentally, how much does your own career mean to you?'

She hesitated. He meant the stage. Soon, once lambing and her valuation of the antiques were over, and Theo and Lucy had departed, she would have to tell him who she was and what she was. She didn't want to add more lies. She said, sincerely, 'I'm not obsessed by my career. I enjoy it. I mostly enjoy whatever I'm doing. Like after Dad died, and Mother had to go fulltime nursing to pay off our mortgage. I housekept for two years. Some jobs I found a bit tedious, but then there are tedious parts to all occupations. I loved keeping house, mostly, and adored the garden.'

'So if you were married and unless you needed two wages, you wouldn't be bored just keeping house?'

She answered sincerely. 'I'm very rarely bored. And to keep house for the one you love ought to raise it from the prosaic anyway. But we're getting off the subjects. Dermid. We ought to be looking for possible pitfalls in this new complication. I know Theo hasn't been able to sit up to play cards, but today he was definitely less stiff. I said my mother was a bridge-playing fiend, and to be candid she hardly knows one card from another, she's a real duffer. What'll we do if Theo improves and asks her to play cards with him?'

'Don't panic. She won't stay more than three days. I don't see him improving to that extent. He can't reach forward too much. We've seen it through this far, we'll see it to the end.'

'And as soon as is reasonably possible, when he and Lucy go home, we'll stage a row and I'll depart.'

There was a silence. Was he thinking how soon? Oh, if only he would show some regret that she must go! When he spoke he seemed to be considering it rather clinically. 'Let's play that one by ear. Theo's bound to ring up from time to time over there and he'll want to speak to you. Apart from being grateful because of your supposed presence that night at the motel, I think he's quite fond of you.' His tone held an amusement that chilled her for some reason.

She said slowly, 'You know I said, when I was asked by the TV people what firm I worked for, that I was a freelance, buying antiques on commission?'

'Yes.'

'Well, before Theo departs, I'll say regretfully that I've had to promise the firms I sell to that I'll be bringing them some goods soon, so I'll have to go off on a tour round old homesteads in the Te Anau area. Then it won't matter when or where we stage the break. He doesn't have to know every last detail when we do.'

'Well, leave it meanwhile. Till after your mother goes.'

He didn't object to that, then! He added, 'That's about as

many pitfalls as I care to anticipate at the moment. We're nearly there. Stay in with Stephie this afternoon and help create the atmosphere in front of Theo that you're so het up about your mama arriving that you want to impress her.'

At first Stephie wrung her hands. 'You must run the feather duster over those banisters and round the lounge. What on earth can we have for dinner? I was just going to serve the last of that mutton heated up. It's too late to thaw chickens. We can have apple pie for dessert, I've got the apples stewed already. But the main course?'

'Stephie, you've got that lovely beef casserole already cooked in the freezer. It's delicious. We could add a swirl of yoghurt to the top of it and some paprika and make it Stroganoff. And with all that mashed potato you've saved up, I could put it through the forcer and we'll have Duchesse potatoes—it saves time.'

Stephie hugged her, chuckling. 'She must be a sport, and for her own sake I'd like to put on a good show. We don't often bother with entrees, but you know I showed you how to make pancakes—well, make some now and I'll keep them hot and fill them with cream sauce and mushrooms. Oh, yes, we have loads of mushrooms. We had a moist warm autumn and had so many I fried them in butter and froze them on foil pie-plates, inside plastic bags. They're in the small freezer, bottom shelf.'

When Theo came shuffling through on his painful way to the bathroom he was amazed at their air of preparing for a critical guest. 'It puts us on our mettle,' said Stephie. 'We're hoping Mrs Blakeney goes home thinking that if we can put on a meal like this in the middle of lambing, her darling daughter isn't going to live like a barbarian.'

Theo guffawed, then said amazedly, 'It didn't hurt. Lucy, I'm rapidly coming right. I can laugh suddenly without groaning!'

So he would go home sooner, thought Veronica.

CHAPTER NINE

DERMID came home early and told them he'd dropped this
afternoon's crop of weaklings at the men's quarters for
looking after. 'Now it's me for a shower and some decent
clothes. Not every day I have my future mother-in-law to
dinner, and apart from her wondering if Veronica really can
take the existence, she's not a bad old girl really.' He winked
at Veronica. 'I'll go across for her in the Rover.'

Veronica too showered and changed, so did Stephie.
Veronica slipped into an almond-green velvet dress with a
high-standing collar, and long sleeves fitting tightly at the
wrists. She brushed her hair till it shone and belled out into its
hyacinthine petalled locks about her shoulders, and looped
the front tresses back as Maude had done, with a scarlet
ribbon, clasped a scarlet bone bracelet over one wrist and
slipped in matching earrings, beautifully carved, a treasure
she'd picked up and kept for herself. They swung and glowed
translucently at her every movement. She used more lipstick
than usual, in the same shade, and added polish to the nails
that had suffered a little with the ewes this morning. A touch
of white rose perfume at throat and wrists and she was ready.

Stephie could evidently set out an elegant dining-table
when she had time. Some of these dishes and the crystal
Veronica hadn't seen before. Two tiny posy bowls held violets
that perfumed the room deliciously and wouldn't hide
opposite diners from each other. Apple logs from the old
orchard burned aromatically in the grate.

'I'm so glad to meet you at last, Mrs Blakeney,' murmured
Stephie for Theo's benefit.

Mrs Blakeney smiled, 'Do make it Marian . . . I've got so
used to thinking of you as Stephie from Veronica's letters I
can't stand on ceremony now. I hope my girl realises how
fortunate she is, some women wouldn't like another fussing

round her kitchen, but you get on splendidly. So this is the wounded hero. I believe you were the reason for the TV people coming up here, Theo. I read a bit about it in some television news-sheet, about programmes to come. It was called *The High-country Doctor Calls In*. How exciting to have one's daughter on TV, and all due to you. You looked so sweet on the photo, Lucy. I shall tell all my bridge friends to watch.'

She gazed appreciatively around the table, then the room with its beautiful furniture and the aerial photographs of the estate, the gilt-framed long-ago ones of Euphemia and Findlay, who looked most impressive in his kilt. 'I must say, Veronica, if you had to fall in love with a farmer, you chose well. If that's your man's background, you might as well have it as glam as possible. Those friends of mine began to commiserate with me. I shall tell them they don't need to. I think Mrs Dermid MacBride of Tordarroch Station, Lake Wanaka, sounds very impressive. Do get some letterheads done, Veronica. I shall show them your letters.'

Oh, dear, Mother was starting her flibberting and gibbeting with a vengeance! Veronica hoped she wouldn't lay it on too thick. Once she got going she was a prankster. Dermid's eyes were alight with laughter. 'Be careful, *belle-mère*, I could develop an inferiority complex, thinking she was marrying me for the estate!'

'As if you could think that,' she retorted 'when you look like a cross between Gary Cooper and Richard Burton. Oh dear, that rather dates me! But you know what I mean. When I first met you at the engagement party, I was afraid you were only a handsome face! I thought Veronica might never take the life you were offering, that it was sheer infatuation. By the way, what did you call me?'

'I called you *belle-mère*. It's what the French call their mothers-in-law. How do you like it?'

'I like it very much, dear boy. Mother-in-law sounds so dragonish—though I had the most delightful mother-in-law myself. I suppose it's because of all those music-hall jokes. But *belle-mère* is just sweet. I do wish I'd known it in time to call mine that. She was a gay Gordon before she married and lived up to her name to the end.'

Veronica helped serve the meal, very much the prospective bride; they praised her filled pancakes, and the casserole that had become beef Stroganoff, so the honours were even between the cooks. Then Stephie set out the huge apple pie.

'My favourite dessert,' said Marian Blakeney, pouring cream on hers lavishly, 'perhaps because it has such happy memories. Veronica, have you ever played your own composition on the apple pie poem for them?'

Veronica had an instant flashback. That was the night that till she had played and sung that wretched song, had been so happy. Dermid's black mood had descended upon him so quickly after that. Pity Mother had mentioned it. She gave a deprecatory laugh. 'I played it at Chattan House the other night. It's hardly a masterpiece, Mother, just a tinkling little tune.'

Her mother said firmly, 'Considering you were only seventeen when you composed it, it's a splendid little piece.' She informed the company, 'With my husband being captain on one of the Pacific Service ships, we had him away weeks at a time. We always had apple pie for his first dinner home. I found this poem, and as a surprise to us both, Veronica set it to music.'

There was a crash as the wineglass Dermid had just raised to his lips descended into his apple pie, spraying cream widely over the white damask cloth, himself and Veronica. He took it extremely casually, wasn't covered in confusion and embarrassment as he should have been. True, he said instantly, 'Oh, sorry, love. I do hope that velvet won't be ruined. My things will wash, as well as the cloth. Excuse us, folks, I'll sponge it off her. Come on, darling.' Laughing, the two of them made for the kitchen.

Stephie called, 'Whatever happens, don't let him use the dishcloth, I mopped up some melted butter with it. Get a clean hand-towel out of the third drawer down, then use another and sponge it with clean warm water. I'll fix the table.' She slid a plate under the wet patch, mopped with Dermid's table-napkin, then began to chuckle. 'Well, I daresay even Cooper or Burton could have an accident at the table. 'I hope you won't put him down as a clodhopper, Marian!'

Dermid was making a very good job, out in the kitchen, with the mopping-up, even seemed to enjoy it. She finally said, 'My skirt got more of it than my bodice, idiot!'

His mouth twitched at the corners. 'You're always doing it . . . spoiling my sport. It's not every day a man gets a chance at this sort of thing!'

She looked at him exasperatedly. 'You're quite mad! None of this is for real, and the last few days you've been as approachable as a . . . as a Californian thistle!'

'Yes, I know. But then I had a reason for being sore.'

'What? Not something I did, surely?'

He looked rueful. 'I was jealous—I might as well confess it.'

'Jealous? Now I *know* you're mad! There's no one here to be jealous of—besides——'

He looked her straight in the eye. 'It was your song. You sang it with such feeling. I thought you'd composed it for the man in *your* life. I thought your—your boy-friend, if that's the correct term, was on the sea. I realise now you were remembering your father coming home from sea.'

Veronica gazed at him wide-eyed, her nose wrinkled in puzzled fasion. 'But—but this is all a fake. It's not for real. You——'

The laughter and audacity died out of his eyes. The green of them darkened almost to brown. His tone was serious. 'It gets more real to me every moment. Veronica, don't you——'

She put up a hand to stop him even though gladness was breaking over her in a flood. 'Dermid, they're waiting for us. That door isn't even closed. Stephie will be dishing you out a second helping.'

'Well, let her. It'll keep her happy. I know this isn't the time or the place to discuss this . . . we'll have to wait till Theo's gone . . . then we can be gloriously natural. Meanwhile, what's wrong with this?' She was caught and held against him, then kissed with a fervour she had not known before.

A voice floated to their ears from the dining-room. 'They're taking a long time, aren't they? Do you suppose they've gone to change? There's not a sound out there.' Her mother's voice.

They didn't hear Stephie push the door open. She had the dish in one hand and the dripping glass in the other, holding it over the pie on Dermid's plate. She stopped dead in the doorway and said back into the room, 'I think he's apologising for showering that lovely dress with cream. A silent apology, in the very nicest way possible. Don't move, you two. Such a pity to break that up!' She retreated, and somebody, laughing, possibly Lucy, banged the door before Veronica could disentagle herself.

They were both shaken with delicious laughter, then Veronica said, 'How can I go back in there, blushing, and with my lipstick smudged? Isn't Stephie awful?'

'How can you *not* go back in there? They'll be terribly disappointed if you don't show signs of being kissed. Especially Theo.'

She looked mocking and said, 'What you'll do to convince Theo!'

He caught her then in a grip that hurt. 'Theo's got nothing at all to do with this, and you know it. He was out of sight, out of hearing. It was Stephie who proclaimed it to them.' He kissed her again, gently, sweetly.

Veronica laughed, took out her handkerchief and said, wiping his lips, 'You're showing signs too. I was rather lavish with the lipstick tonight. Come on, muggins, your apple pie will be getting cold!'

There was a strange, wondering look on her mother's face that had nothing whatever to do with the part she was playing so ably. Veronica glanced swiftly from one face to the other. Theo looked more relaxed than she'd ever seen him and Lucy had a serene air. Was she thinking that this pretence was probably going to become permanent, that Theo would never need to be upset when she and Dermid parted? There was no doubt that this time of extreme pain for Theo had had great compensations. It had been proved to Theo that life didn't have to be all tough grind and unrelenting work, that his men, in an emergency, could manage without him, and the patient hours Lucy had spent at his bedside reading, and her tender care as she tried to assist his every movement had brought them very close.

Veronica's spirits kept rising. Why wouldn't they? Dermid had shown jealousy, of some imagined seafarer in her personal life. The absolute idiot! She looked at her mother, sparklingly gay, enjoying this break from her nursing routine, and entering wholeheartedly into the escapade once she'd got over the shock of it. Now she knew that her loved youngest child hadn't dealt her an uncaring blow by becoming engaged to be married without telling her. A wave of love for her mother swept over Veronica. She said, across the table, 'Oh, Mother, it's just heavenly to have you here!'

'Lovely to be here, darling, and to see your future surroundings. It puts my mind at rest.'

Veronica's heart did a double flip. She had been so miserable only yesterday, and now not only the acting was making her feel as if this was the real thing, but Dermid had said so, in a fleeting moment that would surely be repeated at a more suitable time. And when he did ... if he did ... then Mother would approve.

Theo said humorously, 'And if ever you get to thinking again that Veronica is giving up a good career for a rather primitive existence, remote and cut off by usual means of access, come and see us! We do have a telephone now, but no television. It would cost the earth. But even when you've crossed Hawea, you have to navigate a river. Then there's a drive of a few miles by truck, into the valley itself. But we've got a good air-strip for emergencies and of course helicopters are proving a great blessing. But it would make you feel Tordarroch was practically on a highway, with tourist launches going up and down the lake, even if they make no regular calls here. But I'm determined to make my old derelict station as famous as this one in time.'

Dermid's eyes held real affection. 'And you'll do it, Theo. I'd always yearned after Hunters' Peak Station. It was so remote, so away from it all. But with Gerald living and breathing veterinary work, I just couldn't let Dad down. When things have eased off here a bit, say just before Christmas, I'll get Fiona and Edward to bring us over in the 'copter. I'd love to see it now.'

'Oh, do. It'll be lovely for Lucy to have Veronica dropping in from time to time. And Fiona. That's what killed the Peak Station years ago, no wife could take it. In the very first days there were just two bachelors running it. Perhaps that's why they stayed single. It's different now, with air transport. We just need a few good seasons like this, and, please God, good world markets and no disastrous industrial situations here, to make a go of it. It's so vast that with a bit more capital behind me, it could provide a lot of work for men who love the high country. You've got about four hundred or so Hereford cattle, haven't you, Dermid? Yes, I thought so. So far I've only a hundred. I'll build them up. Well, if you two have the sense to get married before Christmas, we could get the Campbells to leave you with us for an extended visit. Otherwise I suppose Veronica will have to get on with her job, hunting antiques.'

Marian took the heat off that proposal by asking Theo if their access river was the Hunter River. Theo shook his head. 'No, but that's a natural surmise. I'll show you ours on a map when we've finished. Hunters' Peak wasn't named for that, but for a mountain top that was a landmark for deer-hunters. It wasn't even called that in the old days. Just known as Black's Place, after the men who took it on first.'

Lucy wasn't put off, though. She said, very deliberately, holding Veronica's eye, 'I've a feeling that wedding is getting nearer every moment, especially now it has the maternal approval. After all, if Veronica starts roaming all over Central and Southland, you two aren't going to see much of each other. And an engagement is an awful waste of time.'

Theo gave his wife an approving look. Oh, the poor darling, thought Veronica, he feels that if Lucy wants Dermid married as soon as possible, there just can't have been anything in her rushing to him for comfort when she and Theo quarrelled.

Dermid turned to survey Veronica. 'How about it, darling? It's over to you. Talk things over with your mother. Good opportunity while she's here, otherwise it'll cost a fortune in toll-bills.'

She pretended to consider it. 'I'll have to consult my firm first. I may not be on the payroll, but I do draw commission. Dermid, do behave yourself. Fancy asking a girl to fix a wedding date in public!'

'We aren't the public,' said Theo, 'we're practically family. When one's been so dependent upon others for as long as I have, it's not possible to remain like I was for years ... as prickly as a porcupine. I feel so much better today I reckon I'll be off your hands in a fortnight. Surely you won't take longer than two weeks to make up your mind, Veronica?'

She said lightly, 'I shouldn't think so. Oh, listen, those lambs are at it again! Thank goodness you left the last lot with the men. I must make up some bottles—come on, Dermid.'

On the verandah she said rebukingly, 'Do try to rein in Theo's bright ideas, not encourage them. We're getting in deeper and deeper.'

'Yes, aren't we?'

She gave an exasperated sigh. 'You aren't taking this seriously enough! It isn't going to be easy to finish it up, with Theo making plans to get us over there. He'll just have to depend upon other womenfolk dropping in from the skies, not commit me.'

'I don't think you realise how much it means to Theo to have *us*. Fancy him saying he feels practically family. If you'd known him the way he was, about as approachable as a landmine, you'd know. He's always felt he didn't have the respect of the community. We've got a head start on the others, but I'll see they come in on this. I'm not going to squash him on anything.'

She gave up, grabbed a lamb and said, 'Steady, little one, you'll choke! There's plenty more where this comes from. Here, take a breath.'

Dermid was struggling with a reluctant feeder. It was too

weak to be enthusiastic. Veronica watched, fascinated, his hands with the coppery hairs on the backs of them, held the lamb gently but firmly, till the warm milk, reinforced, touched its tongue and it found it good. Shepherd's hands. Hands that had held her, caressed her. At the thought a remembered tide of physical delight swept over her. Was any of this for real? Was it, with him too, heading that way?

She said a little breathlessly, 'We must be very careful not to overplay our hands. The more we build up, the more to demolish later when it's time to end.'

His hand was under the lamb's chin, holding it firmly, as it pulled. He glanced up from where he was squatting. 'Can't we let it ride, just now? While Theo's here? I've discovered a lot of things about myself lately. Things that were black and white to me once, so that any compromise about them was unthinkable. I'm not so sure any more. I'd no idea when I got my sister to rope you in all it was going to mean. It was any port in a storm, and I didn't expect a girl like you.

'I know you've got something to tell me, but I think it had better wait till Theo's gone. We don't want any spanners in the works and I'm not quite sure yet how I'll react. It's the first time in my life, Veronica, I've been so unsure of myself. I've got to try to understand your world, which is so different. Will you do that? Mark time till they go? If it so happens we don't come to an understanding of each other I don't want the need for any play-acting in front of Theo to cloud the issue. I want it clear-cut. Have you any idea what I'm driving at?'

Her second lamb had finished drinking. His wasn't finished. But she still stayed squatting beside him. She kept her voice low. 'I think so, Dermid. I'd rather wait till they've gone and we can be ourselves. This is such an artificial atmosphere. I've something to confess all right, but this isn't the time and the place.'

With a swift change of decision he said, 'Is it hurting you to bottle it all up? If so, like the other night at Distaff Bay, we could find an hour.'

She shook her head. 'No, I'd rather not be doing any more

roaming in the gloaming. That way I find it hard to think clearly. For instance, I can't imagine how you'll react to what I tell you.'

'Why should roaming in the gloaming affect your thinking?'

He saw the crooked smile flash out, the endearingly curved lips part, a hint of mischief flash in her eyes. 'Put it down to the alchemy of moonlight on the lake, Dermid MacBride. Let's face it, we're both aware we're physically attracted to each other. That could cloud our judgment. At the moment of telling, because of this, we might let our feelings hold sway. Later doubts might set in.'

She looked at him sharply. 'Dermid, you've gone quite white. I've never seen you that way before. What's the matter? Too big a day? Too much happening? Too much play-acting? It's becoming a strain, isn't it? Mother arriving was the last straw. But we couldn't know it was going to last as long or that we——' She stopped, confused.

To the indignation of the lamb who, contrarily, was now bent on getting every last drop, Dermid rose, cast the plastic bottle from him, took her hands, as sticky as his, and said whimsically, 'I'll finish your sentence. We couldn't have known how we were going to feel about each other. It's been a powerful combination, thrust together in a situation like this. All right, we'll have our talk when the Barings leave. Oh, speed that happy day! But if you want it cut and dried, with no false scenery, like soft spring airs and moonlight, we'll have the interview in my office. Come to think of it, there won't be another moon in time. Meanwhile, I'll content myself with the tamer affectionate moments when Theo is around. Don't look so tense, Veronica. I've told you I'll try to understand.'

He must have had very strong suspicions to talk that way. They filled more bottles and finished the round.

There weren't so many dramatic moments the rest of the time her mother was here. Marian very cleverly forestalled any of those hideous coincidences that can happen, in case any of her friends ever met Theo, by telling him how suddenly she'd got tired of her meaningless existence and had gone back to the nursing she'd been trained for. 'So I'd like you to let me have a go at a bit of massage. I'm sure I'm better at it than Dermid and Lucy.' It came at the right moment, and by the time the third session was over, Theo was able to walk almost without pain. He still couldn't sit for long, but was improving fast. Marian rang her hospital, got an extra couple of days' leave, and as she rubbed and kneaded the stiffened muscles, Theo confided in her in a surprising way—told her he felt he owed a terrific lot to Dermid and Veronica. She hid a smile when he almost floundered, nearly having told her of Lucy's flight, and Veronica's subsequent night at Dermid's motel. He remembered just in time that her mother wasn't supposed to know. He very kindly assured her she need have no further fears about the life at Tordarroch for Veronica and added, 'You can see what they mean to each other. I hope they make it soon.'

'So do I, now,' said Marian. She wondered if Theo knew how passionately she wished it, but she wasn't at all sure how Dermid would take Veronica's deception of him, pretending to be Anne's friend. Her reason for being here. Buying antiques from a large family was a dicey business at any time. She supposed the whole thing would have been exposed long ago had it not been that the company Anne was touring with was travelling all round Australia. She thought bleakly, this was something the two of them would have to work out for themselves. It wasn't easy being a mother . . . even when adult, your children's pains and disillusionments and follies became your pain too. She went on massaging Theo, who, all unknowing, had been the cause of it all.

Dermid decided that when she left he'd take Veronica's mother down to Wanaka in *MacBride's Lass*. 'That will give you a whole day off the place, Veronica. You've seen nothing of our lakeside town at all. Our garage man will let us have a car. We'll have a few hours there, though it's three hours down-lake, three up, sometimes shorter or longer either way, depending on the wind.'

Marian said happily, 'It will be lovely for Veronica. She's

like her father, at home on a boat. She's never seasick. It's her element. Of course, growing up in Auckland that was natural.'

Veronica looked forward to the return trip. There would be just the two of them. It could be the ideal time to confess, with no possibility of interruption. Not even a phone to ring, to destroy a mood. The Fates were against her. Maude and Adelaide decided it was too good a chance to miss. 'If you go early, Derry, and show Marian and Veronica that view of Mount Aspiring from the Glendhu Road, we could use the time to see ever so many people, and drop some sheets in at the crib, and air it a bit. It couldn't be better.'

Dermid's look across at Veronica said it couldn't be worse. It seemed as if he'd had the same idea. It would have been heaven. She came out of those thoughts to hear him say sharply, 'You can't go to the crib, Aunt Maude, some friends of the Strongs have got it. You know they keep the key. I hate butting in on tenants. You're sure to catch them sitting down to a meal, or the place untidy, and it makes them feel under observance. But you can certainly see your friends. But I must pick you up at two-thirty. Marian's bus goes at one, so we'll get away at three and be home by six. I've got supplies to pick up too. I was hoping for the chance.'

He said to Veronica on the quiet, 'That was a close shave. The crib is sold, the money paid over through the lawyers to settle up for the other house, and some of the furniture is gone. I did it all by phone. I want to have a look at the new place too.' Mrs Blakeney was with them, so Dermid explained and he added, 'I've had a shady porch put on the new place for them. Wanaka can be bakingly hot in summer and they're so mad on pot-plants, the aunts, they'll need one cool room. I'd like to see how they've progressed.'

Marian said, 'Then when your parents set up Tordarroch House as a guest-house, that will leave Chattan House empty, won't it? I find that rather sad.'

His mouth twitched, Veronica noticed. 'We won't let it deteriorate. Besides, I'm pretty sure it won't be empty for long. A young couple might be in it.'

Veronica saw her mother look at him sharply, and she herself turned away smartly. There had been a smile in his voice. Oh, how she loved him in this sort of mood! She knew a longing that was a physical pain. Don't be stupid, Veronica! He might mean exactly that. Another couple coming to work on Tordarroch. But that was a family house, a Shaw house, named after clan Chattan. Too darling a house for strangers.

In many ways it was a day to remember, with a summer warmth. The lake was its glorious cornflower blue, the contours of mountains and hills had been carved out in the dawn of time by a loving finger. The friendliness of the shopkeepers as they picked up various goods had a village flavour. That magazine had done the trick—Veronica was recognised by most people, seeing she was in Dermid's company, and greeted warmly as one soon to come among them. Only once did she have a chance to say anything. Her mother walked away from them on the road to take a photo of Aspiring in all its shining Matterhorn-like splendour across the lake and valleys that lay between. 'We could never have believed it could lead to all this, Dermid, when we first embarked on what we thought would be a fleeting deception. It just grows and grows.'

'Not to worry. Another month or two and it will be history.'

'You mean like a nine days' wonder?'

'No, I didn't mean that. Hush, here's your mother.'

It was tantalising. They were so hemmed in by aunts and mothers here on this day they might have had to themselves. Back home they had to be so careful not to arouse suspicions in Theo. Even if they took to the lonely gullies, if Dermid was furious with her about the antiques, Theo could sense a rift in the lute. Better wait.

They had a quick look at the little house he'd bought for the aunts with its annexe for the convenience of those from Tordarroch wanting lodging in Wanaka. 'That was why I snapped it up. It was hardly likely another with such an ideal combination should fall vacant. I'd have liked them to choose their own, but daren't risk it going. It was pricey and I didn't want them to know that. Even though the aunts in most ways have moved with the times, *belle-mère*, they simply can't comprehend today's prices and they'd have been terrified I was burdening myself with too much. I did have to raise money.'

'*And* postpone the building of the woolshed,' added Veronica. 'Who says the young people of today don't care about the aged?'

Dermid went a dusky red. 'Come off it, Veronica. It's not a sacrifice, you know. It's a darned good investment.' She laughed at him.

Marian said, 'I like it. It means that you hand them a dream they've always cherished. That way they know they're loved dearly by the young. I can imagine what it'll mean to them.'

'They deserve every bit of it. They've given their whole lives to the station. Now, I must get you to the bus and pick them up.'

They were there, however, to say goodbye to a new friend. Marian kissed them warmly, said, 'Thank you for being so good to my girl,' then she kissed Veronica and, surprisingly, put her hands about Dermid's face, said, 'Goodbye and God bless, dear boy,' and said something else in a whisper nobody else heard, and to which he just said, 'Thank you.'

A strong wind was blowing down-lake, so it was choppy, and cold, but when they turned into Tordarroch Inlet, it was a haven of spring twilight. They'd left the Rover at the jetty, unloaded their stores, took the aunts back to Tordarroch House for their meal because they'd had a long day, and it saved them cooking a meal.

As they turned the last corner, Dermid threw on the brakes in sheer surprise, for here was Theo, walking along the path towards them. 'Surprise! Surprise!' he called, grinning all over his face. 'I can hardly believe it. I haven't had a twinge all day, and my hips feel as if they've been oiled. I've rung the doctor and he says if I stay like this the next three days, I can get Fiona to fly me down to Wanaka, with Lucy, and we'll spend a week in a motel, under his supervision, before flying in to Hunters' Peak.'

So she had three days left then. How short a time ... how long a time before she need confess who she was and why she was here. She must get those things valued before then and keep her fingers crossed for herself and the aunts. And for Dermid, who had raised money to make their other dream come true. What a complication!

Those three days were happy ones, as if there was an unspoken agreement to make those days as happy as possible for Theo who, till now, had known such physical pain here. Now, in a sensibly restricted sort of way, he was enjoying being on another station. He was only stiff in the mornings, or when he'd been too long in the one position.

Veronica admired the way Dermid left the more distant work to his men and spent hours with Theo nearer home, not so much demonstrating to him the excellence of his own station, but sharing experiences and even asking advice occasionally. Lucy had more time with Veronica, glad to be less confined. There was a great difference in her. With her newly-won confidence her voice even deepened and she ventured more opinions. She had far more colour than she used to have.

They stood on the threshold watching the men cross to the woolshed. Lucy said, 'Isn't it great to see Theo like that and for him and Dermid to become such friends? You and Dermid must come whenever you get the chance.' Then she clapped two hands to her mouth and said, 'Oh, Veronica, we've played this for so long, I keep thinking it will continue.'

To her great embarrassment Veronica felt a vivid blush rising from below her throat in a wave of vulnerable feeling. Lucy caught her hand and said fiercely, 'It *mustn't* end, Veronica. It's so right! I've never seen Dermid like this with anyone before ... he's been in many ways, austere and aloof. He's had the odd fancy, but never seriously of late years. He's not austere by nature, I'm sure. He's warm-blooded and vital ... I feel he's come into his own since you've been here. I've never seen him like this. Don't stage a break, Veronica, don't go away, give Dermid time to——'

'Give him time to what?'

'To make up his mind that even an actress could take this sort of life, if she loved a man enough, like I do Theo, now.'

Veronica checked the impulse to tell Lucy she wasn't an actress. Lucy might not be able to resist telling Dermid, and that wasn't the only obstacle. It would mean confessing she'd come out on the launch, to spy out the ground for acquiring antiques. No, not yet.

Lucy shook her arm. 'What is it? You've gone into a daydream. I know ... you're in love! Come on, Veronica, admit it. Oh, do play it by ear. Don't hurry away. It would be lovely to have you for a friend and neighbour ... within helicopter reach of my man's isolated estate. You just mustn't leave here. You belong to the lake,'.

Veronica turned, caught Lucy's hands in hers and squeezed them. 'Thank you for saying just that. I'm rather a mixed-up person myself just now. I hardly know myself at all. Don't worry about me, Lucy. I don't know what's ahead. I'll play it by ear like you said. We dare not break it off too soon after you go. Theo could wonder.'

'You don't have to hurry back to Dunedin, do you? I mean, actresses do have long rests between engagements. Have you anything in mind?'

'I might give the stage up, go back to my first job— which was in an antique shop.' That was an inspiration. A safe one.

'Of course. I thought you sounded very knowledgeable. But you will come over and look at what I thought was junk in Theo's loft, won't you? He'd be tickled pink if that gave him some ready cash. We're living on borrowed money. One of the Stock firms has financed us. Don't go out of our lives. Oh, bother, the men are coming back.'

Veronica said swiftly, 'Lucy, don't embarrass me in front of them, will you? Dermid is just playing a part.'

Lucy laughed. 'Is he? I won't embarrass you, dear friend.

But when it ceases to be make-believe, and becomes truth, promise me I'll be the first to know.'

'You would be, Lucy. If . . . and it's a very big if . . . it ever does. It's not as clear-cut as it seems to be.'

CHAPTER TEN

THREE days later Lucy, Theo and Dermid set off across the lake, Dermid at the wheel of Theo's launch because he wanted to spare him all he could, and Geoff following them in *MacBride's Lass*. Dermid had arranged for someone from Hawea to meet them with a truck and boat trailer on the far side, to transport them across the Neck, and a friend of Theo's would be with it to go right across Lake Hawea with them and up-river to the homestead.

They would have sent Theo home by helicopter except that he didn't care to be without his own water transport. 'The men have been there without a break all this time and may want out for a long weekend by now.'

Veronica declined to go. 'Stephie and I have only skimmed through the housework during the lambing, plus having Mother here and Theo and Lucy. Besides, we've used up all the emergency stuff in the freezers, so we must stock up on fruit cakes and pies and cookies, Steph says. Far too much for one woman to do.'

Dermid had nodded. 'That's so. You can see it another time. Anyway, Geoff will be with me coming back. We wouldn't be on our own.'

What significance had that? Her heart beat faster at the implication. That this could be the time they talked frankly with each other? But if Dermid did want to suggest their present status should be carried on into a shared future, she didn't want him at the wheel of a boat. Because when it happened she'd have to tell him she'd come up here intent on a deception. Besides, now that Lucy and Theo were going, they would have other hours, blessedly alone, please God, in which to confess and to confide.

Theo kissed Veronica goodbye quite tenderly, at the jetty.

171

'This is where I came in,' he said whimsically, 'with a black rage in my heart. I feel a new person now, and a good deal of it's due to you, dear girl, so goodbye for now, and don't keep Dermid waiting too long. The single life is nothing compared with marriage. I've a feeling you and Dermid will start off on a better footing than we did.' He added, sincerely, 'God bless you both.'

Veronica had to blink away tears, but was able to say mistily, 'And God bless you both in return. Theo, that was so nicely put. I don't think Lucy will have any reason from now on to think you inarticulate.'

Dermid kissed her briefly, but on the lips. The launch started up and they headed out of the inlet into the lake. Adelaide and Maude, who never missed a welcome or farewell, said, 'Come to our place for morning tea,' but Veronica shook her head. 'No, Stephie needs me. I'll come over tomorrow to go on with the attic, or the next day.'

They baked and brewed, dusted and scrubbed, stripped Theo's bed and the fold-up one Lucy had occupied, restored the little porch to its accustomed tidiness, and decided the upstairs floor, with its seven bedrooms, could wait till another day. The main thing was to have cupboards and freezers full again.

Stephie heard Veronica singing her tuneful little ditties to herself as after lunch she dusted and tidied the farm office. She smiled to herself. Those lilting tones betrayed the happiness of a girl in love. When Stephie heard the men coming up from the lake shore, and saw Geoff go over to the quarters, she slipped away herself.

Veronica, cheeks flushed from the warmth of cooking, and clad in a stylish modern apron with frilled shoulders over her oatmeal slacks, was bending over the table, carefully icing Stephie's orange cakes and sprinkling lemon jelly crystals over them. Dermid came behind her, put both arms round her waist and caught her back against him, hard. One of his hands came up before her so she could see what it was holding . . . a couple of sprigs of little purple flowers surrounded by leaves. 'Your namesake, Veronica, the native *koromiko*. A bush of it was leaning out from the bank where we beached the launch on the far side.'

It really was veronica. She was delighted. 'What unusual flowers you bring me, Dermid! Scarlet pimpernels, wild veronica. Thank you.'

He turned her about and kissed her lips lightly. 'Reward for a dangerous adventure, that kiss, to bring my lady-love her namesake!' His voice was mocking. He stuck a leg out for her inspection. 'I couldn't quite reach it, so I stepped on the launch seat and slipped over the edge when it rocked. The others thoroughly enjoyed the spectacle, damn 'em.' His trousers were plastered with lake-slime and moss and mud from the knees down. 'Sorry I can't bring you orchids or a dozen roses in a florist's box, but here in the wop-wops, our women have to put up with what they get.'

'I like the wild flowers best,' said Veronica simply. 'Wattle blooming on the Cashmere Hills and ranks of foxgloves that spring up on dry creekbeds and river banks.'

The green eyes held the brown. 'Some day I'll take you to see the Queen of all wild-flowers . . . the Mount Cook lilies blooming lusciously on inhospitable-looking shingle on the lower slopes of Mount Aspiring. Remind me, come December. Not a lily really, you know, but the world's biggest ranunculi. They have great fleshy green leaves like deep saucers, and to drink mountain dew from them on a thirsty climb is like supping in Arcady. The flowers are great waxen cups, white with orange and green stamens.'

'I've only ever seen pictures of them.' It was only when he'd gone away that she realised he'd said, 'Come December.' That was the first month of the New Zealand summer, weeks away.

That night Veronica woke to hear a storm battering at the windows, swirling round the house in tremendous gusts, whistling eerily among the many chimney stacks that were so necessary here to warm the house in winter when the power plant could get overloaded so much that the voltage dropped the lights to a glimmer.

Dermid was up at the crack of dawn and out with his men

and soon the verandah was full of cold, bleating morsels, some beyond even bleating, but often reviving with a good rub down after a warm bath. There was a pathetic heap of lifeless bodies in one of the pens, but they kept their minds off that and saved all they could.

Their immaculate kitchen of the day before had a barricaded corner by the big purring stove, spread with old blankets and sacks, and packed round with hot water bottles from the rubber kind to the copper and stone jars of the early days. Stephie had even heated bricks and wrapped them in old sweaters. 'Nothing is ever wasted here.'

When at last they were able to relax and sit down they just stayed in the warm kitchen and the very good television programme was wasted on them, because all three fell fast asleep, wakened only by the piteous bleats of far too many hungry lambs demanding a late supper.

At last there were only two left. Stephie said, 'I'll leave that pair to you two. One privilege of getting older is that one can leave the most hateful chores to the younger ones.'

They finished. Dermid's face was drawn with fatigue, but he grinned. 'I'm damned glad that at last you've seen it at almost its worst. I knew that was a false spring. But it continued so long I thought you might easily think it was always like that, a sort of pastoral idyll. Might as well get the true picture.'

She said quietly, 'I think you're forgetting those holidays I had on farms as a child. I'm not completely a city girl.' That was as far as she could go in encouragement.

She rinsed out the bottles, then said, 'I sincerely hope they're Plunket trained. No feeds in the early hours.'

'If they do, I'm sure I won't hear them. But if they do wake they usually settle again.'

However, in the wee sma's, Veronica it was who heard the bleating. She was snug and warm and had faith in what he'd said. They'd settle. She pulled the clothes over her head to shut out the sound. If she went down to pacify that one who was so strangely loud, they'd all waken and rouse the household. Suddenly she pushed the clothes away, sat up. It sounded so near. But that was absurd.

It was cold out of bed. It had been so deliciously warm snuggled down on the electric blanket at first, she'd not bothered to find a warmer nightie than this bit of rose-pink nonsense she'd been wearing the last week of unseasonable weather. She wouldn't put her light on. She knew the stairs well enough by now to venture down them in the dark and because of the private power plant, there always had to be some lights on downstairs.

She clutched her rose-coloured gown about her, girdled it, and opened the door. She could see the chink of light in the room beyond the stairs and began to feel her way down. Strange that the bleating had stopped as she opened her door. But she was certain that last bleat had come from the downstairs passage. It would be disastrous to have a lamb, certainly not house-trained, loose for the rest of the night, when they'd been so meticulous in their house-cleaning!

Three steps from the bottom it happened. She stepped on to a small woolly body, and nothing could have stopped the scream that rose in her throat as it moved. She clutched, missed the banister and rolled the rest of the way down. She heard the thud upstairs as Dermid leapt from his bed, followed a moment later from Stephie's room.

Dermid's hand found the landing switch, the whole scene was flooded with light and revealed to the two startled people above the sight of Veronica picking herself up and bounding along the passage in pursuit of a lamb to which she was apologising.

Stephie, laughing, looked over the rail and said to Dermid, 'It's over to you. I'm too old for these sort of capers. Oh, listen, the whole darned lot are awake now!'

Veronica stopped apologising to the lamb and began apologising to them. Dermid said, 'I'll be with you in a moment,' and appeared to dive into his room again. Presently he was with her and took the lamb from her. 'Where was it?'

'On the stairs, a few steps up. It had stopped bleating, so I thought it was below in the hall. I was going to be so noble and stop it disturbing the whole household. Oh, Dermid, it felt horrible . . . woolly and warm, and *it moved*! Now I've ruined your night.'

'Don't you believe it. My door was open, yours wasn't. It would probably have come right into my room. It's full of pep. Once they revive you can't keep them down. Or in. But it must be some high-jumper if it could leap that barricade. For goodness' sake, give it to me—your dressing-gown will be indescribable!' He took it off her. He'd got himself a mohair robe.

They opened the kitchen door and stood aghast. The lamb must have got out the far door and come right round, but when it first made its escape it had knocked the entire barrier down and now the room, still warm with that purring stove, was filled with lambs going full bore. Veronica closed her eyes at the state of the floor.

'Just a moment.' Dermid strode out to the scullery and snatched a three-quarter coat from a hook, came back in, slipped out of his own robe and handed it to her. 'I'll use this coat. Put that on before you do anything more.'

She hesitated, remembering her wispy nightie, then modestly slipped into the hall, hung her own garment on the banister knob, and got into his gown, thankful it was a short one, and tied it firmly. She came back, met his eyes, found them full of laughter. 'As usual, the perfect spoilsport! You could have thought you owed me something for waking me up.'

She said quickly, 'I thought it would look rather odd if Stephie came down after all. It's a stupid garment for a night like this.'

He came across, put his fingers about her cheeks and said, 'I'm not calling you prudish. I like that attitude. At least I like it at this stage in our . . . in our progress.'

She pulled back, saying hastily, 'Let's get on with the job.'

And job it was, but at least with that thrice-blessed fire range the kettles were warm. They made up the mixture, filled four bottles and started, after they'd made sure that this time the barricades were secure. Veronica finally said, 'We could get away with just mopping that floor, couldn't we? I'll hand-scrub it tomorrow.'

Dermid looked at the clock. 'It's already tomorrow. You mop and I'll follow, scrubbing. Where's Steph's kneeler?' The clock struck four as they went wearily upstairs. A faint bar of light from some watery-looking stars shone through a break in the clouds as they passed the landing window. It fell across Dermid's features. He touched her ruffled head in a sort of goodnight gesture. 'I know you've got something to tell me, Veronica, that you dread. Don't be too afraid. I may not like it, as you said, but I promise you I'll try to understand. I hope that in the telling, you can put paid to the whole thing and forget about it. Now . . . back to bed.'

She felt muzzy with tiredness. It had been nicely said, but she really couldn't understand it. But if he had an inkling things were not what they seemed, it could help when she confessed.

It was three days before the storm blew itself out and every moment had been filled to the brim. It had been unrelenting, unglamorous and demanding work, but satisfying, and it hadn't been as disastrous as it might have been with so many lambs having arrived earlier.

By sunset on that third day the lake was calm again, and blue. The peaks back in had emerged, though they carried much more snow so that the air was colder, but gloriously exhilarating. 'It will be a lovely day tomorrow,' Dermid prophesied, scanning the sky above the mountains, blood-red and amber, weather-wise in his own territory. 'We'll let you off foster-mothering tomorrow, Veronica. The aunts would like you over there for morning tea. Do go. It gives them the variety they need. Take the Rover, we're using the bikes. Stephie says you've worked like a Trojan. I thought Anne was a bit crazy when she spoke about you. I thought she could have picked someone more suitable, more credible as a fake fiancée for a high-countryman, but she knew you, of course. Gosh, she's the limit—never a word from her! She might have written you.'

Veronica felt slightly hollow. Dermid had relieved her mind a bit earlier by saying Anne rarely wrote when on a tour like this, where they just had three-night stands at most places, but that 'She usually sends cards. She'll probably write when they finish and she reaches Mum and Dad in Queensland. She won't say anything to them about this lark, of course. Mother would imagine me co-respondent in a divorce case and would be back here to tackle Theo and tell him he was a damned fool.'

Nevertheless, now this bad weather lambing crisis was over she must make the time and opportunity to tell Dermid. That she'd done him an injustice, thinking of him as a crabby middle-aged nephew, denying his aunts their cherished dream. She still felt apprehensive, because you never knew how Dermid would take anything. But he'd said she wasn't to be scared, he'd understand, so she was halfway there.

She would finish the classifying and valuing of the aunts' treasures tomorrow, and tell Dermid that night. Where? How?

It was awkward with Stephie in the house, liable to interrupt them at any moment. The snow on the peaks put paid to roaming in the gloaming. She didn't want to fill the aunts with apprehension by suggesting they invite Stephie over while she told Dermid. Could she say she wanted to see him in the farm office? But what an atmosphere! Oh, she'd think of something.

Next morning she came down dressed in an emerald green lightweight suit. She felt like dressing up and the aunts always loved it. It took so little to make their day. Dermid had come back for something. She was sure his eyes lit up at sight of her. It gave her confidence. He said, involuntarily, 'I've not seen you in that shade before, love.'

Love. The endearment he'd used so often to hoodwink Theo. But Theo was miles away. It gave her courage to say, 'Dermid, it's been so hideously busy, we've not had time for our talk. I'd like to get it off my chest soon. Will you make an opportunity shortly?'

She saw a muscle in his left cheek twitch. She said, 'I believe you're as nervous as I am.' She put up a hand to his cheek in a spontaneous gesture. He held it there and said, 'Yes, I won't deny it. I only hope I won't spoil anything. I can, at times, blow my top at the wrong moment. But, Veronica, be completely honest with me. I won't settle for less. Oh, let's have it out now. Steph's feeding her fowls.'

'Dermid, I can't. There's something I have to finish first.'

'Finish? You don't mean you have to get in touch with someone first? By phone, say?'

'No—oh, please, Dermid, leave it till tonight and we'll make time for it. I'm too frightened of being interrupted now.'

'Right, it's a date. Watch that track as you drive, it's a bit scoured out.' His eyes held a smile. 'Till tonight.'

The aunts loved her in the emerald green. Maude immediately fished out a piece of matching ribbon and tied the two wings of hair behind her head with it. The loops fell gracefuly down against the polished brown locks. 'But you could get dusty in the attic. I know we've dusted most of it off by now, but you must have an overall. Maude, you know those ones of Mother's that were used when we had the nineteen-twenties fashion parade in Wanaka? Aren't they in the chest in the hall? They'd cover everything but her sleeves, and she could roll those up.'

Veronica could have laughed her head off as she saw the garment. There was a back and a front and it tied each side of the waist. Their mother must have been slim enough, so she didn't feel quite out of her generation. It had probably been dashing as a pinny in its day. It was black, with huge orange poppies splashed all over it. Laughing helplessly, she let them tie it. The phone rang—Rena. Maude turned from it, 'She wonders if we'd like to bath Rebecca this morning. But——'

Veronica made them go. She'd get on with the valuing far faster if she didn't have the aunts twittering at her telling her stories with every piece. They rang later to say Rena had asked them for lunch. Would it be awful if——'

'I'll be candid and say it would suit me beautifully. Your list has helped me so much, and I'd like to finish this and tell Dermid the whole story pretty soon. One of these days I'm going to get found out, and I'd much rather tell him myself. I'll cut myself a sandwich and work on. It would take just one letter from Anne to blow the whole thing sky-high.'

By two it was all finished. She didn't think Dermid would blanch at the thought of what she'd like to offer her firm. These things weren't in the top class. They were not being displayed here, or even used. Some things the aunts wanted to sell she'd put aside. These would appreciate in value, much more assets than stocks and shares. Inflation couldn't touch these. It was a crime, even, that some of them should have been hidden away here. Of course, the aunts had lived with them all their lives.

She heard them coming. They had driven the Rover over. She went to the doorway and called out, 'I'm still up here, my dears. You're going to get a very good price for this stuff. I don't think you had any idea how much these things have gone up in value. My firm will give you good prices for them, prices which I'm jolly sure will soften Dermid's heart and he'll give his consent.'

There was a quite appreciable silence. She called out, 'Did you hear what I said, Maude, Adelaide? Come on up.'

Then a voice, not theirs but Dermid's, said in a tone of suppressed fury that was worse than a shout, '*I heard all right. And certainly I'm coming up!*'

Instinctively Veronica retreated into the middle of the attic where they had cleared a big space. Dermid positively bounded into the room. Theo might have said he crossed the lake with a black rage in his heart that day, but MacBride of Tordarroch had a matching rage in his right now!

Inwardly Veronica quailed, outwardly she stood calmly, one hand on her wad of lists, but her face whitened. 'Yes, Dermid,' she managed, 'you've come up. What can this be all about?'

'All about?' he barked. 'As if you didn't know? You cheat! You underhanded little money-maker, sneaking in here, getting the aunts to deceive me . . . they're babes unborn when it comes to money value . . . they were cheated once before, and what's more you knew about that! Oh, very clever, wasn't it? I suppose you twisted Anne round your little finger. She'd never suspect that you really wanted to get up here to see what you could diddle us out of. I expect Anne, all unknowing, filled you in about the treasures we have! I thought you were damned clever when you invented a career in antiques to Theo. All your smug talk about saving a marriage and how important it was and worming your way into our hearts ... just to think how I've lain awake night after night trying to fight my desire to keep you here despite what I knew about you ... and this is what you are ... *in addition to that* ... a liar, a cheat! Oh, you certainly were clever, told your boss not to write, that mails were irregular ... never thought he'd *ring* to see how you were getting on, did you? Or that he'd get me? Oh, yes, he spilled all the beans. I didn't let on ... no, I pretended the greatest of interest. I'm going to have real satisfaction in ringing him back and telling him I'm sending you home with a flea in your ear!'

Veronica held up her hand and it stopped him dead. She said with icy calm, '*This* is what I was going to tell you tonight. Oh, what brave words you uttered just a few hours ago ... how understanding you were going to be. I just wonder! You warned me you could blow your top ... you certainly can! Now I give you at least this much credit, you've heard only half the story. My boss, as you call him, doesn't know it either. Only that I was coming up here hoping to find some antiques you might want to sell. No, not you—the aunts. They belong to the aunts and it was the aunts who approached me.'

He looked staggered. 'What——?'

'Let me finish. That was my *sole* purpose in coming up here. I came in answer to a letter they wrote me. And you are *not* to perform like this in front of them. I could tell when they wrote to me that they were just terrified of you. Didn't want to let their nephew know, they said. I imagined a real curmudgeon ... much older than you. I didn't know you were a great-nephew. But it makes no difference. I can see now men can be curmudgeons at any age! They were *rightly* scared of you. I changed my mind about you when I knew you were planning that modern house for them in Wanaka ... I thought therefore you'd be sure to understand when I told you *why* they wanted to sell some of the antiques. Not your antiques either, but the ones their mother left to them personally. Not MacBride possessions, nor Shaw possessions, but their very own. I wouldn't have touched them if they hadn't shown me their certificate of possession. I wouldn't dare. That firm I used to work for, and freelance for, is one of the most reputable in the business. Even then, I told the aunts they must have a second opinion after I told you. Ask them!

'Their mother left those things to *them*, and she'd be the first to want them to be the means of her darling younger children realising the dearest dream of their lives. What's more, I'll do everything I can to help them. They only need their fares and they didn't want to ask you for the money because they know your overheads have gone up so much. They only need their return fares for Italy.'

The colour of anger in the coppery skin had subsided, leaving him curiously pale. He said in a sort of winded way, 'Their return fares to Italy? *Italy?*'

'Yes. To visit the graves of their lovers who fell at Cassino. And what's more, although my firm would have leapt at it, there's stuff over there,' she pointed, 'that belongs to them too, but I wouldn't take it from here. It *must* stay here. It would be a crime to separate it from Chattan House. That other pile is what I'm offering to buy. It's not my favourite period. Some Victoriana, though not all, is just plain hideous, but it's fetching colossal prices. And seeing it was stowed away like old junk and never saw the light of day, I just don't see why those darling women can't kneel where they want to kneel.' She choked.

MacBride of Tordarroch said. 'We never knew. They never said. They could have gone long ago. But why didn't you tell me?'

'I didn't dare. Look how you behaved when you did get to know! I dared not risk it when Theo was here—you'd never have been able to hide your anger with me. I did what I did for his sake, to save a marriage, and I'd do it again, even if I didn't know if I was on my head or my heels when I got thrown into the arena. You and your talk about how understanding you were going to be. Just because you found out first you're beside yourself. *Understanding!*'

Dermid seized her, but she stepped back with a positive recoil. 'Don't touch me!'

So he stood, his hands hanging by his sides, and said in a different tone, 'But I *was* going to be understanding. About the other matter. Though it's nearly killed me to arrive at even being able to contemplate trying to be tolerant about ... about the other thing. You've seemed so sweet, so home-loving. I tried to understand you'd really gone overboard for this man—told myself you had so great a capacity for loving and comforting that you'd want to make a home for this chap who'd spun you that hard-luck story. What a line ... a wife who'd walked out on him years ago and who'd never been seen since! So he couldn't marry you. And all the time he was living up to the image of the sailor with a wife in every port ... though in his case it was just two ports, Sydney and Dunedin. I didn't *want* to love you, Veronica. *But so help me, I couldn't stop myself.* I'd got to the stage where I felt I could understand, because you're so loving and giving that in a case like this, you'd have to give all. But to think you'd deceive me in this, on top of everything, is the last straw. I feel I can't know you at all. Veronica, what are you looking like that for?'

She swallowed. Her throat was dry. 'Dermid, what are you talking about? What wife? What sailor? I——'

He said savagely, 'Don't give me that! Don't, don't. You can't lie your way out of this one. Anne told me the whole story. Said it would do you good to get away from Dunedin, to be in an inland place where his ship couldn't dock. Gosh, Anne must have been in it too. She must have known you bought and sold antiques as well as acting, or she'd never have said that about you liking only modern stuff. That was to pull the wool over my eyes. My own sister! Is that how the aunts heard of you? From Anne? *But don't pretend to me you never lived with this man.* What did you say?'

Veronica said slowly and clearly, 'Will you listen? And try to take it in? Then I'll go. But you must know the truth. I'm *not* Anne's friend. I've never met Anne. That girl *was* Victoria—you didn't mistake the name. The aunts know I'm not. I'm just a buyer of antiques they heard of through their Christchurch friends. They wrote me saying they were keeping it dark from you because then if the things were valueless they wouldn't have upset you. I was to arrive as this young friend of their friends, for a holiday. I was to leave my car at that garage. So was Victoria, evidently.

'Unfortunately the garage man mistook me, and shot me over to the launch, saying we mustn't lose any time. I couldn't think what the rush was, but I accepted it, and there were two parties of people on the launch for Minaret, so Gus couldn't explain, then he tried and completely mystified me, but before I could work out what was happening Theo was coming across the lake, quite close. Gus pressganged me into doing it—substituting for Victoria. And I was going to tell you I wasn't her, when you'd turned round to see if Theo and Lucy were coming and Gus hissed at me not to say, that if you thought I wasn't an actress, you'd have no faith in my ability to act, to carry it off.'

She swallowed and rushed on, 'I thought it no end of a lark. I even thought that if I carried it off till Theo and Lucy were gone that day, you might be so grateful you wouldn't mind a bit when I offered a price for those things. But then Theo slipped his disc and——' she felt her voice faltering and her reaction was to feel angry with herself, so she continued fiercely, 'and at first I was terribly cross to think I'd been pitchforked into such a situation not knowing what had really happened, and now I was helping someone I thought was a male chauvinist . . . that you ruled this place like the Lord of the Isles . . . MacBride of Tordarroch! That you'd taken after the aunts' father who wouldn't let them marry. Then I found out *he* had a heart of butter, that he'd only been concerned for their ultimate happiness, and I began to find out nice things about you, like postponing the building of the new woolshed so the aunts could live out their last years in the place they love . . . in Wanaka . . . so I changed my mind about you . . . and you promised me you'd be understanding and—Dermid, what are you shaking me for? It'll be all right. You hate and despise me, so I'll go as soon as you can take me to Wanaka ... stop shaking me!'

Dermid said, 'Veronica, Veronica ... don't you see what a wonderful thing has just happened to us? Nothing else matters except that! You aren't Victoria. You aren't that poor forsaken girl who was pitched that tale about a disappearing wife ... don't you remember how furious I was when you played and sang that song about the apple pie? I felt that night when we'd returned from that dander in the moonlight as if you had suddenly slapped my face. That you were remembering *him*. I was so sure that night when you kissed me so beautifully that you too were falling in love. So that it nearly killed me to think of that other fellow. So I went all in on myself. I'll never forget that wonderful moment when your mother said you wrote that music for that poem, for her to welcome your father home. Remember how I droppped my glass into my pie? Veronica, my darling, don't you see none of it matters now? It's just like my darling dilly aunts to foul up my love-life. I admit I was furious that they got diddled by that other shark, but with him, not them. That simply doesn't matter. It was just that revelation, from your boss, coming on top of the other thing. I thought you must have no principles at all. Sweetheart, you're the most wonderfully clever girl in the world, to be positively hurled into my arms, with about five seconds' warning, and act like that. No wonder your knees caved in on you that day! Veronica ...' he gave her another shake, 'aren't you going to say anything?'

She said quietly with her slow smile coming, 'When are you going to give me the chance, MacBride of Tordarroch? Oh, Dermid, Dermid, Dermid!'

She was gathered to him and kissed in a way that he had never kissed her before ... because till now there had always been misunderstandings. Presently he held her off from him. 'Let me just look at you,' he exulted. 'Really look at you, and know you're mine.' Then his face changed and he said bewilderingly, 'Darling, what in the world have you got on?'

She looked down and her eyes danced. 'It's so fitting for an antique buyer. I'm wearing your great-grandmother's pinny.'

He gave one of his great guffaws. 'I'll tell *our* great-grandchildren that, some day, what you wore when I proposed! It *is* a proposal, by the way. But you can take it off now, and I can see my Veronica in her contemporary dress . . . you look the very spirit of spring itself, love.'

Veronica was overcome by delicious laughter as he began untying the side bows. 'Dermid, when you came bounding up those stairs with all of Theo's black rage in your heart, could you have imagined that in twenty minutes' time you'd be calling me the spirit of spring?'

'If ever you tell anyone *how* I proposed, I shall slit your beautiful throat, my sweet.' He kissed it, lingeringly. She kissed him back, and any man would have been satisfied with that kiss. 'By the way, Veronica, your mother knows. I told her I was going to make this engagement stick if I could. She gave me her blessing when she said goodbye to me. Tell me, who knows beside Gus?'

'Just his wife. Gus told me one day I was helping unload stores when you weren't there that this Victoria had never turned up. I don't suppose we'll ever know why. Oh, I do hope she meets someone worth loving and makes something of her life.'

'Gus's Mollie is a sport, lending us her ring. Wasn't it funny when Theo thought it a little modest for the owner of Tordarroch?' Dermid held her hand out, twisted the dainty ring and said, 'What do you fancy for a ring, my love? Perhaps a ruby. I love the pink shades on you. Or an emerald, like this suit, ringed with diamonds?'

'Don't you realise, dear idiot, that we embarked on this tissue of lies to save a marriage? You're going to have to get an exact copy of this ring made for when we visit Lucy and Theo in Fiona's helicopter. Not locally though, or the secret will get out.'

'Oh, yes. It will have to be Dunedin. We're stuck with a modest one. Shall you mind?'

'Mind? I'd never feel properly engaged with anything else. I *love* this ring. I used to twist it at night and wish it was for real.'

He kissed her for that, then lifted his head and said, 'I hear the aunts. Let's go down hand-in-hand, see if they guess.'

Together they came down the staircase that was only just wide enough for two, the staircase Euphemia and Findlay Shaw had been so proud of when at last they could build a second storey on to their home. The aunts looked up as they came into the hall and heard descending feet ... saw the linked hands, and they lifted aged faces towards them, aglow with love.

They held out their hands, Dermid kissed them, they kissed him back, then folded Veronica to them. There were tears in their eyes. Dermid's eyes danced, 'It was a grand plot you hatched, aunts, when you decided to write to the young antique dealer you heard about.'

They gasped. 'You know? How did you know?'

Dermid's eye flickered to Veronica's. 'Did you really think I was deceived, surely MacBride of Tordarroch wouldn't be so gullible? I can keep a secret better than most ... though I did reveal to Veronica my own secret the day we went to Wanaka.' He told them.

Their response was overwhelming. He didn't mention that he'd had to raise money and had postponed the new woolshed. Then he twinkled, said, 'I'll book your flights for Rome almost immediately. As soon as Veronica and her mother can decide on a date for our wedding. It must be soon, because we must have you there. But you can be in Italy for the Northern Hemisphere summer.'

A thought struck Adelaide. 'Dear boy, you'll be living here with Veronica in Chattan House. How fitting, with her love of antiques. I feel Euphemia would be pleased, and our mother. Maude, we can tell them that other bit now, can't we? Gus slipped into Distaff Bay one day without sounding the hooter. Anne had rung him from Australia. She was worried, she'd had a letter from Victoria. It seemed Victoria had only got as far as packing to come up here when she was offered a good part in Wellington, in an emergency. She had to catch the next plane. She tried to get us on the phone and was told the line was out. There was nothing she could do, especially when she knew it was all hush-hush. Gus reassured Anne, said a substitute had been roped in. She nearly died, promised not to tell her parents when she saw them, and was really thrilled when Gus said he was practically sure the engagement wouldn't be terminated.'

Veronica said, 'What? How could Gus have thought that? He's only unloaded stores here ever since.'

'We told him,' said Maude. 'It was sticking out a mile.'

It was much later that night. Stephie had been told by phone and had come across to congratulate them. Then she had taken the aunts off to Tordarroch House for dinner, leaving Veronica to cook Dermid's in the lovely old home that would soon be theirs.

When the day was completely done, and the fire was glowing red to its heart, the hour was all their own, all alarms and misunderstandings over. They were sitting together on the velvet couch in the sitting-room. After a while Dermid said dreamily, 'Some day I'd like you to compose a song for me. Set one to music, I mean. We'll find some suitable lyrics.'

Veronica said softly, 'I sometimes compose lyrics myself. Not often, just when the spirit moves me. I did the other day, when you brought me the veronica that grows wild on the far shore. I remembered you bringing me the scarlet pimpernels. Nobody else has heard it yet.'

He was moved. 'How personal a gift! Veronica, would you play it for me now, as a tinkling little tune on the goblets?'

'That's how I composed it. Just as my grandmother taught me.' As before, she set the goblets on the piano-top, took the silver fork out of a green-baize lined drawer, and used it once more as a tuning fork, a rippling cascade of sound. Then she moved to the upright piano, sat down and began to sing:

> 'Behind the window-glass they glow,
> ... Proud tulips in a crimson row,
> Pale orchids, delicately wrought
> And early roses, dearly bought,

Great pansies, purple, blue and gold,
A myriad blooms shop-windows hold,
... Then why should I whose life is stayed
In city streets, in city trade,
Dream wistfully of flaming gorse
By tussocked hill and river-course,
Of lupin tapers by the sea,
Of wattle blooming goldenly,
Of scarlet pimpernels that pass
Their lives amid the wind-blown grass,
The dear wild flowers that bloom for God
In distant hills, in unturned sod ...

These stir with nameless ecstasy
This strange, untamed wild heart of me.'

When she had finished singing there was a silence, a sharing silence of appreciation. She returned to his arms.

Dermid lifted a coppery eyebrow. 'An untamed heart?' he asked. Veronica put her cheek against his, looked into the dancing flames. 'A committed heart,' she said dreamily.

Discover the secret of Gypsy

CAROLE MORTIMER

Gypsy

Gypsy – the story of a woman they called Gypsy, a woman with raven hair and a fiery, passionate nature.

Four brothers try to tame the Gypsy. Read their story – and hers – from 8th November 1985, at just £2.25.

Gypsy. A longer, more involving romance from Mills and Boon.

Mills & Boon

The Rose of Romance

ROMANCE

Variety is the spice of romance

Each month, Mills & Boon publish new romances. New stories about people falling in love. A world of variety in romance — from the best writers in the romantic world. Choose from these titles in November.

RETURN TO WALLABY CREEK Kerry Allyne
PILLOW PORTRAITS Rosemary Carter
THE DRIFTWOOD DRAGON Ann Charlton
TO CAGE A WHIRLWIND Jane Donnelly
A MAN WORTH KNOWING Alison Fraser
INJURED INNOCENT Penny Jordan
TOUCH NOT MY HEART Leigh Michaels
SWEET AS MY REVENGE Susan Napier
SOUTH SEAS AFFAIR Kay Thorpe
DANGER ZONE Madeleine Ker
***THE GARLAND GIRL** Liza Manning
***MacBRIDE OF TORDARROCH** Essie Summers

On sale where you buy paperbacks. If you require further information or have any difficulty obtaining them, write to: Mills & Boon Reader Service, PO Box 236, Thornton Road, Croydon, Surrey CR9 3RU, England.

*These two titles are available *only* from Mills & Boon Reader Service.

Mills & Boon
the rose of romance

 **ROMANCE**

Next month's romances from Mills & Boon

Each month, you can choose from a world of variety in romance with Mills & Boon. These are the new titles to look out for next month.

FINDING OUT Lindsay Armstrong
ESCAPE ME NEVER Sara Craven
POINT OF IMPACT Emma Darcy
SILENT CRESCENDO Catherine George
THE MAN IN ROOM 12 Claudia Jameson
THE HARD MAN Penny Jordan
HUNGER Rowan Kirby
A LAKE IN KYOTO Marjorie Lewty
PALE ORCHID Anne Mather
NEVER THE TIME AND THE PLACE Betty Neels
***LEGACY** Doris Rangel
***FOREVER** Lynn Turner

Buy them from your usual paperback stockist, or write to: Mills & Boon Reader Service, P.O. Box 236, Thornton Rd, Croydon, Surrey CR9 3RU, England. Readers in South Africa-write to: Mills & Boon Reader Service of Southern Africa, Private Bag X3010, Randburg, 2125.

*These two titles are available *only* from Mills & Boon Reader Service.

Mills & Boon
the rose of romance